BUCKET LIST

'Rarely does one read a novel that so nourishes the soul and completely restores one's faith in the inherent goodness of mankind. Jones is an exceptional writer'
TENDAI HUCHU

'A poignant, entertaining and uplifting read as loneliness, larceny and a lottery win lead to the unlikeliest of friendships'
OLGA WOJTAS

'There is pathos and poverty, brutality, and a longing for connection that sings throughout this book.
I could not put it down'
JANE YOLEN

ABOUT THE AUTHOR

Russell Jones is an Edinburgh-based writer and editor. He was the UK's first Pet Poet Laureate, has published six poetry collections, three fantasy novels, one graphic novel and has edited three writing anthologies. Russell was the deputy editor of Scotland's only sci-fi magazine from 2015–2023, organises literary cabaret nights in Edinburgh and has a PhD in Creative Writing.

BUCKET LIST

Russell Jones

Polygon

First published in 2024 in Great Britain in paperback by Polygon,
an imprint of Birlinn Ltd

Birlinn Ltd
West Newington House
10 Newington Road
Edinburgh
EH9 1QS

9 8 7 6 5 4 3 2 1

www.polygonbooks.co.uk

Copyright © Russell Jones, 2024

The right of Russell Jones to be identified as the author of this work has been
asserted in accordance with the Copyright, Designs and Patents Act 1988.

All rights reserved. No part of this publication may be reproduced, stored, or
transmitted in any form, or by any means electronic, mechanical or photocopying,
recording or otherwise, without the express written permission of the publisher.

ISBN 978 1 84697 654 4
eBook ISBN 978 1 78885 637 9

British Library Cataloguing-in-Publication Data
A catalogue record for this book is available on request from
the British Library.

The publisher gratefully acknowledges investment from
Creative Scotland towards the publication of this book.

Typeset in Bembo Book MT Pro by The Foundry, Edinburgh
Printed and bound by CPI (UK) Ltd, Croydon CR0 4YY

For Margaret and Jean
— two great old gals

01

A Leap of Faith

Lottery number 29 (Dot is twenty-two years old)

'A bloody leap year, you're crazy!' Dot's mum protested, pouring too much tea into Dot's cup. 'Getting the date in everyone's diary was a nightmare, you know. And how are you meant to celebrate your anniversary every year?'

'We'll celebrate every four years,' Dot said, taking her teacup before her mum purposefully added an excess of milk to punish her. 'And hardly anybody gets married on the twenty-ninth of February, which makes our day more special.'

'It's done now, I suppose.' Her mum heaped sugar onto a teaspoon and moved it towards Dot's cup.

Dot placed her hand over her tea. 'Not for me.' She fluttered her eyelashes. 'I'm sweet enough already.'

'Move that hand – you'll need all the energy you can get today.'

Dot relinquished control and her mum slid four heaped teaspoons of sugar into her cup as if sliding muck from a spade, filling the cup to its brim.

Dot sipped the tea down to a safe, manoeuvrable level. She

stared at the mounds of wedding gifts, partly excited to open them and partly despairing at the sheer volume of crockery she knew she would uncover.

'How are you feeling?' her mum said, softening. 'Nervous?'

'Actually, no. It's strange, but it feels like any other day. Except for *this* thing.' She looked down at her pearly cheese-cloth wedding dress. 'I feel like a meringue.'

'Well, you look like an angel,' her mum said. 'And don't worry about the presents. Your cousins will all be getting married in the next few years, so you can just give away any duplicates or tat. If anyone asks where their present went, just tell them I borrowed it.'

'I already peeked at a few.' Dot took another sip of her obscenely sweet tea. 'There are at least six casserole dishes. I haven't made a casserole in my whole life.'

'Me neither, dear.' Dot's mum took a tarnished golden pocket mirror from her posh purse and flipped it open, checking her lips. 'I'll redo our lippy once we're finished. We ought to look our best – people will remember today, and all eyes are on the mother of the bride.' She added another stealthy sugar to Dot's cup. 'And you're sure, aren't you? Because if you're not sure, now's the time to change your mind. I mean, you can't *really* change your mind because your aunts have already taken the sandwiches and trifles to the social club for your wedding breakfast, but if you've any niggles then now's the time to tell me.'

'I'm sure,' Dot said. 'Charles is wonderful, Mum, there's nothing to worry about.'

The doorbell rang and Dot's mum bolted up, checking her watch. 'He's early, that idiot! Stay here!'

Dot's mum marched downstairs and opened the front door. Dot, half-listening to her mum's agitated mumbles and her uncle's muffled apologies, finished her tea and picked up the bouquet that her best friend, Grace, had made for her. She sniffed the pink and yellow roses, imagining herself lying in a country garden, bathed in sunlight as birds twittered amongst the branches.

'Right, time to go!' Dot's mum shouted as she climbed back up the stairs to Dot's room. 'There's a road closure and a lorry crash, so there are diversions. Today of all days! You'll have to take the long way round, and Uncle Brian stinks of whisky and cigars.'

Dot took a deep breath, hoping that her bouquet's scent might be enough to mask Uncle Brian's shortcomings. No, it wouldn't do. She didn't want to sit in his stinking, cramped car and take the long way round.

'Tell him to meet me there,' Dot called back as her mum reached the landing.

'What?!' The wedding antics had turned her mum's face so red that blusher was out of the question. 'What do you mean?'

'I'll get there by myself. It's not far and it's a really nice day. For February. I'll cycle – I can cut through the lanes in the housing estates. It'll be quicker than taking the car through diversions.'

Dot's mum placed her fingertips on Dot's forehead. 'I'm sorry. I thought maybe you'd lost your mind. What about your hair? What about the dress? It'll get caught in the wheels, I know it.'

'I'll manage, I've cycled in dresses before.' She stared into her mum's frantic eyes. 'Relax, okay? It's me getting married, not you. What happened to the unflappable woman who raised me to be as cool as I am?'

Her mum took a long, deep breath. 'All right, it's your day.

But arrive on foot, won't you? The town will talk if they see you arrive at your wedding on a push bike.'

Dot grasped her mum's hand and shook it. 'Deal. You ride in the stink mobile and bring the favours.' She gestured to the box of silver-papered cardboard horseshoes, pastel-coloured confetti and plastic silver bells on her bed.

Her mum piled their bouquets on top of the box of favours and kissed Dot on the cheek. 'Don't be late.' She picked up the box and scurried down the stairs.

Dot watched from her bedroom window as her mum (her head now topped by a huge lavender-shaded flying saucer-shaped hat) continued to berate Uncle Brian until they clambered into his car and drove away.

Dot checked she had everything she needed, walked downstairs and locked the back door behind her. She placed her purse into the bike's basket and sat on the saddle, hitching her white dress over the handlebars so that it wouldn't snag in the wheels or trail on the dirty ground. As she rode through the quiet lanes towards the church, she smiled to herself and thought of Charles in his suit and wondered just how many casserole dishes they might have inherited.

A few people waved to Dot as she passed, congratulating her on her happy day. But most of them looked utterly confused at the bridal effigy that flew past them, and she couldn't care less.

Dot left her bike near the back of the bakery, taking in a lungful of yeasty air before walking the final two streets to the church. Uncle Brian's stink mobile had indeed beaten her to the venue, but she wasn't late and the bike ride had kept her warm despite the crisp February air.

She watched her guests from afar, catching her breath while hidden behind a bush: Grace looked the best in her short skirt as she smiled at Dot's elderly relatives and ushered them into the church; her mum pretended not to look around nervously for Dot as she chatted to Uncle Brian, partially eclipsed under the brim of her hat; Dot's nurse friends clung to the arms of their wide-tied, mane-haired, moustached men; flower girls ran in excited circles around Dot's good-looking kilted cousin; and the younger boys stood awkwardly, gawping in second-hand suits, their hands disappearing into the overlong sleeves of their jackets.

Dot's mum caught sight of her. She whispered into Uncle Brian's ear and shoved Dot's bouquet into his hand. Uncle Brian ushered the guests inside and, when the coast was clear, Dot joined him.

'You nearly gave your mother an aneurysm,' Uncle Brian said, taking Dot's hand. 'But you look crackin'. Charles is inside, sweating like a glassblower's arse crack. Ready?'

Dot smiled, threading her arm through his. 'Absolutely.'

★

The photographer's camera flash blinded Dot as the newly weds left the church in a shower of pastel-coloured confetti. As bulbs danced in Dot's vision, an ominous grey cloud lurked overhead, threatening to unleash its load and leave confetti-shaped stains on her wedding dress.

Don't you dare! Dot thought with her best menacing voice, psychically scowling at the cloud.

The photo-taking was a hazy, dull chaos of family members coming and going in overly specific combinations. Dot just wanted to push on to the social club for a cheese sandwich and a bag of ready salted crisps, but Charles appeared to be enjoying the attention.

'Dotty, you've hooked yourself a good fish, there,'

Grace said, standing next to Dot for a photo. 'I suppose we won't see you at work for much longer.' She smiled for the camera.

'What do you mean?' Dot whispered to Grace.

'Well, you've got your honeymoon in the Highlands, right? Then nine months later you'll be stuck at home.'

'No, I won't.'

'Did I get it wrong? Are you already . . . ? You know. Is that why you didn't wear a veil?'

Dot continued to smile, trying not to ruin the photos. 'No!'

The photographer lowered his camera, he grinned, eyeing Grace's leg. 'I know you want to natter, ladies, but the faster we get through this, the faster you can get to the buffet. All right, sweethearts?'

Dot wanted to smoosh her bouquet into his face, but she simply nodded. She could feel her tethers wearing thin.

'Let's talk at the social club,' she whispered to Grace, readopting her photo pose. While she found the photographer to be intrusive, demanding and slightly pervy, he was right about the buffet.

With the photos taken, sky darkening and guests mumbling about the chilly weather, Charles opened his car door and held out his hand to Dot. Dot approached, kicking a couple of the tin cans that were strung to the bumper.

'Wifey . . .' Charles said, his best man and friends chuckling nearby. 'Shall we?'

'Yes, husband,' Dot said playfully, taking his hand and inspecting the inside of the car. She looked up to the guffawing groomsmen. 'I'm ninety-nine per cent sure there's a booby trap in here, but just reassure me that it won't damage my dress or my ego.'

The men looked disappointed.

6

'You're safe,' the best man said. 'There's nothing fishy going on.'

Charles sighed. 'You didn't?' He peered into the car and pointed to the heater, where a kipper's tail protruded from the vent.

The groomsmen burst out laughing.

'As it happens, I love the smell of smoked fish,' Dot said, sitting in the passenger seat. She pulled the kipper from the vent and sniffed it. 'Beautiful. We'll see you geniuses at the social club.'

Dot closed the car door and waved to her guests as Charles sat in the driver's seat. Outside, the best man tossed huge handfuls of coins into the air, and children appeared — as if from another dimension — to collect them.

'Thank goodness that's over!' Charles said.

'It looked like you were enjoying yourself,' Dot said.

'Looks can be deceiving. I wanted to wallop that photographer.'

Dot laughed. 'Me too! I think he had the hots for Grace.'

'I think most of the men there had the hots for Grace.'

'Most?' Dot raised an eyebrow.

'Not me, of course. I've only got eyes for one woman . . .' He leaned in and kissed her softly. 'Your mum. She looked so good in that giant purple hat. Like a Lazy Susan that had come to life.'

'Well, I suppose I can't stop true love. Or true lust. It was a short marriage, but good while it lasted. Please promise me that you'll make my mum happy.'

Charles laughed, started the car engine and revved it. The kids scattered like startled birds, their pockets heavy with gathered coins.

'Do you want to go to this wedding breakfast?' Charles

asked. 'Why don't we just drive off and live in the hills?'

'It's almost dinner time and I've only had a cup of sweet tea, so we're going to that party.'

Charles eased the car away, the tin cans rattling behind them. The guests cheered, waving goodbye. Dot wound down her window and put her hand outside, rolling it in circles as though she were royalty. As they drove into the distance, Dot's stomach rumbled.

'Forget it,' Dot said. 'It's our wedding day, let's do what we want.' She switched on the car radio and 'Get Back' by The Beatles played. She cranked up the volume and loosened her shoes, tapping her feet to the music. 'I'm hungry, and a cheese sarnie won't do it.'

'Fish and chips?' Charles asked. 'Or did the kipper trap put you off?'

'Now I know we were meant to be together.' Dot leaned her head on his shoulder. 'Fish and chips with plenty of sauce, please. The rest can wait.'

02

Old Crones & Tiny Trees

Dot refused to believe that she was the same age as the two old crones at the next table. She'd seen them at the garden centre café several times recently, and every time they had lists of complaints to share with one another, each as long as their faces.

This time, while waiting impatiently for their tea and scones, they muttered to each other while berating the young waiter: his T-shirted arms were too bare for the icy skirl of a true Scottish October; he was too chatty, or he wasn't chatty enough; he once wore stained trousers; he didn't smile enough; his smile wasn't genuine; he was almost certainly giving other customers preferential treatment while leaving *them* to rot. And so the two old women droned on, and Dot tried her hardest not to hurl a cup of tea in their faces.

Dot took a breath of chilly air while heating her lips and fingers on a cup of hot sweet tea. She tried to ignore the two crones, but she really wanted to flick sugar in their eyes, to give them a good, bone-rattling shake.

It was times like this that Dot felt like a little girl trapped inside an old woman's body.

'Oh, here comes Linford Christie, at long last!' the larger of the two crones cackled under the cowl of her winter coat.

'Don't hold your breath, he's going nowhere fast,' the smaller one said, snorting like a horse.

The young waiter delivered their tea and scones with a sweet smile, but they scowled at him.

'You forgot the sugar. How are we meant to drink tea without sugar?' the larger crone asked.

The waiter apologised and hurried back through the café's maze of plastic trees towards the kitchen.

Dot couldn't help but watch the women as they nibbled their cakes while spouting bitter words. She squirmed in her seat at how their suckling lips tightened like a cat's arse when they bemoaned the youth of today. They yacked on about how the garden centre, Edinburgh and the whole of Scotland had gone to hell in a handbag, and how nobody cared about tradition and good honest values anymore. In a word, Dot decided, they were *fusty*.

She gulped her cup of tea and gobbled her cake. Even though her mood was crummy today, she wasn't going to waste cake and risk hellfire. She scrambled through her shopping bag for her big purse, took out her tarnished golden pocket mirror and checked herself. Her eyes were bright and, most importantly, her lips looked nothing like a cat's arse.

Her purse was almost empty but she left a few coins on the table to try to compensate the waiter. She smiled at him as she left and said: 'Thank you, dear, there's a little something on the table for you. Have a nice weekend.'

'Thank you,' the waiter replied, hurrying to Dot's table.

Dot left the café, grabbed a trolley and wheeled it into the flowering-plant aisles. Her knee, which had been giving her an increasing amount of gyp lately, soon began to ache. She stopped and leaned on her trolley with a groan, staring at a row of small trees labelled *Bonsai*.

If Charles had been with her, she wouldn't have let the crones and knee aches get to her. But alone, she tended to ruminate on life's little inconveniences and irritations, which had a habit of stacking up, mounting on top of one another like circus acrobats. She didn't want to admit it, but she felt the weight of her years. She had nobody to complain to, nobody to share her aches and pains with, nobody to share her time with, nobody to laugh with. It was all amounting to be about as much fun as a clown at a funeral. Or a clown at any social gathering, really – as far as Dot was concerned, clowns could get in the bin and stay there.

She looked amongst the plants to distract herself. A sign amid the forest of tiny trees read:

Bonsai (Indoor, potted)
Bonsai trees symbolise harmony, peace, balance,
order and all that is good in nature.

Well, that was a lot of things to symbolise. The poor trees must be frantic with the symbolism and the pressure to bring balance to the world, Dot thought. In comparison to a bonsai, Dot considered, her problems seemed relatively minuscule. But then again, they didn't have iffy knees to worry about, did they?

Fake birdsong sounded from the ceiling speakers, trolleys trundled along the paved paths, children screamed and the archaic moans of the two crones grew nearer. So much for peace and harmony.

'This one's damaged!' The whinnying voice cut through the birdsong. It was the smaller crone from the café. She gripped a bonsai in her talon-like leathery hand.

A slight young man turned to face the two crones. He wore

a puke-green garden centre shirt with a badge that said: *Justin, happy to help – just ask!* He looked at the two women as though they had just trudged out of the ocean covered in seaweed and barnacles.

'Well, can you discount it? The leaves are coming off, look!' The larger woman tugged on a leaf of the bonsai and it snapped off. She shoved it under his nose. 'Look!'

'I . . . er, I can't,' the young man muttered, his face almost as green as his shirt. 'You'll have to ask a manager.'

'You ask him for us,' the smaller crone said, pushing the bonsai into his sweaty hands. 'Thank you.'

The young man walked hurriedly away with a look of relief. The two miserly women searched for more disfigured plants, or plants to disfigure, each smiling as though they loved the smell of their own farts.

'I've changed my mind,' the larger crone said to the other, once the employee had disappeared from sight. 'These little trees won't look right in my lounge. Don't you think?'

'I did think that,' the other replied. 'Let's go, before he gets back.'

Dot wondered whether she had ever been so miserly, so pedantic, so bloody annoying as those two. She prayed that nobody thought so badly of her as she thought of that draconian duo.

Someone ought to put them in their place. Someone ought to say something. Someone ought to *do* something. And Dot knew exactly what that something should be.

*

The tills rang out like church bells as Dot followed at a distance which exuded innocence, whilst still being close enough to oversee and overhear everything.

She didn't want to miss this.

The two crones shuffled past the conveyor belts at the tills, and Dot felt sure that they were chirping about how much free tea they'd managed to swindle from the café this time. They hadn't bought a thing from the shop, the cheap old gits. Not that Dot had either, but she at least hadn't been so impolite to the staff, and she had paid full price for her tea and cake.

Dot tapped a security guard on the elbow and he looked down at her.

'Excuse me, but I've seen someone trying to steal from the garden centre,' she said sweetly, adopting a slightly nervous lilt to her voice. 'I don't want to cause a fuss, but . . .'

'Thank you,' the security guard said. 'Can you show me who it is? We won't let them know you're involved.'

Dot looked towards the crones as they meandered towards the exit, chatting to each other. 'Those two women. They took some small trees and hid them inside their big shopping bags.' She prepared to put a tremble into her voice. Old women were timid, after all, weren't they? 'I . . . I think.'

'Thank you,' the guard said, walking hastily towards the exit. He waited for the crones to take a step outside the store and then intercepted them.

Dot followed, overhearing the crones shriek and grumble at the guard. He opened their bags and asked to see a receipt for the two bonsai trees in their shopping bags. But, of course, they had no receipts to show.

'Please step back inside the store,' the guard said firmly.

The crones looked thoroughly confused but obeyed the

guard, their faces as red as birthday balloons, while customers watched them and whispered to one another.

Dot held her shopping bag loosely at her side, her own stolen bonsai tree safely nestled inside it like a babe in a cot. This wasn't her first heist, after all.

She smiled as she passed the crones and the guard and exited the garden centre without a moment's fuss. A good job done.

03

The Mayor of Christmas Town

Dot placed her new bonsai amongst the other plants. Half of her living room was submerged in green leaves, and the little tree would have to work hard to be remembered, though she tried not to forget anyone.

They were all equals here, although perhaps some were more equal than others: the banana plant, for example, had started life as little more than a timid child, but had grown so tall that it touched the ceiling and had begun to spread sideways. Dot worried that, if left to its own devices, it might consume her entire lounge or even seek expansion out of the window and into the street. But she couldn't bear to part with it, and the plant was proof of her misdeeds. If plants could talk (especially to the police), she was screwed. She tried not to ignore the potential threat of Triffids.

The plant half of her living room was not the only growing problem Dot had. The left side of her lounge was also the depository for her ever-increasing Christmas village. It had started out innocently enough: Charles had bought her a light-up gingerbread house one Christmas, as a mantelpiece decoration to show off during the festivities. It was partly a joke, because he'd never really been much of a Yulephile (or a Whovillian or Santarian or Noelian – or whatever else a Christmas enthusiast might wish to be called), but he knew that Dot enjoyed it. So, perhaps rather than a joke, the light-up gingerbread house had been Charles's concession to Dot's enjoyment of Christmas. But that, too, had got out of hand.

Since Charles's passing, Dot had saved what she could to buy more Christmas centrepieces from Mini Christmas, the local all-year-round Christmas shop (yes, she had thought that was bizarre too, at first). She was the self-elected mayor of Christmas Town and, despite her best efforts to cease and desist, was hell-bent on expansion. The people of Christmas Town needed a candy cane factory. Where else would they work? The next year, the town required an ice-skating rink with tinkling music and banners of lights. After all, the residents of Christmas Town needed exercise, not only to prevent seasonal affective disorder, but also to work off some of the weight gained from eating all the candy canes from the candy cane factory.

And so it went. Piece by piece, more locations were added – more snowmen and tinsel-topped cats and rosy-cheeked children took up residence in Christmas Town, and their needs had to be met.

But Christmas Town, much like the Amazin' Rainforest on the right-hand side of her living room, didn't come cheap. And Dot didn't have many spare pennies to rub together, let alone many pots to tinkle into. So, she had to be a little more frugal. And if she was honest, really honest with herself, she liked stealing. At first, she was afraid and thought – maybe even hoped – she would be caught. At the very least, being caught would have broken the monotony of life. At least it would have made her feel like she'd done something, and it would make people notice her again.

But she wasn't caught. By her third or fourth successful theft, it had become a game to her. Over the years, the stolen items became larger, then more expensive. She'd test the perception of guards by stealing when they were nearby, or challenge herself to remove a security tag in record time.

Once, she had even managed to walk out of the garden centre with a stolen peace lily under her arm while a much younger and gruffer-looking woman was having her pram searched by the security staff. It was one of the few times that her old-lady appearance had felt like a blessing. It had made her feel superhuman, though she felt bad for the woman who'd been searched. Appearances were deceiving.

But yes, a part of her liked the rush she felt when she took something and got away with it: it was like she'd cheated the system, like she wasn't another drone in the hive – she was the bear, taking the honey. And it tasted oh, so sweet.

So, every now and again, whenever she felt downtrodden or belittled, whenever she was missing Charles or felt angry with the world (it really was a mess – she didn't remember it being so messy when she was young and felt that someone really ought to sort it all out, pronto!) she would pop out with her trusty shopping bag and take something. It was easy, and any bad feelings she had about it were quickly washed away by the thrill of it all.

But she had to be careful, too. She knew that, sooner or later, even the greatest thieves were likely to be caught. And her framing of the crones might only draw more attention to her illicit activities at the garden centre. She'd been careful to avoid the CCTV, but there were only so many risks she could take. She had to be smart.

And, unfortunately for Dot, the realisation that she should stop stealing was at odds with her desire to continue. The inhabitants of Christmas Town were very demanding – they wanted more and more from her – and the talented artists at Mini Christmas were making it hard for Dot to refuse her people's demands.

Mini Christmas had many unmonitored corners, many pocket-sized items that were easily misplaced or that had been forgotten by the staff. It made for low-hanging Christmas fruit.

'Just one more, then,' Dot said.

She fired up her computer to scour the shop's selection, which they regularly updated on their website. It was good of them to advertise their wares online, Dot thought, her eyes lighting up with the computer screen. Her heart skipped when the words *New Arrivals* appeared.

*

The microwave sang out: 'Dot, your bad lasagne is ready! It's hot on the outside and cold in the middle!'

Dot creaked up from her comfy chair, damning her knee for no ... defying gravity and medical science. Lately her kitchen had ... some more of a bacterial breeding ground than a gourmet's ... dream – she used to enjoy cooking with Charles, or for friends when they had dinner parties, but now there was no point. Dot wanted to eat great food, but the weeks-old stains on her pots and spoons were too much of a chore to bother with.

Was she depressed? *Depressed* felt a bit overused in recent years. But yes, she was depressed. She knew all the signs – she'd seen so many of the patients on her ward exhibit them, back when she was working in the hospital. She found herself in her memories and felt like she was someone almost unrecognisable now. The stains of time were on her clothes and skin, in her

18

shoes and nostrils – they distorted her view. Sometimes they were pleasant, but even a pleasant smell could turn sickly with overexposure.

Dot had noticed that she'd been sleeping more and more, and that she lacked enthusiasm for things she used to enjoy. And she missed Charles, she really missed him. She missed him so much that she could almost think of nothing else when she was alone, and so she would turn on the radio or the TV, or go to the garden centre to stew over other people, just to drown out her own thoughts and how dreadfully hungry she felt.

When Charles died, their friends had been good to her at first. They hadn't had many friends, admittedly, as they were the kind of couple who mostly kept to themselves, happy in each other's company and often irked by the habits of others. But those friends she'd held on to would drop by to see how she was coping. Not well. The visits then grew further and further apart – some visits morphed into phone calls, but those calls became briefer and briefer until they became non-existent. A few friends still invited Dot out to play cards, or to go to the cinema or for walks with the dogs, but she felt like she was an imposition. She knew she was bad company, moping and obsessed with what she'd lost, and didn't want to burden them.

And so, soon enough, Dot was alone.

Dot peeled the plastic lid off her lasagne, cursing under her breath when the cheesy béchamel steam burned her fingers, as it always did. She grabbed a slice of not-quite-stale bread and took her evening meal to her comfy seat, turning up the volume on the TV.

'Tonight . . .' the high-street-chic presenter on the television said, standing in front of a wall of numbers, 'we're visiting an iron pipe museum with a bad case of rust, and finding out how juggling can help alcoholics to recover. All this – and, of course, the big weekend lottery draw – is coming up. But first, have you ever wondered how our lottery balls are made?'

No, Dot hadn't ever considered how lottery balls were made, or how juggling might help with addiction, or why iron pipe museums were even worth saving. And, frankly, she didn't really care. It seemed to her that the lottery draw was so stretched for additional content that it was verging on becoming surrealist performance art. Why couldn't they just give money to hospitals or schools and draw the damn balls?

She blew on her forkful of overly hot, flavourless lasagne and stared down at the lottery ticket on her armrest. She'd played the lottery every week since it began, winning the occasional barely-worth-it prize, and dared not calculate how much she'd lost overall. Given the rising price of her heating bill, and the various broken things around her small house, Dot could think of a dozen things she would rather have spent the lottery ticket money on. But she always held on to a tiny slip of hope. It was possible, wasn't it? She *could* win, and then . . . well, what? She had nobody to share her winnings with anyway. Maybe she'd expand Christmas Town or buy nicer lasagnes. Maybe she should stop playing.

Dot ate her lasagne, resenting almost every bite. She mopped up the last of its sauce from the plastic container using her slice of dry bread, just as the filler segments on the lottery came to an end. She picked up her ticket and, despite not truly believing in good luck and charms, crossed her fingers.

Five of her six numbers were always the same: 5, 10, 17, 29, 50. They were her lucky (or, in reality, not particularly lucky) numbers. But she always let kismet decide the sixth number, because she didn't like the idea of repeating the same thing exactly each time. So, tonight, her sixth number was 2, because she'd foiled two old crones with two bonsai trees at the garden centre.

The balls flew around their machine of chaos and shot out of a tube. The presenter read them out.

Dot had hit one number: 29.

What a bleedin' waste.

She scrunched up her ticket and tossed it into the overflowing bin, then poured herself a big G&T and changed the channel to a horror movie, in which a killer hunted down victims with an iron pipe.

Shame the iron pipe wasn't in that museum, Dot thought: it might have gone rusty, and that would've saved a few lives.

04

Park Life

Aside from Mini Christmas and the garden centre, Dot liked to visit the local park that her dad used to take her to for picnics when she was a little girl. It had a mostly pleasant pond in the middle (though it was sometimes home to shopping trolleys) with little wooden jetties where burly men fed the ducks bread with their little girls and boys. She was sure that the pond had been larger all those years ago. It had seemed like a duck-laden ocean, ripe for exploration on a raft or canoe. A concrete path circled the pond, and there were trees around the perimeter of the park.

It was hardly the Hanging Gardens of Babylon – Dot didn't imagine that one of the Seven Wonders of the Ancient World had been littered with broken vodka bottles, loaded nappies and occasional used needles – but it was usually a nice escape from the bustle of the city and the quiet of her home.

Dot took her usual route around the pond, picking up the occasional safe piece of litter as she walked. Edinburgh's notorious wind whipped at her face, but she'd mummified herself in her thick winter coat and faux-fur-lined boots. It was only on the coldest days that the weather managed to penetrate her cocoon.

She passed the burly men and their small children feeding the ducks, smiling at the memory of doing the same with her dad. Some things hadn't changed too much, had they?

Dot's first lap of the pond was a clean-up lap. She'd collected three crisp bags, two chocolate wrappers, a beer can and an empty soft drink bottle, but left a mystery plastic bag that swarmed with flies. Whatever was inside the bag, she'd decided, couldn't be good. There was far too much litter for Dot to collect, but she liked to do her bit.

Her second walk around the pond was just for pleasure. She passed dog walkers, hoping the cutest pooches would come and say hello. She carried a few treats in her coat pockets just in case they were hungry, and they usually were. The dog owners rarely said much, if anything, though, and it seemed to Dot that they were always in a hurry. So, instead of talking to them, she would stroke their dogs and imagine their lives.

The Dobermann's owner, a tall woman with a fringe, was a party planner because she wore glittery false nails. And she must have been strong to keep her big, excitable dog under control, so she probably worked out. Yes, this woman lifted weights. Big ones.

The Jack Russell's owner wasn't much younger than Dot, but she looked like a miserable git who smoked like a stack of Victorian chimneys. She always hurried her dog along, not even letting him stop to wee and sniff and do other important dog duties. She was an ex-dinner lady, Dot imagined, who used to eat the chips when the kids weren't looking. The dog was a yappy little blighter, but then Dot would be too if she had to live with such a sour-faced woman.

It was true, Dot thought, what folk said about owners and their dogs: they were similar to one another. She didn't blame the dogs, though – she was sure that the owners' traits rubbed off on the pups over time. Nice owner, nice dog. That was usually the rule, and the inverse was almost certainly true.

The winter air took it out of Dot, so she stopped at her favourite bench to catch her breath and to give her dodgy knee a break. Like all the other benches in the park, this one had a bronze plaque to indicate that it had been dedicated to the memory of someone who had passed. Dot enjoyed the whimsy of this bench's dedication:

In memory of John C
Who liked ducks more than most people

It was hardly the joke of the century, but Dot liked the double meaning.

The ducks were a pleasant bunch – she didn't have a bad word to say about them. Not like the swans. She regularly watched the swans chase and attack the geese, willing the geese to fight back. She wished the geese could form a union to fight against the swans' oppressive regimes. But they never did. And today was no different, as the swans were rampaging through the water to terrorise the foreign visitors. Those mean white hoodlums really had it coming to them, sooner or later.

Dot dipped her hands into her pockets to keep them warm, and her fingertips rubbed against a slip of paper. She took the incomplete lottery numbers form out of her pocket. Of course, her usual numbers (5, 10, 17, 29, 50) had already been chosen for this week's draw, but she had yet to decide on her final number. She considered choosing the number 7, recalling the Christmas song in which seven swans were *a-swimming*, but didn't want to give the swans the satisfaction.

Musing on her potential final number, she saw something she'd never seen in her park before: a group of six young men and women, each around fifteen to nineteen years old, at a guess. Each wore a fluorescent yellow bib that said *Community Service* on the front and back.

The bibbed teens looked highly unimpressed with their outing, scowling and checking their phones. They reluctantly followed a Buddha-bellied bald man in his mid-fifties to the edge of the pond, where he handed them each a thick black bin bag and a litter-picker. He watched them in silence as they searched the perimeter of the pond, occasionally placing pieces of rubbish into their bin bags.

'Oi, sir,' a hoop-earringed girl said, her face screwed up like she'd been chewing on vinegar-soaked hornets. 'We've been cleaning this place for ever and it's Baltic here. I can't feel my hands!'

'Keep working, you'll soon warm up,' the bald man said.

'What about you, then?' a lanky boy with an oil spill of a haircut called out. 'Why are *we* doing all the work?'

'I didn't get caught breaking the law,' the bald man said. 'But you can moan in court instead, if you prefer.'

'Siiiir,' the hoop-earringed girl moaned. 'Didn't get caught, aye? I bet you've been up to some right dodgy stuff, haven't you, sir? Come on, tell us.'

'I've got to make a call. Keep working,' he replied sternly, turning away and holding his phone to his ear.

They searched the pond-side, but Dot could tell that they weren't really working. Two girls walked together, chatting and laughing. Two of the boys waved their litter-pickers at the swans, and the birds hissed at them.

One boy – a tall, nice-looking lad with a soft, almost sorrowful expression – walked alone, doing as he had been told. He was only wearing a red football shirt underneath his yellow bib and had a black woollen hat on his head. He occasionally glanced at the others from afar, turning away from them whenever it looked as though they might catch him looking.

Dot kept her hands warm under her armpits, watching the boy in the football shirt fill his bag with rubbish. The other teens returned to their starting point, huddled together and moaned to one another.

'There's a bike in the pond here,' the boy in the football shirt shouted back to the group. 'Can someone help me get it out?'

'Errr, nah, mate! You do it!' the boy with oil-spill hair shouted back.

The gaggle of teens laughed, and the boy turned back to the submerged bicycle in the pond, staring at it.

'Oi, Max!' the hoop-earring girl yelled.

The boy turned, his worried expression fading as his eyes brightened. 'Yeah?'

'Is this yours?' the girl said. She held her litter-picker high in the air, a worryingly heavy condom dangling from its metallic hand.

Max shook his head and turned away, a cloud of white water vapour erupting from his mouth as he cursed under his breath.

The girl drew her raised litter-picker back like a tennis racket, preparing to serve. 'Tidy up after yourself, Max, you beast!'

She swung her raised arm forward, releasing the litter-picker's grip. The filled condom flew through the air towards Max.

Dot opened her mouth to warn him, but she was too slow. The condom fell just short of Max's head, slopping on the back of his jeans and falling to the ground.

Max turned and looked down at the condom, his face filled

with horror. He glared at the girl, his nostrils flaring.

'Bitch!' Max shouted.

The girl laughed like a hyena on nitrous oxide. The others followed suit.

Max's handsome face turned ugly. His hands balled into fists. He tossed his rubbish bag to the floor, spilling its contents.

'All right, that's *enough*!' the bald man snapped, putting his phone into his pocket. 'Tanya, that's your second red mark. One more, and you're out. Got it?'

'It's not me who's leaving johnnies in the park for little kids to find!' hoop-earring girl said. 'It's Max, he's a dirty beast, sir!'

'I've had enough of you lot,' the bald man said. He looked at his watch. 'Well, we covered enough of the park for today, and that's time anyway. I'll see you all tomorrow – don't be late again.'

Dot watched Max. He took long, deep breaths, and his fists slowly unfolded as if he'd been rehearsing how to de-escalate himself. Dot had seen similar practices on her ward, often with ex-soldiers who struggled with stress.

Good lad, Dot thought, hoping the swans would take umbrage with earring girl and peck at her feet. A good old swanning was what that girl needed.

Aside from Max, who remained where he was, the teens de-bibbed and tossed their fluorescent tops at the bald man. They placed their litter-pickers into his backpack and dropped their almost-empty rubbish bags next to a park bin before walking off together, their laughs echoing from afar.

The bald man approached Max. 'You can't let them get to you. You're doing well otherwise. Just control your anger, okay?'

Max bowed his head, his nostrils still flared. He took another deep breath. 'Okay.'

'Good. Now pick up this mess, and you can head home. You live nearby, right?'

Max nodded. He removed his bib and handed it to the man along with his litter-picker.

'I'll see you tomorrow,' the bald man said. 'Be on time, or it's an automatic red mark.' He walked away, putting his phone to his ear again.

Dot watched Max collect the rubbish he'd dropped on the ground, including the condom. He tied his bulging bin bag and placed it beside the others at the bin.

Show's over, Dot thought, feeling her incomplete lottery numbers form in her pocket. She prepared to stand up from the bench, her knee aching with the cold, but stopped when she saw Max open a small metal gate in the fence surrounding the pond.

Max stepped through the gate and reached into the pond, pulling on a bicycle wheel just under the water. He grunted, swearing to himself as he walked backwards and drew the bike out of the pond. He wheeled the bike out of the gate and leaned it against the fence. He looked around cautiously.

Max caught Dot's eye. She didn't look away.

'Need a bike?' Max asked. 'It's a bit broken.'

'No, thanks,' Dot said.

Max nodded. 'Maybe some kid will take it, then.'

He turned away from Dot and began walking, and she read the back of his football shirt:

Ronaldo

7

She took a miniature blue pen from her pocket and chose her final lottery number for the week's draw: 7.

Max whistled to himself as he continued to walk away. Perhaps it was something about his gait, or his soft manner, or his work ethic, or the way he tried to control his anger . . . she couldn't be sure why, but something about Max reminded Dot of her dad, and she liked him all the more for it.

05

Lucky Number Ten

Lottery number 10

(Dot is ten years old)

Dot had barely slept a wink. She'd counted sheep, whispered to God (who didn't respond – perhaps He was trying to sleep, too) and even closed her eyes as tight as she could to pretend she was dead. None of it had helped, and so the night felt like a thousand dull-as-dishwater nights rolled into one.

When the sun finally peeked through her curtains, enough was enough. She flew from her room and climbed into her parents' bed, shocking them awake with cold feet on warm bellies.

'There's something special about today, isn't there? I can't quite remember . . .' her dad said, his face so serious that for a dreadful second she thought that he'd truly forgotten. But his mask cracked and he let out a cheeky monkey grin. 'Ah yes, Dotty's birthday. The big one-oh. My little girl's hit the lucky number ten.'

He tickled her, his fingers like sausages on her thin arms, and she screeched with laughter.

Dot's mum got up to make a special birthday breakfast of eggs and soldiers. Dot dressed quickly and sat at the table. She and her dad arranged the soldiers by rank, helmeting their heads in the yolk before they got too cold, then Dot opened her cards and presents: a red tasselled scarf (doubly disappointing, partly because it was spring, but mainly because she'd been hoping for one of the polka-dotted dresses she'd seen on television), a chocolate bar (YEEEESSSS!) and a mystery gift that her dad rooted out from the sewing box.

'You're ten now, and that means you have to help around the house a bit more,' her dad said. 'That's why we got you this grown-up present, okay?'

He'd asked, as though the present would only be given to her if she agreed to his terms. She would have agreed to anything to get the present – she would even have agreed to clean his big black work boots.

'Okay then,' her dad said, handing her the box and smiling.

Dot peeled back the sticky tape and unfolded the flowery paper like the delicate wings of a butterfly.

The box was black with a gold trim. It was the kind of box that very posh ladies might keep in a drawer, or inside an even lovelier box that played tinkling music when you opened it. It was the kind of box that she knew must contain something very precious. Something just for her.

Dot opened the box.

Inside was a silvery oval attached to a chain. The surface was smooth, and Dot almost didn't want to touch it for fear of tarnishing it with her fingerprints, but she did.

'Open it,' her dad said. 'There's a little clip on the side.'

Dot pushed on the clip and her gift opened to reveal a tiny

photograph of her dad in his smart army hat and uniform, his jacket heavy with medals.

'It's you!' Dot said, rubbing her finger over the thin glass that covered the photo.

She expected him to say something, maybe to crack a joke or ruffle her hair, but he just sniffed quietly and had a glazed look on his face, like he'd turned into a ventriloquist's dummy for a few seconds.

'It's a locket – put it on her,' Dot's mum said.

Her dad placed the chain around Dot's neck and the locket hung heavy on her chest. When she stood up or walked, or leaned in a certain way, she felt it thud against her like a second heartbeat.

'Now, get ready,' her dad said, his face returning to normal again. 'We're going out, just you and me.'

Dot jumped up excitedly, running to put on her shoes. 'Where are we going? Why just us two?'

'It's a father–daughter day out,' he said. 'Mum has . . . things to do. She'll see us when we're back.' He wrapped a coat around Dot, even though it was springtime and too warm for her thick coat.

'Don't fill up on rubbish,' her mum said. 'We'll get fried fish tonight.'

Dot squealed, almost drooling. 'And chips and sauce?!'

'And chips and sauce.' Her mum kissed her on the forehead, then hugged Dot's dad and whispered: 'It'll be fine.'

★

Dot often took the bus to her aunt's house, or to see her gran, or to visit the shops. But this bus was different – it was heading out of the city, away from her usual stops at the museum or gallery, or the impossibly long gardens along Princes Street where beautiful girls had picnics together and boys played guitars.

Her birthday locket *rapa-tap-tapp*ed on the window as she peered out at the people outside, who walked in busy lines like ants looking for jam sandwiches. The bus got fuller and louder with kids and parents, and Dot couldn't help imagining what kind of place they might be going to: perhaps to the beach, where she'd dig the deepest hole and build the grandest castle; or to the woods, where she'd capture insects to take home as pets and frighten her mum.

But soon enough she had her answer. She heard the playful music first, then saw the white- and red-striped pointed hats of the tents. Her heart beat so fast that it felt like a bird was trapped in her chest.

'Roll up, roll up!' a moustached man said, juggling balls and wearing a hat so tall that it reminded Dot of a chimney.

Dot's dad held her hand as they marched towards the wooden kiosk. He paid to pass through the big golden gate, taking a few papery ticket stubs from a smiling woman.

They walked into a field where kids screamed on rides and pretty ladies in stripy dresses ate pink clouds on sticks. The air smelled of sugar and sounded like happiness.

'Happy birthday, Dotty,' Dot's dad said as a big pink cat strolled behind him, waving to kids and speaking in meows.

It was the best place Dot had ever been. Turning ten really must be a big deal, she decided.

Dot watched the rollercoaster fly along its rickety wooden slats-on-stilts with a mixture of excitement and dread.

'Do you want to try it?' her dad asked, holding out a ticket for her to take.

Dot shook her head. 'Not on my own.'

'Then I'll come, too,' he said, looking around. 'But I need the toilet – just wait in the queue and I'll be right back. And, Dotty, I'm a bit afraid of this coaster, so hold my hand and sit close, all right?'

Dot nodded.

Dot's dad walked to the toilets as she stood in the queue to board the rollercoaster, surrounded by tall, rough boys.

She listened to the music and screams, trying not to think too hard about how fast and rickety the ride might be, and hoping that her dad would get back soon. The rollercoaster pulled into its station and a new set of passengers jumped into its seats. Dot moved forward in the queue, looking back for her dad as more older boys joined behind her.

'This ride isn't for little girls,' a large boy ahead of her said.

'I'm ten,' Dot said defiantly. She stared directly into the boy's eyes, like she had once stared down a mangy dog who'd wanted to eat her sandwiches at the beach.

The boy shrugged, turned to his friends and lowered his voice: 'I bet she screams.'

The boys laughed, looking down at Dot.

'She'll ride whatever she likes,' her dad said, standing beside her. He held her hand a bit tighter than before, and his face was red. 'Got it?'

The boy's face turned school-chalk white. He nodded. He and his friends were silent as the queue shortened and they loaded onto the coaster.

'Ready?' Dot's dad asked, squeezing in close to her.

Dot wrapped her arms around him. 'I'm afraid.'

'Me too. But we just have to be brave, and in a moment we'll be enjoying ourselves.'

Dot nodded and thought that her dad really was the best person she'd ever known. The rollercoaster shook and flew like a rocket, and as it turned the sharp corners Dot was crushed into the side of her dad. But she didn't mind, she loved the speed and that it took her breath away, and she laughed when the boys from the queue screamed around the fastest corners.

The ride was over all too soon. Dot ran straight back to the end of the queue.

'Let's go again!' Dot beamed at her dad as he followed behind. He was a little wobbly and his face was pale.

'That's enough for me.' He put an arm over her shoulder. 'Aren't you happy you didn't listen to those boys, that you tried it for yourself?'

Dot nodded, smiling at the boys as they passed her, each of them even wobblier and even paler-faced than her dad.

He leaned down and whispered in her ear: 'Never let anyone else tell you what to do. Okay? I've always got your back, I'm always here.' He tapped the locket hanging around her neck. 'Even if I'm not at home.' He stared into her eyes. 'I have to go away for a while.'

Dot felt herself sinking into the ground, and the happy buzz of the fairground shrank.

'Where? Why?' she asked.

'Abroad, for work. People need our help.'

'Is it dangerous?'

He stroked her hair. 'Sometimes. But I'll do my best to make it safe again. While I'm gone, I need you to help your mum, okay? She has a lot of work to do, and you're ten now. Lucky number ten.' He ruffled her hair and kissed her cheek. 'Keep the house shipshape and Bristol fashion, that's an order.' He smiled, saluting to her.

She saluted back. 'Aye, sir!'

'Good.' He straightened back up, pulling her towards the

carousel where painted horses leapt through the air. 'My turn to pick the ride.'

They rode rides until the sun began to fall, eating popcorn and candyfloss but not ruining their appetite for the fish and chips with sauce that would be waiting on the table for them when they got home.

And that was the last day Dot and her dad ever spent together.

06

Fish Day

The midweek passed as monotonously as any other for Dot, but she had something to look forward to because it was Friday, and – as tradition happily dictated – Friday was Fish Day.

Dot put on her cocoon of clothes, locked her front door and walked towards the old chippie (the very same shop her parents used to buy from when she was little). She could almost smell the fat in her nostrils, almost taste the salt and vinegar on her tongue, almost feel the grease in her veins and the shooting pain down her arm. Glorious. Had Dot been a dog, she would almost certainly have been drooling and wagging her tail.

The chippie sat at the top of the hill. It was along a pot-holed road, and the incline made the journey a little harder each year for Dot, and even more so if the pavement was slippery. But almost nothing would prevent Dot from getting her Friday fish.

Dot puffed and panted her way up the hill as though she'd been smoking twenty roll-ups a day, even though she had barely touched cigarettes her whole life. She'd held the hands of far too many heavy smokers on her ward.

Walking up the hill, she imagined a hook in her mouth and a fishing line pulling her onward. Cars sped past her, breathing clouds of noxious fumes into the cold air. A car would have made her weekly commute so much simpler, and she used to love driving to the countryside with Charles, but cars were expensive – and Dot wasn't convinced she was cut out to be a car thief.

She stopped for a breather at a set of traffic lights, waiting for her turn to cross. Her old primary school watched her from across the road. A group of teens loitered in the school playground, passing a glass bottle between them and taking swigs and shouting swear words at the cars driving by.

Dot wasn't scared of the teenagers who hung around in the streets, but she knew they bothered other people – she regularly perused the local neighbourhood forums online, and teenagers were frequently a hot topic, usually for all the wrong reasons.

Part of Dot wanted to tell them to move on and find something worthwhile to do, to tell them that they were wasting their time and that time was precious. But Dot knew there weren't many options for kids their age – the council had cut funding to parks and youth centres, rejected plans to build a cinema and even abandoned a skate park when it was half-completed.

The usual 'money doesn't grow on trees' excuses were given, but then a forest of money trees was suddenly found when it came to private housing projects and wage increases for more senior members of the council. Dot had started to write a letter of complaint but gave up, sure that the words of a random older woman would amount to diddly-squat.

So, she couldn't blame those teens for loitering, could she? If a few swigs of vodka and a few shared profanities made their lives a little more bearable, she understood. In fact, she might have joined them if she wouldn't have seemed insane, and if the smell of freshly fried fish hadn't drawn her away.

Dot placed her order (cod and chips, salt and vinegar and plenty of sauce) and sat at a table near the window. Warm, chip-scented air swam around her, and a neon fish sign flashed blue light into her face. She closed her eyes and drew the aroma deep inside, to prepare her stomach for salty, saucy heaven.

She estimated that the man who had owned the fish shop when she was young, Mister Fish − was that his real name, or just a nickname her dad had made up? She'd never know − would be over a hundred years old now, but either way, his retirement was legitimate. She would allow it. The new owners, an Eastern European couple who seemed much too thin and attractive to run a chippie, were polite to her, even if they lacked the friendly familiarity of Mister Fish.

Dot opened the locket around her neck. Her dad's picture had barely faded in all those years.

She felt like a little girl again whenever she was in the chip shop. She felt a rush of excitement when the chips were poured into the fat and let out a raucous sizzle. She enjoyed seeing the week's newspapers stacked on the windowsill, and she liked turning to see who was entering whenever the bell above the door tinkled, hoping it would be someone she recognised. Despite its changes, the chippie felt like a portal back in time, a safe place.

The bell above the door rang. Dot tucked her locket under the padded collar of her coat and looked up to see two men, both around twenty years old and each with a hazy, drunken look. They were tall, with shaved heads and heavy bags under their eyes which made them look like they'd risen from the grave. They lurched towards the chippie counter, having left the door open behind them, causing an Arctic air to prowl through the shop.

Dot stood up and closed the door behind them, biting her lip to prevent herself from asking whether they'd been born in barns. She returned to her seat, hoping her passive-aggressive door-closing had been duly noted.

'Two cod and chips, large,' the more muscular of the two men said, slurring his words slightly.

'It'll be a five-minute wait. Is that okay?' the owner asked.

'I'm starving. What about that one?' Muscle Man pointed to a battered fish that rested in the heated counter, glistening in its golden light.

The owner shook his head, then nodded in Dot's direction. 'It's taken.'

'Well, we're in a hurry,' the man said. He opened a can of beer he had in his coat pocket and took a swig from it. He glared at Dot. 'You don't mind, do you darlin'?'

'Let's leave it, let's wait,' his thin, denim-jacketed friend said.

'No, I'm fucking hungry! You wait, I'll have this one that's ready, all right?' the man growled as his friend retreated to an empty table .

'As I said, it's a five-minute wait,' the owner said firmly. He took Dot's fish from the heated counter and placed it on a plate.

Muscle Man downed the rest of his beer and tossed the can at an open bin, missing it. The can clattered on the floor. He burped and went to sit at the table with his friend.

The owner shook his head and sighed.

'You should clean this place up! It's a fucking state, mate!' Muscle Man said, laughing to himself.

The owner continued to dish up Dot's meal.

'You hear me?' Muscle Man snapped at the owner, turning in his seat.

The owner ignored him and continued to work.

Dot stared at her tabletop, her hands shaking. She'd seen men explode over nothing before, especially after they'd had a few drinks. She willed him to be quiet and to leave. She willed his friend to intervene before the situation escalated, or for the man to laugh and apologise.

'I said you should clean this fucking place up!' the man repeated, louder. 'You're a fucking mess. Don't you fucking ignore me – I pay your wages, mate! Pick my can up and give me that fucking fish.'

'Leave,' the owner said. 'Or I'll call the police.'

Muscle Man stood up, marched over to the chip shop owner and slammed his fist on the counter. Dot noticed that the knuckles of his right hand were tattooed poorly with the letters *D.A.D.*

The owner shuddered and the till rang. Muscle Man looked as though he might reach across the counter and take Dot's fish from the plate with his bare hands, but he sniffed and turned to his friend, who was still sat at the table.

'Fuck this place,' Muscle Man said. 'I'm not eating here. It's filthy. Let's fucking go, I want another drink.'

He walked to the door and looked at Dot. Her heart felt like it had stopped, and she took a shallow breath and held it, avoiding the man's eyes. 'Don't eat here, love, it's shit.'

The two men left, slamming the door behind them.

Dot heard the men's muffled laughter through the closed window as they walked away from the shop. She could barely breathe. She took out her locket and pressed it into her palm, closed her eyes and counted slowly to ten.

'I'm sorry for that,' the owner said, placing her meal on the table. 'Thugs. Are you okay?'

'Yes, love,' Dot said, not wanting to seem as shaken as she

41

was. 'I'm sorry you had to put up with that nonsense.'

'It happens.' He smiled, clearly a little shaken himself. 'Too often. But they're all talk.' He pointed to a small plate of bread and butter. 'That's on the house, and I'll get you a cup of tea. Do you like milk and sugar?'

It was kind of him. He didn't have to do any of this, Dot thought. She shouldn't deny his kindness – it felt like a rarity lately.

'Yes. Thank you,' Dot said.

The owner returned to his counter and turned on the kettle.

Dot hated how she felt, how those men had made her feel. She wished she had done something, that she'd stood up to them. But what could she do?

Dot let her meal sit for a while, until she felt more settled. She tried to eat, but she felt sick with nerves, worrying that the two men might return. She hated them for what they'd done, for the power they'd held over the owner, and for ruining the one part of her week that she looked forward to.

07

A Night to Remember

By the time Dot had managed to finish her meal (she wasn't going to waste it, no matter how little appetite she had left), it had turned dark outside. She thanked the owner, and he asked if she was okay and if she wanted him to call her a taxi, but she refused. She wasn't about to be frightened into avoiding the streets she grew up on – not by a couple of bullies, not by anyone. She zipped up her cocoon and stepped into the glow of the flickering streetlights.

Dot had never been easily scared – it was something she prided herself on. When the other nurses had recoiled at the sight of blood and bone, Dot had been the first to a patient's side with calm words and bandages. She'd held the hands of dying men who cried for their mothers, seen surgical wounds unstitch themselves and release all manner of horrors, treated glassed faces and hammer-beaten women. She'd faced them all with a smile, false or otherwise, because she knew that under all the bravado and show, everyone was just a frail human brimming with fears and insecurities. They were no different to her: probably no worse, and certainly no better.

And so Dot walked towards home at her usual pace, purposefully making sure she didn't rush or slow, that she stayed on her usual path near the road, looking down the hill at the busy houses with their brightly lit windows staring up at her.

She reached the crossing near her old school. The teens were gone now, and it bolstered her to think she'd stayed out later than them. What a rebel.

The traffic lights changed and Dot crossed, making good progress. A quiet screech sounded above her and she thought she caught sight of a bat flapping through the sky, but it was too quick for her to be sure. Even a winged rat of the night couldn't shake her steely resolve.

Halfway down the hillside, she neared the gates of the cemetery. Charles was elsewhere because this ground felt far too close to home. She had friends buried there, though, and her parents were laid together, deep inside, behind iron gates and past rows of stone. They were there if she needed them.

Up ahead, in the shadows cast by the stone arch of the cemetery gate, Dot could hear someone speaking.

'Don't take it all, you greedy shit,' a familiar voice said. A ghoulish face with tired eyes turned, half-caught in the lights of a passing car. It was the thug from the chip shop. He whispered: 'Shh, quick.'

She couldn't stay put. She couldn't turn back. Dot continued to walk down the hill.

Muscle Man turned as she walked by, his shoulder knocking into hers.

Dot held a shriek inside and continued to walk.

'Oi!' the man shouted after her.

She could hear footsteps quickening behind her. She picked up her pace.

'Oi, you!' the man yelled.

His hand gripped her shoulder and she froze. He stepped in front of her.

'You're from the chippie!' he said, not entirely unpleasantly. 'Did you eat there?' He wiped a finger under his nose and sniffed.

Dot knew the elsewhere look on his face. She'd treated plenty of drug-users before.

'I . . .' she started, her heart pounding. 'I'm on my way home now. To my son.'

'All right, don't shit your pants,' the man said, his pupils so large that his eyes looked black. 'On your way, then. Watch out, there are some nasty sorts around here.' He looked to his gaunt friend and smirked.

Dot stepped around Muscle Man, catching the friend's gaze as she did so. He looked at her purse and she clutched at her neck, where her silver locket nestled beneath her coat. His jaw was slack and eyes vacant.

She walked on, trying not to stumble or look panicked, trying to breathe normally, but the cold air felt stagnant in her lungs and throat.

She heard whispers and footsteps behind her.

'Hold on,' Muscle Man said.

But she didn't stop, she carried on, choking out the only words she could muster: 'Leave me alone!'

Dot felt the crook of a strong arm wrap around her neck, and she gasped for breath. She tried to call out, but no voice could escape, and she was dragged backwards into the shadows, her feet sliding along the ground.

She kicked but struck nothing. She tried to fling an elbow out behind her, but the impact was too soft to register. Her body wouldn't respond properly, and they dragged her through the gateway into the cemetery, out of sight.

Dot tried to shout, but a hand covered her mouth and then a fist cracked her ribs. She crashed to the cold ground and felt a sharp pain on her forehead, a warm liquid running down her face as she lay gasping on the grass. A heavy weight pushed down on her back, squeezing the last air out of her.

Aside from the distant hum of traffic, the only noise Dot could hear was the men's deep, calm breaths, their muffled grunts like those of hungry dogs as they searched her.

She could only feel the pain of her injuries, the strap of her handbag slipping from her shoulder and, worst of all, the chill of their fingertips on her neck.

They snapped the chain of her locket and took it, leaving her utterly alone as they fled into the dark night.

*

The world was cold and bible-black.

Dot wondered whether she was dead – but then if she was dead, would she be able to wonder about it? So, she was either alive or in Limbo or Hell, because this couldn't be Heaven. Then she felt the sharp pain in her chest return and spread through her bones. It was like having a tooth extracted, but through her entire body.

She screamed but could only hear herself cry and wheeze.

Damn, so she was alive after all, and in bad shape. She took a few deep breaths, and the pain subsided a little. She opened her eyes and could barely see the ground in front of her nose, but she felt sure she was still in the cemetery and it was still night-time.

She tried to bend her fingers but they were too cold to respond at first. Eventually, despite the sporadic pain and numbness, she managed to dip her hand into her pocket to find her mobile phone.

But the thugs had taken that, too.

There was no way she was getting up from such a beating on her own, and she knew it. She had to get help, because if she stayed on the cold ground all night, she was done for.

She focused on catching her breath, on trying to calm herself. She told herself that she was alive, none of her injuries were likely to be critical, and she was in a public place near a road. All she had to do was to be found.

She tried to move her body but it refused. This damn sack-of-potatoes body! Do something, move!

But it wouldn't. She was trapped inside it as it throbbed and stabbed with a terrible pain that made her wish she'd pass out.

Dot took as deep a breath as she could, her lungs pushing against her broken rib as they inflated, then screamed: 'HEEEEEELP.' She was dismayed by how quiet she sounded, however, and how loud the cars on the road were. Unless someone was close by, the traffic would probably drown out her call. And even if someone heard her, they might not respond.

Dot's vision blurred and she felt sleepy. She wanted to just lay her head at the foot of a grave and take a nap, but she knew she shouldn't, she couldn't . . .

She passed out.

★

Warmth and light covered Dot like a blanket. She felt no pain, no fear.

'Hello,' a familiar voice sounded. Charles's voice. It was him! He was here! His face appeared in front of hers, wreathed in a golden halo. He smiled.

She smiled back. 'Hello.'

Charles's hair lengthened. The white light around him began to change colour, turning aquamarine, then electric blue. He looked so angelic. Had she made it to Heaven?

'I've got her!' Charles said, his voice deepening. 'Can you tell me your name?'

What kind of question was that? Of course she could. But had he forgotten her? Was that what happened when you died, your memories were altered or erased?

'Dot. Charles, I—'

'We need the stretcher,' Charles said, his voice taking on a Jamaican lilt. His face was much darker than she remembered, his eyes were much browner. 'Dot, listen to me. We're going to help you.'

The blue light expanded around Charles, and Dot could see other angels around him, all of them dressed in dark green. Their wings shrank into their bodies.

'What . . . where?' Dot uttered.

If this was a trick, she'd be having words with God.

'Charles?' Dot asked.

'No, love,' Charles said, but he looked nothing like himself now. His hair was long and brown; his face was someone else's entirely. 'I'm Ben. You've had an accident, we're going to take you to the hospital.' She felt a mask being placed on her face. 'Breathe normally.'

Dot's vision began to return to normal, like someone was adjusting the contrast on her TV set. The paramedics rolled a stretcher towards her and placed their hands softly under her. As they lifted her, Dot's body filled with pain again and she grunted, trying not to scream out.

A woman and her little dog stood beside the ambulance, its blue light glowing on their faces. Dot recognised the dog first: a Jack Russell. The dog's owner was the sour-faced, chain-smoking, miserable git she always saw and disregarded at the park.

'Will she be okay?' the woman asked, a concerned look on her face.

Dot didn't hear the paramedic's response.

'Thank you,' Dot uttered to the woman as the paramedics began rolling her stretcher into the ambulance.

08

White Sheets

Dot had thought about her death a lot, perhaps more than most people. Not in a morose way, usually, but just that death was inevitable – she wondered how it might happen, and what might follow. Now that she was laid up in a hospital bed, she had plenty of time to think about mortality.

When a new patient was wheeled onto the ward, Dot guessed what their medical problem was and, if she later overheard something about their condition, would reward herself with a jelly baby (the ward staff had handed out bags of the candied infants as a special weekend treat) for each correct guess and vaguely correct guess.

In films, people die in extreme ways: gunshots, sunken ships and broken hearts. But in reality, most people get old, go to sleep and just never wake up. Seeing so many people die had made death seem much more normal to Dot, much more like a regular, natural thing to happen. And it was.

In comparison to the fiction, the reality of death didn't seem so bad.

Her real problem wasn't with death, but with living. With so much time in bed to reflect, she couldn't deny that her life was unhappy and she wished it could change. She was poor, for starters, and that made even simple things more difficult: she couldn't travel, couldn't buy her favourite foods or even turn the heating on for long when it got cold at home. She certainly couldn't afford to spend a day in a luxury spa to let her troubles melt away under a lemon-scented face mask, which she'd heard some of the doctors talking about when they passed on their rounds.

And she was lonely, too. Her parents were gone, her husband was gone, her friends were mostly estranged or far away, sick or busy with their own families and problems. Though she didn't really want anybody to see her like this either, bruised and beaten, vulnerable.

It was actually nice to be in a hospital filled with busy people, where friendly professionals took care of her and took an interest in her for once. As pathetic as that might seem to some people, Dot enjoyed being in hospital. It was something *different* and, in a bizarre way, it was exciting to her, especially when the police visited.

'How are you feeling?' the police officer asked, smiling warmly but not too warmly, like she was making sure she looked concerned rather than happy. 'Can you tell me what happened?'

Dot reconstructed the scene and told the officer every little detail she could recall about her attackers. She couldn't quite remember their clothing as it was dark, but perhaps the chippie had CCTV or the owner could give extra details.

'I think they were taking drugs,' Dot said. 'And they liked battered fish. A lot. Maybe even more than battered women.'

She laughed to herself, but it hurt her ribs. She wasn't sure that the fish detail would prove particularly helpful but it couldn't hurt, could it?

The officer nodded, taking notes and asking if Dot could remember their accents, anything about their size, if she knew them, if they said anything that stood out, what items they took from her.

Her locket. They'd taken her dad's locket. And her purse and mobile phone, but she only cared about the locket. It felt like they'd stolen her childhood – they'd taken her dad from her all over again.

'I just hope you find them before I do,' Dot said, raising a fist and shaking it. She chuckled but winced at the pain the chuckles caused.

'We'll do whatever we can,' the officer said. 'These things take time, but we'll get in touch with you when we know more. Take care, Mrs Hindley.'

Dot liked the officer a lot. She did her job but seemed kind and interested in Dot's well-being. With the news constantly spouting tales of demise and disorder, it was sometimes easy to forget that strangers were people, too, and that kind people existed. Dot enjoyed the reminder.

★

Two jelly-heavy days passed under observation, but Dot knew her hospital clock was ticking. She'd been incredibly lucky – there was nothing seriously wrong with her, despite the ordeal – and there was little they could do about her broken rib.

So, Dot thanked the staff, said goodbye to a few of the friendlier patients who'd not farted too many times in her direction, and checked out with a bag full of painkillers, antiseptic creams and a reminder to take things easy.

Outside of the white walls of the hospital, Dot felt suddenly like a fox being released back into the wild. Her ears were pricked, her tail twitched. Sniffing the air for predators, she scurried to the taxi rank.

'Where can I take you?' the taxi driver asked through the open window.

Dot ached as she got into the taxi and told the driver her address. It was an unusually warm and sunny day for October, and Dot noticed that the streets were especially busy with shoppers. She thought she recognised the gait and silhouettes of her attackers as they drove – she thought she saw the cold eyes of those terrible men – but they were just regular shoppers.

The taxi driver whistled a jaunty tune, occasionally looking back at Dot in his mirror, as if checking up on her.

'Nice day,' the driver eventually said.

Dot opened her mouth but no words came out. Her attackers' faces flashed in her mind – she felt their boots and hands on her, crushing her chest. Her heart began to race.

Speak! Speak! She struggled to catch her breath and felt dizzy.

'Are you okay?' the driver asked. 'Do you want me to stop, or go back to the hospital?'

'I . . .' Dot closed her eyes and took a deep breath, blotting out her racing thoughts. 'I'm okay.' She felt a burning sensation in her stomach rise up her throat and she threw up on the taxi floor.

The taxi pulled over and Dot stared at an interior sign:

Clean up fee: £50 minimum

Oh God, no. She couldn't even afford the taxi fare, let alone the clean-up fee. She'd only just realised her predicament: her muggers had taken her purse and phone; she didn't have a penny on her and would have to cancel her bank cards. Well, she had nothing in her account to steal, at least, so the joke was on the muggers, however unfunny the joke was.

The driver got out of the taxi and opened the passenger door.

'I'm so sorry,' Dot said, hoping he wouldn't be mad with her. 'I'll pay you, I promise, but . . .' She took another long breath and swallowed a mouthful of acidic saliva.

'It's all right, love, relax,' the driver said. He pulled a paper bag from the seat pocket in front of Dot and opened it for her. 'Here.'

'My purse was stolen, and I didn't mean to make a mess,' Dot said, staring into the chasm of the paper bag.

'It's okay. Don't worry about the floor. It's seen much worse, and at least you're not another drunken idiot who's regurgitated a doner kebab with garlic mayo!' He placed a gentle hand on her shoulder, and she felt her nausea fade. 'Are you okay? I'll take you back to the hospital, no charge.'

'No, I'm fine. Thank you. I just want to get home. And I will pay you. Please give me your number, I'll get the money.'

'This one's on me,' the driver said. 'You sure you're okay?'

'I'm sure. Thank you.'

'There are more bags in the seat pocket, if you need them.' He picked up Dot's bag of medication, which had slid onto the floor, and placed it on her lap before returning to his seat at the wheel.

As the taxi pulled away, Dot caught sight of herself in the driver's mirror – her face was pale and bruised, and she had stitches above her eye. Her lips were chapped, and she had red marks on her cheek and nose where her face had scraped on the cemetery ground.

What must the driver think of her? Well, he probably hadn't assumed she was a brawler, so he probably felt pity for her. He probably saw her as a defenceless little old woman, and she hated it.

54

09

Mountains of the Ant God

The chain was on the door.

Busybodies. Curtain twitchers. Fussbudgets. Meddlers. Muckrakers. Pryers. Scandalmongers. Whatever the preferred term was that day, Dot had always been against those people who had their noses in other people's trifle, who watched and judged how others lived. But now, having spent more than two weeks bored and alone in her home – with her bones aching and bruises healing, with nothing much to do, wary of who might be outside and sick at the thought of leaving her home – she watched the street and its inhabitants from behind a locked door:

6.30 a.m.: Lorry passes, man throws bottle of suspicious yellow liquid from window.

6.40 a.m.: Black cat sniffs bottle, recoils, chases shadow.

7 a.m.: Lights on at numbers seven, nine, thirteen.

7.10 a.m.: Young couple with the noisy baby make breakfast. Husband burns toast. Wife calls him an idiot (probably). Baby throws toast.

7.30 a.m.: Black cat returns to suspicious bottle, chases bird.

8 a.m.: Young couple with noisy baby get in car, argue about being late, wife calls husband an idiot (almost

certainly). Baby screeches like a banshee.

And so on it went until about ten o'clock, by which time the entire street seemed to be awake and going about its business somewhere else, completing Dot's own personal (and, admittedly, mundane) morning broadcast.

That dull feeling was an old silent friend by now, because it felt like the world had left her behind. She was alone, despite being surrounded by a city of people.

Deep, deep, deep down inside, she knew they didn't mean to hurt her, but it felt like they'd chosen to leave because of her. They didn't want to be near her. They couldn't bear to be near her. And when she thought about that, if she really allowed herself to think about it – and she often did – she wanted to go with them.

But something in Dot refused to listen to that side of her. She didn't like bullies, and she was a contrarian. If someone told her to sit, she'd stand. If they told her to sleep, she'd punch them in the jaw.

So, when the world seemed to say *don't look*, she peeked through more windows. Right now, however, the people were busy elsewhere, so she turned to the kitchen to make a cuppa and something to eat.

The kitchen cupboards were almost bare. She'd not been to the supermarket since her ordeal, and the last slice of bread was well past its best. She heated a tin of off-brand baked beans in the microwave while the kettle boiled, pondering how she could consume the day.

She didn't feel ready to go out yet. The streets felt noisier, wider, more alien to her than they had ever been before. She had never expected to be hurt by them – and this is where she grew up, so if it could happen here then it could happen anywhere.

But inside her house? She was safe here. She had chains on the doors, locks, a bread knife by her bed. Just in case. She imagined shadowy goons hovering over her bed at night, fleeing in terror when she whipped out her crumby serrated blade, although she supposed the weapon would likely only scare bread-based intruders.

The kettle hissed. Dot filled her cup and watched her beans waltz around the inside of the microwave, popping under the intense heat.

A knock sounded at Dot's front door.

She froze.

Who was it? She should check, but she didn't want to. What if it was her muggers, looking to finish the job? What if it was the police, wanting her to answer more questions? What if it was a neighbour who'd caught her peeking? What if it was the black cat wielding the suspicious bottle of yellow liquid?

There was another knock and the doorbell buzzed like a nest of angry bees.

Her legs jellified and she sat on the kitchen floor, head between her knees, panting.

It's just the doorbell. Nobody wants to hurt you. It's just the door. Get up, don't let them do this to you!

But she couldn't.

⋆

The bell's silence announced the all-clear. But Dot remained where she was, drawing breaths to settle her nerves.

She watched an ant walk across her kitchen floor. The ant moved in seemingly crazed lines and circles, as if frantically searching for a trail. It seemed to be looking for the sugar she was yet to put into her tea, but then she wondered if it was seeking something else entirely – other ants, perhaps, or just another direction, an escape.

Did the ant know that she was watching it go about its everyday life? Perhaps, if it was aware of her, it may have thought she was God.

Dot waited patiently for the ant to approach her. When it neared, she placed her fingertip on the floor, and the ant walked around it. She lay her finger in its path again, and the ant explored her unpolished nail as if exploring a mountaintop, before carrying on its journey towards the tea cupboard.

By the time Dot had regained herself and stood, her beans and tea were cold.

This whole mess was just a blip, she told herself, and she had to keep getting back up, she had to keep fuel in the furnace. So she reheated the beans, remade the tea and checked the front door.

Nobody was there, of course, but a slip of paper had found its way inside:

Need cash?
We're buying homes in your area!
Great prices! Quick sales.
Call 07986511204 for a quote.

Vultures. She'd seen them before: businessmen in bad suits, flying door to door. They circled the old and sick on the street with keen eyes and sharp beaks, trying to buy up property for scraps. Nobody wanted the hassle of advertising and selling their home, especially if they were unwell or desperate for the money, so it appealed to some old folk on the street who struggled to pay the bills and take care of themselves.

But this was her and Charles's home. The vultures could take a hike, then get on their bike, then take a long walk off a short pier. The queen had to defend her castle.

She logged onto her computer to check on the current stock at Mini Christmas, but there was nothing new in stock that she particularly wanted to add to her town, or didn't already own. So, she loaded up the neighbourhood forum, just to see if anyone else had reported vulture sightings, but something else caught her eye: a discussion titled, *Offenders at the park!!!*

The post went like this:

> *BigJohnProud2Bbri69 (30 mins ago)*
> *Anyone been to the park at the crossroad? I saw CRIMINALS (also known as young offenders to the woke brigade) hanging about and shouting and smoking near kids. I saw one kick water at a swan, DISGRACEFUL! NO RESPECT!!! Waste of taxpayer money. Starting petition to clear them out, get them in jail where they belong. We're too soft.*

And a reply:

> *SallyRiley (18 mins ago)*
> *They're practically kids. They're cleaning up and there's not much to do around here. Give them a break!*

Big John wasn't pleased:

> *BigJohnProud2Bbri69 (17 mins ago)*
> *This town's going down the pan, and YOU are the problem. Prison's not enough any more, it's a holiday with TV and xbox. We need to make a stand.*

That reply got a few likes, and one haunting response:

> Beam-Me-Up-Scotty-Too-Hotty *(12 mins ago)*
> *I've got an air rifle.*

Dot's tangle with the thugs from the chippie was hardly a glowing endoursement for the younger generations, and she was on the verge of agreeing with Big John, when she stopped herself. She'd seen a lot of troubled kids in her time, a lot of folk who'd done bad things, and believed that people usually deserved another chance. Doing something bad didn't automatically make them *bad people*; it didn't mean they were disposable.

Plus, she didn't want to become a crazed gun-toting zealot. She didn't even want to be a miserly complainer like the person who posted the original complaint.

She was no angel, either, and didn't want to judge others too harshly. After all, she'd been stealing for years and had never been caught. She'd never even been watched carefully by security guards – it was like she was invisible.

Who would be left if the neighbourhood just shot everyone who stepped even slightly out of line? Those kids weren't the problem, it was the fire-and-brimstone crew who felt that shooting kids (what the actual sweet Jesus?!) was a reasonable reaction to . . . well, anything.

And she'd seen those young offenders first hand, at the park. They were a bit rough around the edges, but they weren't exactly the mob. They were trying their best during a bad time, trying to survive.

She thought of the ant running over her fingertips, how it was undeterred even by a finger mountain in its path. And, before she had time to convince herself otherwise, Dot dropped a rolling pin into her biggest handbag, her coat was on and she was out the door.

10

All the Goslings
Walk in a Line

Dot didn't allow herself to think about the fact that this was her first time out of her home since her assault; she simply let the adrenaline do the walking.

Dot didn't really expect to see Beam-Me-Up-Scotty-Too-Hotty (whatever he looked like – she imagined a keg-bellied fifty-something Territorial Army dropout with all the charisma of a dead wasp) at the park with his air rifle, but the insane forum chat was enough to put proverbial ants in her pants.

Her rib ached as she walked, but it was okay because, in a way, the pain was reassuring – it reminded her she was alive and out there, that she was healing.

She scoured the edges of the park first, looking for crazed gunmen. She was an ant seeking sugar, undeterred. But, as she'd anticipated, the brave warriors on the neighbourhood forums were yet to appear and make their move.

What would she have done if she'd seen them in the bushes, waiting for their hunt? Wielded her rolling pin like a baton and given them a good clubbing? Unlikely. She had no idea, really, but why worry about something that hadn't happened?

Convinced that the area was secure, for now, she continued towards her favourite bench.

As the adrenaline rush faded and her mind took over her body again, she felt suddenly vulnerable but tried to distract herself. She hoped that she might run into the sour-faced woman with the yappy dog. There was a good chance they'd saved Dot's life, and she wanted to say thank you, to make amends (even though the sour-faced woman was probably completely unaware of Dot's now-defunct secret beef with the old girl).

But the woman was nowhere to be seen either, so Dot sat on the bench with the bronze plaque dedicated to John (who liked ducks more than most people), hoping a chuckle might convince her that things were normal and she was safe.

The bike, which had been fished out by the tall lad wearing a number 7 football shirt, was gone. Dot wondered if perhaps the council had taken it, if they had broken the habit of a lifetime and actually done their job. More likely, the bike had been reclaimed by the natives and deposited back into the pond, or migrated to another body of water, like some of the swan-tormented geese and goslings did each year. Dot imagined the bike rolling along the park's paths honking its horn, pursued by a brood of little tricycles.

At that moment, the community service teens appeared wearing scowls and thick black rubber boots, which made them look like farmers with fetishes. The bald man, who Dot decided must be their probation officer, or an equivalent, reached over the fence around the pond and pulled up a plant – a long grassy weed – and tossed it onto the concrete ground beside him.

'These plants are bad for the pond and the wildlife,' the probation officer said. 'So you're going to remove them.'

The usual suspects (hoop-earring girl, oil-spill-haircut boy and tall football lad, plus the others from last time) were all there, with a couple of new morbid faces. They all looked just as motivated to be there as they had been previously, albeit without their phones glued to their hands this time.

'I'm allergic,' hoop-earring girl said, raising her ring-heavy hand.

'To what?' the probation officer asked.

'Dunno.'

'She's allergic to work,' oil-spill-haircut boy said, and they all laughed, including hoop-earring girl and the probation officer.

Dot was almost impressed by the girl's lack of devotion to her own lie. Dot wouldn't want to trudge through stagnant pond water pulling up random weeds either, and she wondered what each of them had done to earn their criminal stripes.

She reckoned that hoop-earring girl had probably been a shoplifter. Maybe she stole hoop earrings and sold them to buy marijuana and posh crisps. And now she was flaunting her crime by wearing hoop earrings in front of them all so that, in some way, she felt like she was giving a middle finger to the system.

Lanky oil-spill-haircut boy looked a bit of a thug, if Dot had to profile him. His jaw was slack, like he'd been chewing rocks, and his eyes were like those of a toddler who'd been denied his favourite toy. Dot guessed that he'd been caught vandalising bowling greens. Specifically bowling greens, nothing else. His granddad had loved to bowl, loved it more than his own family. And so, lanky oil-spill-haircut boy internalised his resentment for the greens and took it out on the finely trimmed grass.

Tall football lad – Max, was his name – was harder to pin down. She'd seen how angry he got before, but she'd also seen that he was a hard worker and clearly didn't like the others. So, maybe he aspired to better things. Maybe his reality filled him with an insatiable rage, and he lashed out at the police, or a banker or a politician. Yes, Dot quite liked that. He was a warrior, fighting against social inequality. He was a revolutionary, and the tight-collared wolves in the office blocks and jail houses wanted to teach him to stay in his place, so now he was pulling up weeds and thinking of ways to overthrow the system that kept him chained down.

Dot rifled through her big handbag, ignoring the hard mints, lottery ticket and lint, and took out her tube of antiseptic cream, applying a little to the scrapes – which had scabbed over rather nicely – on her face as she watched the teens weed the pond. She'd almost forgotten about the lottery ticket she had put into its zip pocket, the very same ticket that football lad's number 7 shirt had inspired. The draw had been made while she was recovering in hospital, and she hadn't checked the numbers, but she hoped she'd at least won a tenner because she really fancied picking up a bar of chocolate and a few cans of stout from the corner shop on her way home.

'Oi, Max!' hoop-earring girl yelled, repeating her phrase from her previous visit, as if caught in a time loop. 'Catch!'

She hurled a handful of pond weeds at Max, but he moved aside and the weeds missed him. He walked out of throwing distance and continued to pull up weeds.

'Hey, Max,' oil-spill-haircut boy called out. 'My dad knows your mum.'

Max ignored him, but Dot could see Max biting his lip as he tore weeds from the water and shook mud from their roots.

'Max's mum's real friendly, isn't she, Max?' oil-spill-haircut boy called out louder, turning so the other community service teens could hear him. 'No wonder he was pulling bikes out the pond – he thought his mum had drowned!'

Max flew through the weeds, all claws and teeth, so quickly that oil-spill-haircut boy didn't have time to defend himself.

★

The teens whooped and jeered at first, until it looked like Max might actually drown oil-spill-haircut boy in the dirty pond water. The probation officer moved quickly, pulling Max away as the others helped oil-spill-haircut boy to his feet.

The boy's nose was bloody, he was drenched and muddy, but he looked okay otherwise. Dot's heart raced with the excitement of it, torn between wanting the violence to stop and the desire to grab a bag of popcorn to better enjoy the fight.

'Psycho!' oil-spill-haircut boy yelled as his pals walked him away and checked his nose, shooting glares at Max.

The probation officer took Max aside, talking quietly to him. It was one of the few times Dot wished she needed a hearing aid, so she could boost its receiver and listen in on the conversation.

Even without enhanced hearing, Dot could predict what the probation officer was saying to Max: cool down, that is unacceptable, you could ruin your future.

And Dot recognised the expressions on Max's face as it returned to its regular colour, his hurried breath began to slow, his shoulders sagged and his fists uncurled. He was sorry or, at least, wished he hadn't gone into attack mode so urgently.

'You lot, back to the meet-up point!' the probation officer called out to the others.

'What about Rocky?' hoop-earring girl replied, thrusting a jab in Max's direction while elbowing oil-spill-haircut boy playfully.

The probation officer turned away from the teens to address Max, talking at a regular volume: 'You finish up here. I'll be back to make sure it's done. Any more trouble, and that's it for you. Got it?'

Max nodded, his eyes pinned on his shoes. 'He shouldn't have said that about my mum.'

'I know. And I'll speak to them all about this. But you can't explode like that – you're going to meet people like them all the time.'

Max nodded again.

The probation officer led the rest of the group away, chatting to them, and Dot could overhear the teens fluctuating between laughter, concern and outrage.

Max sat down on the ground and leaned against the little metal fence that separated the path from the pond. He stared at his knuckles, licking them like a tomcat licks its wounds after defending its garden from feline intruders.

Dot had seen her dad do the same one day, when he came home from the pub with grazed knuckles. Dot's mum asked what had happened, and he said he'd had a scrap with his friend over something stupid. He was angry and hurt and sad, but Dot's mum made him sit at the table with her and talk it through until everything was okay again. And that was that, it was put to rest.

Dot saw in Max the same hurt as she'd seen in her dad that day.

She approached him slowly, retrieved the tube of antiseptic cream from her big handbag and held it out to Max.

'Hi,' Dot said.

He looked up at her, confused.

'Who knows what's in that pond water,' Dot said. 'This helps.'

Max raised an eyebrow. 'What is it?'

'Cream. I got it for these.' Dot pointed to the scabs on her face. 'I don't have the lurgy, don't worry. They're scrapes.'

Max took the antiseptic cream hesitatingly and began reading the instructions on the tube.

'Just rub a bit onto your knuckles,' Dot said.

Max squeezed the cream onto his fingertips and rubbed it onto his knuckles, gritting his teeth.

He replaced the lid and held the tube out to Dot. 'Thanks. It feels okay.'

'You can keep it, I have plenty.'

'No, really. Thanks.' Max's eyes insisted, though they were still tinged with pain and embarrassment. He'd clearly realised that Dot had witnessed his outburst.

Dot took the tube and placed it into her big handbag.

'What happened?' Max asked, staring up at Dot's face.

'I got into a fight. You should see the other guy.'

Max laughed quietly, as if trying to suppress it. 'Really?'

'Not exactly. I saw what those others did – are you all right?'

Max shrugged. 'Fine. I just don't like it when they say stuff about my mum.'

Dot nodded. She tried to bend down to his level but her knee and ribs ached. 'My knees are shot. Why don't we go to the bench?' She gestured to John's bench.

'I should keep working.' Max got to his feet. 'But thanks.' His eyes glanced into Dot's big handbag. 'Is that a baton? What are you doing? Who are you?'

Dot laughed, pulling out her rolling pin. 'No, it's just a rolling pin. I'd tell you I was going to do some baking, but actually I brought it here to smack it across some idiot's head.'

'Seriously? You're lying. You're making pies or something.'

'Seriously.'

A smile broke across Max's face. 'Well, thanks for the cream. I should carry on with these weeds, or he'll report me.'

'Come on, let's sit. I'm good at this stuff. Just a couple of minutes.' Dot gestured to the bench again. 'If he comes back, I'll say it's my fault you stopped working. I'll say you were helping me with something – he can't report you for that. You're here for community service, right?'

'Yeah.'

'Well, I'm part of the community – little old woman who needed your help. Let's sit.'

11

Fence on the Bench

'So what's the real deal with the rolling pin?' Max asked, keeping some distance between himself and Dot, as if he was afraid of catching a virus from her.

'Why are you on community service?' Dot asked.

'You're just going to dodge my question like that?'

Dot nodded. 'Quid pro quo. I tell you things, you tell me things,' Dot said in her best creepy voice, resisting mentioning fava beans and a nice Chianti, sure that the reference would be lost on Max.

'*The Silence of the Lambs*, 1991, starring Anthony Hopkins and Jodie Foster.' Max looked pleased with himself. 'You can't out-movie me, Clarice.' He leaned back on the bench. 'All right, it's a deal. But you seem weird, so you go first. What's with the rolling pin?'

'It's for battering some creep with.'

Max stared at Dot, reading her face for lies. 'Who?'

'Quid pro quo, remember? What did you do to land in community service?'

'I'm a fence.'

Dot flicked through the dictionary of her mind, searching for another meaning for the word *fence*, but came up empty.

'You're planks of wood that divide land?'

'No. Different meaning. I sell things.'

70

'Ohhhh, *that* kind of fence,' Dot said, still not entirely sure what he meant, though she was beginning to think that she recalled the term from old gangster movies, of which she'd seen approximately three. 'What kinds of things?'

Max shook his head. 'The rolling pin . . .'

'Fine. There's a creep on the internet who suggested he might come down here and shoot you. I was going to hit him with this, if I had to.' She took the rolling pin from her big bag and mimed clubbing someone across the head with it.

'Shoot *me*? What the fuck?!'

'Well, not necessarily *you*. But your lot, the community service crew. Just with an air rifle.'

Max looked around nervously and lowered his voice. 'I don't care if it's a fucking bubble gun. Why was he going to shoot us?'

'He's troubled, I suppose,' Dot said. 'I don't know him, he's just someone on the neighbourhood forum. I don't think he really meant it. But it's your turn. What do you sell?' Dot reckoned she could sneak another question in, given how much information she'd just provided. 'And why would that cause you to be here?'

'You know, this and that. Things that fell off lorries that nobody would miss.'

The term *fence* finally clicked in Dot's mind, like a piece of a jigsaw. 'Ah. But someone *did* miss it?'

'Right.' Max cocked his head. 'So, you came here to batter some guy with an air rifle. Why?'

'Why what?'

'Why come here?'

Dot hadn't really thought it through until now – she'd just let the inspiration take her out of the house while she had the momentum.

'I didn't want him to shoot you,' Dot said. 'And I felt like maybe I could stop him.'

'But you said you didn't think he'd really do anything. And, no offence, but you don't look that tough.'

'Hey, I can be tough!' Dot protested. 'Plus, I'm good at talking, remember. If the rolling pin failed, I think I could have talked him out of it. Then I saw you, and I thought maybe I should talk to you instead.'

Max began pulling off his long black rubber boots, but they were suctioned to his feet. Dot reached towards him to help, and he instinctively jerked away.

'Sorry. Thanks,' he said, straightening his legs.

Dot wiggled the boot to loosen its limpet-like grip on his foot and pulled with all her strength. The boot came off with a squelch and a pop, almost sending Dot tumbling backwards.

She repeated the process with the second boot, and Max got up to retrieve a pair of trainers from a nearby plastic bag, putting them onto his feet.

'I was here a couple of weeks ago,' Dot said. 'When you snapped at that girl with hoop earrings.'

Max began to blush. 'Oh. Tanya. She's a mouthy bitch.'

'Hey, please don't. I don't like that, all right?' Dot said sternly.

'Sorry. So why were you here, watching us? You some kind of weirdo?'

'Why would you think that?' Dot asked, a little hurt by the question.

'You're in the park, alone and with a rolling pin to beat up some random gunman. Your face is messed up, and you're just randomly talking to me. That's weird. It's what a weirdo would do.'

'None taken.' Dot took a hard mint from her bag, removed the lint and plastic wrapper and popped it into her mouth, sucking on it. She offered one to Max and he took it. 'I guess I am weird, then. Or . . . just looking for someone to talk to. I was bored at home, and I wanted to get out.'

'Fair enough.' Max tossed the mint into his mouth and crunched it between his teeth. 'So, what do you think of the community service crew?'

'They seem troubled, too, like they need a bit of help. What do you think?'

'Bunch of bastards.'

Dot restrained herself. They'd only just started talking, and she didn't want to discourage him with too many beratings.

Max sighed, running a nervy hand through his hair. 'I mean, they all pretend they're something special but I don't think any of them really believes it. And it comes out like piss and vinegar, like they're just a bunch of bullies and idiots. But I guess I'm not that different: I'm here with them.' He slumped forward. 'Tanya called me a beast the other day. Maybe she's not wrong. We're beasts.'

'I don't think so,' Dot said.

Max glanced up at her. 'They think everything's a joke or unfair, and they won't work for anything. I want to get out of this stupid programme and *do* something.'

'You can, after it's over.'

Max cracked his fingers. 'No. I tried that. I don't want handouts, I just want a chance to do something that isn't shit. Nobody is willing to give me a shot – they won't even let me work a trial day for no pay. They ask about my qualifications, and then I don't hear from them again. One place said they'd interview me to work in a timber yard. Sounded good. All that wood.'

'You like wood?' Dot asked. It seemed a strange thing for a young man to be interested in.

'Well, I'm not exactly in love with it. But, you know, cutting up wood would be better than being stuck in an office with a bunch of ironed shirts with coffee breath. So, yeah, I like wood enough.'

Dot offered Max another mint and he took it like a hungry seagull, practically swallowing it in one.

'So, what happened?' Dot asked.

'They asked about a criminal record. And I didn't lie. I should have lied, but I didn't. I'm too fucking honest for my own good, my mum says.'

'How old are you?' Dot asked, noticing that Max's mum was a recurring theme now. It made him seem young.

'Nineteen. How old are you?'

'It's impolite to ask.' Dot looked faux-insulted. 'Guess.'

'I'm not that stupid. You want me to say you're forty? Just tell me.'

'Seventy . . . something. But I'm hoping it'll start going backwards soon.'

Max stood. 'You're funny. Weird, but funny.'

'I'll take that as a compliment.'

'I should get back to work, but maybe I'll see you around. I've a lot more community service to do.' He groaned. 'It's only just November and I can't believe I have to hang around those idiots until the new year. They drive me crazy.'

'Stay calm – maybe they'll get themselves thrown off the programme soon, the way they're going.'

'I can dream.' He held out his hand. 'I'm Max, by the way.'

Dot shook it. 'Dorothy. But my friends call me Dot.'

'Like in *The Wizard of Oz*?'

'Yeah.'

'I love that movie.'

'Me too.'

74

Max walked through the gate in the fence around the pond. 'You'd better follow the yellow brick road. Or the grey concrete path, in this case. See you around, Dot.' He waved.

Dot waved back and couldn't help but smile. She'd barely spoken to anybody in weeks since leaving the hospital, and Max had helped her to feel much more like her old self again.

12

She Was Just Seventeen

Lottery number 17

(Dot is seventeen years old)

Dot's stomach was a messy knot of tension and butterflies. She stood in front of the vanity mirror, pouting seductively at the woman reflected back at her. She wore a lime and cherry French-boutique-look clingy jersey dress with custard stockings, and her Hepburn-style updo was a masterpiece of modern hair-based architecture.

Twiggy's got nothing on you, sweetie, Dot told herself in an attempted pep-talk. She was impressed by her transformation but didn't quite feel like herself. Charles won't stand a chance.

A *rapa-tap-tap* sounded on her bedroom door, and Dot instantly recognised the tips of her mum's false nails. Dot flicked off the power to her vanity mirror, its bulbs radiating an intense heat that often made her worry about a house fire, and opened the door.

'Dot, you gab up so nicely. You look fab!' her mum said excitedly.

Dot groaned. 'Mum, you're not a mod. Don't talk like that.'

'Well, isn't someone wound up tighter than a nun's knickers?'

Dot turned back to the mirror and stared at herself, feeling like she wanted to throw up. 'Sorry, I'm just nervous.'

'Looking like that? You've no need! Although' – Dot's mum pulled a golden bullet from her pocket – 'some hot lips wouldn't go amiss. Hold still.' She gripped Dot's chin and turned her head, holding it steady as she painted her lips. She ripped a tissue from the box on Dot's dresser. 'Open up and press down.'

Dot obeyed, her nerves a little settled by the fact that her mum was taking charge. Her lips left a pink imprint on the tissue, which her mum balled up and tossed into the bin.

'It's pearl pink – I borrowed it from the shop,' her mum said. 'You're a knockout, honey. It's all in the genes. You got your incredible looks from me.' She fluttered her eyelashes. 'Oh, and I checked your horoscope . . .' She adopted a mysterious, haunting voice: 'You will find someone special and your life will take a new direction.'

Dot wasn't a believer, no matter how much her mum tried to tell her that some women had special powers, and that fate had plans for them all.

'It's good news for your date, right?' her mum asked.

Dot smiled. 'What do I do if he tries to kiss me?'

'You kiss him back!'

Dot had been reading up on kissing, and she'd talked about it with her more experienced friends (without letting on that she was new to it, of course), but their descriptions were hardly encouraging. A peck on the cheek, sure. A kiss on the lips, why not? But tongues intertwined in a saliva-mingling wrestling match – that didn't sound appealing to Dot. It sounded foul.

Grace, from the nursing school, had said her first Frenchy made her feel sick, but eventually she got used to it and now she can't stop herself. So, Dot figured, perhaps she'd also grow to like it. She didn't like broccoli for years, and now she could abide it if absolutely necessary. Perhaps French kissing was like broccoli.

'The secret is just to be yourself,' Dot's mum said, tweaking a strand of Dot's hair back into position with surgical precision. 'Don't let him take advantage.'

'Mum! I won't!' Dot protested.

'I know, but you're a knockout and you've clearly made an effort. Boys aren't very smart and at your age they're all hands and hormones. They get the wrong ideas. Or the right ones, depending on what you're after.'

'Mum, seriously, stop it!'

Her mum took a purse from her pocket and opened its minty mouth wide. She retrieved a few coins from the purse and placed them into Dot's palm, closing Dot's fingers around them.

'Let him buy you something, let him feel like he's treating you special. But don't let him pay for everything,' her mum said. 'Otherwise he'll think you owe him something. And if anything happens and you're not happy, you leave right away. Call me, and I'll come to collect you, wherever you are, okay?'

Dot nodded. 'Thanks.'

'Wherever, whenever. I don't mind.' She kissed Dot's cheek, her eyes watering over. 'My little girl . . .'

'Mum, it's okay,' Dot said, feeling cruel for telling her mum to stop coddling her. But she was pleased to have her mum's protection, her mum's words in her ears, her mum's blood in her veins. She took her tenth-birthday locket from its box and placed it around her neck.

'Your dad would be so proud of you, you know.'

'I know. I—'

The doorbell buzzed and Dot stood up straight, feeling her nausea return.

Her mum ran to the window and peered down at the boy waiting at their front door. 'He's handsome. You didn't say he was handsome! And he has flowers.' She clapped her hands together like a giddy schoolgirl. She smiled at Dot, placing a gentle hand on her elbow. 'Go get 'em, tiger.'

★

Dot smelled her bouquet of flowers as they waited in the queue to the two-screen cinema.

'This place is great,' Charles said. 'Have you been before?'

Dot tried not to stare at the chest hair protruding from the open collar of his orange shirt. The flamboyant shirt didn't match his fitted brown suit, or the rough mechanic's skin on his hands, and she wondered whether he was also putting on a guise for their date. It relaxed Dot to believe that he was as nervous as she was. It put them on even ground.

'No, it's my first time. I wonder if they sell popcorn,' Dot said suggestively.

'They do. I'll buy some for you, for us, if you'd like.' A single drop of sweat trickled down Charles's face, illuminated by the glowing sign above the ticket counter.

Dot smiled. 'So, why's this place so great? Aside from the popcorn.'

'They show one new film and the other's an older one. Do you watch many films?'

Dot shook her head carefully so as not to cause her hive of hair to collapse. 'No, I'm quite busy at the nursing school at the moment. But I love to watch them when I have the time.'

'That's good of you to train as a nurse. And I bet all the guys in the hospital have a crush on you.'

'Yes. Yes, they do,' Dot said. She tried not to giggle but couldn't help herself. 'No, not really. They're mostly old men, so they just leer.'

'Well, it wouldn't surprise me if they had a crush. You look really great.'

Dot felt herself blush. 'Thanks, you too.'

Charles fingered the top button of his shirt. 'My brother lent me this shirt. It's a bit more colourful than I'd normally go for. I was worried it might attract bees.'

'Buzz buzz!' Dot said, pretending to sting him with the tips of her glued-on nails, before fully realising the strangeness of what she was doing. 'Erm, sorry.'

She looked straight ahead to the woman in the ticket booth who gave her a pitying, and somewhat pained, look.

Charles laughed. 'You're . . . different, you know that? I like different. Who wants to be normal?'

'Not me,' Dot said, relieved. 'My mum told me to be myself and . . . well, here I am.'

Charles's fingertips touched Dot's as they stepped forward in the queue. A warm shiver ran through her hand and up her arm. It felt good, like they were on the same page, like she didn't need to worry any more, like she didn't need to hide herself.

'I hope you don't mind . . .' Charles started, nodding to the film posters behind the ticket seller. 'I thought we'd see *The Wizard of Oz*. Because you're Dorothy, and so is she. I thought it was like fate, or, I guess, just a coincidence. And I like the story, and the songs are great. But if you'd rather see the modern film, that's fine too. Whatever you prefer.'

Dot stared at the film poster for the other movie, which

showed a naked woman holding two pistols. The woman's skin was covered in coloured swirls that camouflaged a parachuting man and the numbers 007.

'*Casino Royale,*' Charles said. 'It's a spy movie. James Bond. It's possibly more romantic than *The Wizard of Oz.*'

'*The Wizard of Oz* is fine,' Dot said. 'I saw it with my dad when I was little. I was terrified of the witch.'

'Me too!' Charles chuckled.

'Don't worry, I'll protect you from her,' Dot said, wrapping her arm through the loop of his. 'All it takes is a pail of water.'

Charles paid for the cinema tickets and, following her mum's advice not to allow her date to pay for everything, Dot bought the popcorn.

They sat in the dark heat of the cinema and watched the film. Dot caught him looking at her every now and again, and she was pretty sure that he'd noticed her looking at him, too. When the Wicked Witch appeared, Dot leaned her head on Charles's shoulder and drew a long, slow breath of him inside her.

When the credits rolled, they walked into the night.

'Thanks for looking after me in there,' Charles said. 'May I walk you home?'

'You may,' Dot said, trying to sound playful rather than formal. 'Along the yellow brick road. Or, in our case, along the cracked grey pavement. I love the songs in that film, don't you?'

Dot began to hum 'Somewhere Over the Rainbow' and Charles sang to Dot sweetly and quietly about making wishes to stars, lands beyond rainbows and daring to dream.

She reached out for his hand and grasped it as they walked towards her home. His warm fingers interlocked with hers and squeezed gently, and that was when Dot felt sure that Charles was the kind of boy she'd really like to kiss.

13

Just the Ticket

Dot left the park buzzing like a bee in a jam jar.

Maybe she could have thought it a little sad that she was so energised by a simple interaction, but she didn't care – she'd been completely alone for more than two weeks since leaving the hospital. It felt great to have made a connection with someone new and different, however strange and brief their encounter was. Max seemed like a decent young man, although a little wild at times. But then again, she hadn't seemed completely tame to him, either.

Her big bag was completely *sans* mints, thanks to Max's gobbling seagull technique, which wouldn't do. Dot also knew her cupboards were almost bare, as she'd not been shopping since her attack, and she was in the mood for . . . cake. Yes, cake would make everything right with the world. So, on her way home, Dot diverted to the local corner shop to pick up cake and some nutritional, filling food items for the cupboards. But, mostly, cake.

The door chimed as she entered the shop. The owner looked up from his little TV behind the counter and smiled. Dot smiled back, exploring the rows of chocolates and sweets laid out like a glorious edible quilt. Had she the money, she would have liked to buy them all, but she would have to limit herself today. She had £23.72 in her purse, which was to cover her food budget for the rest of the week, and anything else she might need.

She perused the narrow aisles and placed a lemon drizzle cake into her basket – her favourite kind.

Then came the mundane part: she had to get some proper food, too, which would not go off immediately and that might impart some kind of non-cake-based nutrition.

Having added a can of stout and a few low-cost foods to her basket, she totted up the numbers and decided not to spend another penny. The rest of her money was needed in case of an emergency, such as taking a bus to the doctor's surgery if her knee decided to turn against her again. And if her week was trouble-free, she still owed the taxi driver for her journey back from the hospital, despite his emphatic insistence that her ride was 'on him'.

She took her items to the shop owner at the till, and he scanned them. They came to £16.59, leaving her with £7.13, so she had to make the items last. She could have engaged her sticky fingers (she was seventy per cent sure she wouldn't be caught as the shop owner must know her face by now and trust her), but this wasn't the same as stealing Christmas ornaments or plants – luxuries and trinkets felt like fair game. But the corner shop was owned and run by a husband and wife, and she felt that she ought to pay for food.

Dot counted out her coins and paid for the items. The owner gave her a carrier bag for free, and she felt she'd done the right thing by not robbing him. But her week, as per usual, would be a financial struggle if she had to purchase anything else.

She returned her purse to her big bag and – on her way out – remembered the lottery ticket.

'Oh, I have this. Can you check if I've won anything?'

Dot asked, passing her folded-up ticket to the shop owner. 'I bought it a few weeks ago, and I forgot I had it.'

'No problem, one second.'

Dot crossed her fingers and toes. If she had three numbers, she'd win enough to pay for the taxi and some more stout. She might even have enough to add treats into her basket for a couple of weeks. She waited eagerly as the owner scanned her ticket.

He looked confused.

'Is it scanning?' Dot asked.

'Yes . . . I think so. One moment.' He scanned again. 'I have to check something.'

'It's a real ticket,' Dot said. 'I bought it here.'

'I remember.' He examined the ticket, scanned it again and audibly gasped. He stared at Dot and reached for a fold-up chair. 'I think you'd better sit down.'

'Why?' Her heart pounded.

'You've won.'

She sat. 'How much?'

'A million pounds.'

★

The shop owner checked the details five times. He showed Dot, and she checked them five times again. She'd hit five numbers and the bonus ball (the bonus ball was seven, the number that Dot had chosen based on Max's football shirt).

'What a shame you didn't get the sixth number,' the owner said once Dot's screaming had subsided. 'You'd have won three and a half million.'

'Who cares?!' Dot shouted, her whole body trembling. She'd never had a heart complaint but was now slightly worried that the excitement would give her a heart attack. 'I'm a millionaire!'

The owner called up the stairs to his wife, locked the shop door and turned the sign to *Sorry – We're CLOSED.*

'What is it?' his wife asked, running down the stairs and into the shop.

'This lady won the lottery – a million pounds!'

'Oh my goodness!' The woman hugged Dot, holding both her hands. 'In our shop, too. Congratulations.'

'Thank you,' Dot said, feeling as though she were floating through a dream.

'Are you okay?' The woman turned to her husband. 'Get her a drink.'

'Tea? Water?' the owner asked.

'Champagne!' The woman looked at Dot with slight concern. 'Are you okay? You look a little pale.'

'It's just a surprise,' Dot said, trying to control her breath so that her heart would stop doing the rumba. 'I'll be fine.'

The owner popped a bottle of champagne and poured it into plastic cups, passing one to his wife and one to Dot. They *cheers*ed and Dot sipped her drink. She assumed the champagne had been sitting on the shop shelves near the hot water pipes for a few years, but she didn't care.

A million pounds, was this real?

'I'm guessing you don't pay me from the till,' Dot said. 'So, do you know how I claim the money?'

'I'll have to check.' He looked at his wife. 'This could mean something good for us too, Chaha.'

'Money?' Chaha asked.

'I don't know for sure – I think we might get a bonus for selling a winning ticket. But either way, the papers will want to know.' He placed a hand on Dot's shoulder. 'Assuming you're okay with that. We could use the publicity.'

'Of course,' Dot said, downing her glass of bubbly.

He checked the ticket. 'I think you need to fill out a claim form online, or call them,' the owner said. 'Can you do that, or do you need help?'

'I can do it, but thanks,' Dot replied.

'Keep that ticket safe,' Chaha said, taking a picture of it on her phone and passing the ticket back to Dot. 'Oh, God, imagine losing it.'

Dot placed the ticket into her zip-up coat pocket. 'It's going nowhere.'

'So, what's on your bucket list?' Chaha asked.

'My what?'

'You know, the list of things you want to do before . . .' Chaha's eyes widened as if searching for a way to back-pedal. 'I mean, with this kind of money you could do anything, you could live your wildest dreams. I'd travel the world. We could go to see our family in Nepal. And then to Thailand. I'd never cook again!'

The owner rolled his eyes. 'We've a mortgage to pay off. And the car's on its last legs.'

She punched his arm semi-playfully. 'We're going on holiday!'

'Fine. We'll go on holiday, and we'll visit family. But the rest should pay off the house, and then we'll invest it.'

Chaha giggled. 'Look at us, spending your money for you. What do you think you'll do with it? Invest it, like my boring husband would, or do something wonderful like travel the world?'

'I don't know,' Dot said. 'I have to think about it.'

'Very wise,' the shop owner said.

'I suppose I should spend it,' Dot said. 'One way or another. You can't take it with you when you're gone.'

'Ex-act-ly!' Chaha said. 'You should enjoy yourself.'

'Don't put ideas into her head,' the shop owner said. 'You spend it however you want to. Don't listen to my wife – if it were up to her, that million pounds would be gone within a week.'

'More like twenty-four hours,' Chaha said, laughing while obviously imagining herself jetting away on a first-class flight, potentially on the arm of a younger model of husband.

Dot considered Chaha's bucket list for herself. Would she like to fly from tropical location to tropical location? She loved travelling when she was with Charles, but jetting around from place to place now might be lonely and a bit demanding on her. Perhaps a luxury cruise would be more her speed, and she might meet some interesting people on board. But then again, if she hated the cruise or the people, she'd be stuck with them for the duration of the trip. And some of those trips lasted for months. Then there were the problems of health and sanitation, the abundance of seafood (she liked white fish, but little else from the ocean), the pokey rooms and the fact that she sometimes got seasick. Perhaps a cruise wasn't the ideal option, either.

She had time to think, though. Time to work out what it was that she really wanted.

Dot looked down at her carrier bag of ham and bread, her single can of stout. She wanted something more celebratory, but the reality of her situation was that she couldn't pay for it. Not yet.

'I hope you don't think this too cheeky. Tell me to sod off, honestly,' Dot said. 'But do you think I could open a tab in your shop? I don't have much money right now, you see, and—'

'Of course,' the owner said. 'I mean, we know you'll have enough to pay us back. And perhaps you'd like more than a ham sandwich for your dinner, all things considered.'

'Exactly.' Dot smiled. 'Thank you.'

She stood, a little woozy from the champagne and adrenaline. The news still didn't feel at all real – it was like she was watching a film or reading about it in a book – but she had a ferocious appetite. Dot picked up half a dozen chocolates and sweets from near the counter, plus three more cans of stout and a couple of spicy ready meals from the fridge.

'Is that all?' the owner asked, ringing them through the till and making a note. 'You can have more.'

'That's all. I have to watch my figure now I'm a millionaire. I might have some glitzy parties to attend.'

Dot chuckled. She'd never had a lot of money, even with her nurse's wage combined with Charles's earnings from the factory. But she liked the sound of *I'm a millionaire*, however alien it seemed coming from her lips. It made her feel immediately safer, like she wouldn't have to worry so much ever again.

'I won't keep you any longer,' Dot said, 'I'm sure your other customers are wondering what's going on. But thank you both so much!'

'We're excited for you!' Chaha said, turning the sign on the door to *Come In – We're OPEN*. 'I bet you can't wait to tell your friends and family.'

'They'll be thrilled,' Dot said, hoping they wouldn't detect her lie.

14

Kismet & Caffeine

Dot wasn't going to risk losing her winning ticket. She hurried out, keeping her eyes peeled for lurkers and loomers, meanderers and muggers. Her journey home was quick and uneventful, and she slid her winning ticket between the pages of a copy of *Alice's Adventures in Wonderland* – her win seemed so surreal, after all, that Wonderland seemed the best place for it.

After confirming her details with the lottery officials, Dot made extra-sweet tea to settle her nerves, but she was overflowing with excitement. She wanted to climb on top of her house and shout happily from the rooftop. But there was really nobody for her to share the news with. Aside from the shop owners, she'd only really had a proper conversation with Max today.

It was his number that won her the million – was it just coincidence that they'd met again recently and got on so well? It felt like fate.

She checked her watch: 4.40 p.m. – Max might still be at the park. Maybe he'd think that she was insane, but she wanted to tell someone, just so it would feel real. And what the hell did she have to lose? He already thought she was a weirdo, and now he'd think she was a weirdo with a million pounds.

Dot was in such a giddy daze, and so eager to share the news about her win, that her body moved almost as if by itself. Even her knee didn't ache, such was her overriding kid-at-Christmas glee. How could she possibly spend so much money? She needed inspiration, she needed ideas!

Having walked at a hefty pace, she reached the park, huffing and puffing.

She rushed towards her favourite bench (maybe she would pay to have all the benches revamped; or erect a set of new benches, each with a duck-based quip; or install a gold-plated bench – or, perhaps not), but Max was nowhere to be seen. A huge pile of the pond's weeds sat beside the fence – testament to Max's hard work – and the pond looked all the better for his efforts. A family of ducks quacked happily in the newly created space.

Dot checked her watch. It was approaching five and getting dark already, but the park's lampposts were flickering to life, as if trying to shed light on her mission.

She walked the perimeter of the pond and soon spotted the fluorescent glow of the Community Service bibs in the park's lamppost light.

Could she just walk up to them? She didn't want to embarrass Max but couldn't see him amongst the group, so he might be nowhere nearby. She walked steadily towards the group, catching her breath.

'I'm looking for Max,' Dot said. 'Have you seen him?'

'Who're you, his girlfriend?' hoop-earring girl asked with a grin.

Oil-spill-haircut boy chuckled, but nobody else in the group did.

'He's gone home,' the probation officer said. 'Are you a family member?'

'No,' Dot said. What explanation could she provide for

wanting to see him? She predicted a taunt on the tip of hoop-earring girl's tongue and intercepted it. 'I'm his step . . . gran.' That was a thing, right? A step-gran was surely a thing, though she didn't know what the common term was. 'He moved recently,' Dot said, impressed by her ingenuity. 'Do you know which street he lives on now? I've not been to his new house yet.'

'Did he?' the probation officer said. 'Sorry, but I can't give out addresses, even if I knew.'

'Dock Road,' hoop-earring girl said. 'I don't know which number exactly, one of the early ones. Near the betting shop.'

'Tanya!' the probation officer exclaimed.

She shrugged. 'He only left a few minutes ago and he's a slow walker – you might catch him if you hurry.'

'Thank you,' Dot said. 'And you've all done a great job in the park, well done.'

The probation officer smiled. Dot wondered if he intended to add her praise to some kind of targets-achieved list and crow about it to his co-workers.

'We aim to please,' the probation officer said.

Dot walked quickly. She knew Dock Road – it was one of the longest roads in the area. And one of the roughest ones. So many small things had changed since she'd last ventured down some of these streets. They had familiar names but they felt unfamiliar to Dot, like incomplete memories.

When she was little, the city was very different to how it seemed now. The bricks were the same, but its spirit had shifted – not necessarily in a bad way, but she sensed its difference, she knew it in her bones.

The docks had once been lively with foul-mouthed sailors and tricksy traders, but the ships had disappeared and the docking machinery was either gone or left dormant. It felt like a ghost that couldn't quite let go of its life. Conversely, some of the previously poor parts of the city had been given a facelift and were now filled with new apartment and office blocks, trendy cafés and overpriced merchants of holistic medicines, organic vegetables and handmade pottery.

Dot didn't feel particularly welcome in any of those areas, and it made her feel like a bit of a relic. The city suddenly felt less like unchanging bricks and mortar and more like a living creature, changing its patterns, morphing in the shadows.

Those were the obvious differences in her city, but there was a less obvious change, too. Once, and for a long time, Dot had felt like she knew people, like she was part of the fabric of life. People used to stop and chat to her in the street, but now they tended to have their heads down, looking at their phones or listening to their music, privately. She didn't entirely blame or bemoan technology as it obviously improved people's lives in a lot of ways. But — whether it was society that had changed, or merely her own relationships, or a combination of both — she felt that people were much more isolated than they once were, and that she was much lonelier than she had been.

Was this why she was chasing down Max, Dot wondered. She'd seen something of her dad in Max, and she'd connected with someone for the first time in months, maybe years. She wasn't a huge believer in mysticism, but it felt like fate had introduced them for some purpose — after all, Max had led her to a winning lottery ticket.

She didn't stop. She kept walking, because it felt like she was meant to find Max. Given what she knew of Dock Road and what she expected of its reputation, Dot walked more quickly, hoping to catch Max before he disappeared inside his home.

Don't think about the muggers, Dot told herself as she raced along.

She arrived on Dock Road and it wasn't nearly as intimidating as she'd imagined. The streets were well lit, there were chip shops and pubs open, and festive lights (snowmen, snowdrops, bells) were being strung between the buildings.

She saw Max sauntering down the street, tapping his leg rhythmically.

She pursued him, shouting: 'Max, wait!' But he continued to tap and walk, turning to a block of flats and taking out a key. 'Max!' Dot shouted louder.

He turned in Dot's direction as she stumbled forward, her knee giving way with a shooting pain. She bent, stopping herself from tumbling completely, and Max ran towards her.

'Dot?' Max asked. 'Are you okay?'

Dot reached up and he helped her to stand up straight.

'Bloody knee,' Dot growled.

A few passers-by had stopped to check on her, but continued on when they realised she was okay. The initial pain quickly subsided, and she felt stupid for making such a scene.

'I'm fine, thanks,' Dot said to Max. 'I was just trying to catch up to you.'

'Why?' He took his earphones out.

Dot didn't want to stand in the street and blurt out her news – he'd definitely think she was a maniac. She needed to calm things down, to make it seem more normal. She looked along the road and spotted a neon coffee cup in a glass window – a café.

'Not here,' Dot said. 'How about a cuppa, over there?' She nodded to the café.

'I . . . I'm not sure. You're being weird again.'

'Oh, come on, I promise it's good news.'

94

He peered into her bag. 'You still have the rolling pin. I'm beginning to think you're an assassin, and I'm one of your targets.'

'If I was here to kill you, you'd be dead already.' Dot smirked. 'You must be tired after pulling up all those pond weeds. And it's cold. How about a coffee?'

Max sighed. 'All right, but I'm keeping my eye on my cup. You'd better not James Bond me.'

★

'You're a . . . millionaire?' Max blew on his syrupy coffee and took a sip. 'I don't get it.'

'Don't get what?' Dot asked, enjoying the aroma and heat of the café.

'The joke. What's the joke?'

'No joke. I choose the same five numbers each week and leave the sixth to chance. I picked seven because it was on your football shirt. Seven was the bonus ball.'

'You're having me on.' He sipped the coffee again, wrapping his hands around the mug to keep them warm. He stared at Dot's mugless hands. 'Aren't you going to have a drink?'

'I'm telling the truth. And no, I've got no money at the moment, so can't afford an overpriced so-called *coffee*.'

Max placed his mug on the table with a *thud* and his eyes widened accusingly. 'Wait, I thought you were buying me this coffee.'

'Why would you think that?'

'You invited me for a drink.' He quickly checked his wallet. 'Jeez, at least I've got enough to cover it. You're quite the host, you know that?'

'Buy your own coffee! I thought you didn't want handouts.'

'I don't, but . . .' He stared into his mug with a hint of frustration. 'Anyway, you said you're a millionaire now. But you can't afford a coffee, so clearly that's bullshit.'

'Could you not swear quite so liberally, please?' Dot admonished. 'I'm not used to it. And I *am* a millionaire.'

'Then *show me the money*, Jerry Maguire!'

'I don't have the money yet, the lottery has to pay me. So, for now, I'm broke.'

'That makes two of us.' His face softened. 'I'll buy you a coffee if you want one. You look cold and poor for a millionaire.'

'That's kind of you.'

Max smiled, clearly thinking that she was declining his offer. But Dot signalled to the waitress and ordered a latte with hazelnut syrup.

'I meant a cheap black coffee or a cup of tea,' Max said after the waitress left, checking his wallet again. 'You ordered the most expensive drink on the menu!'

'Well, you offered.' Dot chuckled. 'You shouldn't offer if you didn't mean it.'

'Did you just hustle me?' Max asked. 'You canny old bird.'

'You know, I think I did. I hustled a fence – that sounds wrong. Anyway, less of the *old bird*, thank you very much.'

'Fine. Well, maybe you can buy the next round, if I ever see you again. I get the feeling that's a possibility – I've talked to you more today than I have talked to anyone else in weeks.'

'I wanted to tell someone the news, and I wanted to pick your brains,' Dot said. 'On how to spend my money.'

Max resisted showing interest, but his raised eyebrow gave him away. 'I don't believe you, and I think you're at least a little bit insane. But okay, I'll bite. A million pounds . . .'

'What would you do with it?' Dot asked.

'Are you offering it to me? By the sounds of it, you only won because of me.'

'No, don't be silly. I might be old, but I'm not senile. But if you had a lot of money, what would you do with it?'

'Well, I'd have to pay this massive coffee bill first.' He shot her a glare.

'And then?'

He hummed. 'And then I'd get the hell out of here. There's nothing here for someone like me – no jobs, nothing interesting to do if you're poor, nobody worth sticking around for. Except my mum. I'd buy her a place somewhere nicer, where she'd be away from the shi— some people who make things harder for her. I'd take her away from here.'

'You're just a little darling, aren't you? I knew you were a good one.'

'Not really.' Max squirmed a little with the compliment.

'Buying old women coffees, helping your mum. And you rescued that bike from the pond – I noticed it has gone, by the way, so maybe a kid took it, after all.'

'Yeah, they did. I found a boy and showed him how to fix it up. I considered keeping it for myself – I don't have a bike right now – but it was too small.'

Dot's drink arrived and she sniffed it. The hazelnut scent instantly sent her back to roasting nuts on the fire with her dad one Christmas.

'You just get sweeter and sweeter,' Dot said playfully.

He blushed but looked a little hurt. 'Don't make fun.'

'I'm not! Well, maybe a little, but not in a mean way. You've a good heart, I can see that.' Dot sipped her drink to allow the awkwardness to dissipate. 'So, how do you know how to fix bikes? Did your dad teach you?'

'Him?' Max snorted. 'No. I learned it myself. I watched

YouTube videos, borrowed some books from the library before it was shut down and I bought some tools. I made a bit of money fixing friends' bikes, and bikes that . . . well, you know.'

'No, what?'

'Bikes that were *lost*.'

'Ah, I see. You fixed up stolen bikes and sold them?'

Max nodded. 'I thought I could do something like that, but it didn't work out.'

'Why not?' Dot asked.

Max shrugged. 'I got caught. But it was a legit business idea, if you ignore the crime bit.'

'Yeah, to be honest, I'm not too keen on the crime bit,' Dot said, feeling hypocritical. She'd got away with her crimes, but Max had been punished for his. She wasn't quite ready to admit her criminal history to him. She touched the scabs on her face and tried not to think about her recent attack. She wanted the conversation to change direction. Max had a less than enthusiastic response when she mentioned his dad, and that piqued her interest in him. 'What does your dad do, then, if he's not teaching you to fix bikes?'

'He's gone,' Max said. 'Screw him.'

'Dead? Mine too.'

'No offence, but I'd assumed both your parents were dead at your age. Wouldn't they be, like, a hundred years old by now?'

'True. I can't fault your maths skills, can I?'

Max tapped his temple and winked. 'I may have flunked every subject at school, but I'm not stupid.'

'I can tell that. I can see you've a few cogs whirring up there.'

'But no, my dad's not dead,' Max said. 'He's in jail, since I was ten. I didn't need him then, don't need him now.' He took a long, solemn drink of coffee.

Dot sensed Max didn't really want to talk about his dad and felt a little guilty for pushing the subject.

'My dad died when I was a little girl,' Dot said. 'And then my mum died much later. But she was younger than I am now.'

'Sorry.'

'Well, we've something in common. Both our dads were gone when we were young.'

Max smiled weakly. 'I guess.'

'You'll be fine. I can tell. Like you said, you just need a chance.'

Dot heard a voice in her head reminding her that Max was, at least in part, the reason she won the lottery. Maybe she ought to give him a break, give him some of her winnings. But another voice piped up, telling Dot that she couldn't just give a fortune away to someone she'd only just met. And anyway, she needed that money and she wanted it. It would change everything.

Max's phone rang and he answered it. 'Hi. Yeah, I'm nearly back, they made me stay late. I won't be long.' He hung up and then downed the rest of his coffee. 'I have to go. You were kidding, weren't you, about being a millionaire?'

'No.'

Max shook his head. 'I thought you were cool, but I don't like liars.'

'I'm not lying!'

His demeanour turned cold. 'Whatever. I have to go.'

He checked the bill and left money on the table.

'Why do you think I'm lying?' Dot protested, not wanting him to leave in a bad mood with her – not after they'd been getting along so well.

'It's too good to be true. Good things like that don't happen

99

to people like us. Maybe see you around, Dot.' He zipped up his coat and left before Dot had a chance to respond.

15

Hack

'Okay, hold it a little higher!' the photographer said. His voice sounded merry, Dot thought, but somebody needed to tell his face because he looked about as cheerful as a goth on death row. She figured he was probably bored of taking banal photos of lottery winners, miracle babies and oversized-vegetable growers.

Dot raised the giant cardboard cheque up to her chest and smiled, blinded by the camera flash.

'And now one with the shop owners,' the photographer said.

The corner shop owner and his wife, each dressed as though they were about to attend a royal wedding, stood either side of Dot.

'This will be one for the family album,' the owner said.

'Oh yes,' his wife, Chaha, said through grinning teeth. 'We will have to show my aunties in Nepal when we go!'

The photographer fiddled with his camera, and the shop owner broke his composure.

'Chaha, I've told you, we're not going to Nepal!' the owner said. He turned his head to Dot. 'She's been dreaming about Nepal, talking non-stop about Nepal, ever since we had champagne in the shop. I think she's still drunk.'

'I wish!' Chaha replied. 'You know, there's more to life than paying off the mortgage.'

Dot was beginning to regret doing the photo op at the shop, but she also didn't want to do it at her house, for two good reasons: she didn't want anybody to know where she lived, and she didn't want anybody to see Christmas Town or her Amazin' Rainforest. Not only would people think she was peculiar, but the shops she'd taken from might realise that she'd been stealing from them.

The couple stopped arguing to pose and smile for the camera. Photos complete, Dot placed the large cardboard cheque on the ground.

The shop owner offered the newspaper crew and Dot a cup of tea.

'Chaha . . . ?' The owner looked expectantly at his wife, but she barely hid her fury, and he quickly scuttled into the shop to boil the kettle.

'Do you have the money yet?' Chaha asked Dot. She gestured to the giant cardboard cheque. 'I don't think you can cash this cheque, can you?'

'Not unless I move to Brobdingnag.'

Chaha tried, but failed, to hide her confusion behind a nod and smile.

'Sorry, that was an obscure *Gulliver's Travels* reference. I just meant *not yet*, but they said it should be with me soon,' Dot said. 'I'll pay you back for the treats I took, I promise.'

'Oh, please, don't worry about that.'

Dot vowed to pay them back, and she planned on throwing in a nice bottle of champagne, or another suitably celebratory treat, to compensate them for their kindness.

'Do you mind if I ask a few questions?' a woman in almost-smart clothes asked Dot. 'I'm from *The Scotsman*. People love these kinds of stories. Rags to riches, you know.'

'Rags to riches?!' Dot blurted out.

She held back on calling the journalist a cheeky git and sending her away with a swift boot up her backside. Dot had promised the shop owner that she'd go along with the publicity stunt, as it might encourage more customers to his shop. He had said that people were strangely superstitious and that his shop might be considered lucky. She felt she owed them something, that she couldn't really refuse.

'Sorry,' the journalist said. 'I meant that people love happy stories about someone in the community coming up trumps. Can you tell me how you felt when you realised you'd won?'

'It was like a dream,' Dot said. 'It didn't feel real. I wondered if I'd died and gone to Heaven.' That sounded right, the kind of clichéd thing a lottery winner ought to say. And it felt not entirely untrue, either.

The journalist made notes in a pad, but Dot couldn't read her scrawl.

'That's great, just great!' the journalist said enthusiastically. 'And what did your friends and family think?'

'Oh, they were hysterical,' Dot said, imagining a group of hysterical people cheering and pulling party poppers.

'And your husband?'

'He's dead.'

The journalist bit her lip. 'Oops, sorry.'

That was strike two in Dot's eyes: *Oops* was really not an appropriate response to *My lifelong partner is pushing up the daisies*.

'So you're a widow,' the journalist continued. 'That's great.'

Strike three! Dot wondered whether the journalist was new to the job, or whether she'd done the job for so long that she didn't give two flying turds about insulting her interviewees.

'Is it?' Dot asked. 'I'm guessing you're not married?'

'Three times, actually,' the journalist said. 'I just meant that people like a story about someone who has had a hard time and then done well. And at least the money is all yours. Nobody to argue over who owns the house and cars, is there?'

'I suppose not. Every cloud has a silver lining,' Dot said sarcastically.

'Exactly. So, you've won a million. What do you plan on doing with it?'

'I really don't know yet,' Dot said, feeling the end of her tether fast approaching.

'Well, how about paying off the mortgage, a holiday and then giving something to charity? People like that.'

'Fine.' Dot resigned. The interview had degenerated into dull lies. She wanted to add a little spice. 'That, and I'm finally going to fulfil my dream of becoming the UK's oldest touring belly dancer.'

The journalist raised a suspicious but hopeful eyebrow. 'Really?'

'No. But please put something interesting in there for me, and let me know what you decide on because at the moment I haven't got a clue what I'll do with the money.'

'You can pay off *my* mortgage, if you like!' The journalist laughed at her own pseudo-joke.

What was it with people and their mortgages? Dot didn't have any grand ideas on how to spend her money yet but she was adamant that she wouldn't spend it on such dull pursuits.

'I'll think about it,' Dot said.

'A holiday, then? Barbados? Florida?' the journalist asked, her pen moving across her paper as though channelling a spirit.

Dot loved travelling with Charles but wasn't convinced it would be fun without him. Perhaps one day she'd feel up to jetting around the world on her lonesome, but not just yet.

'Do you know when the article will be printed?' Dot asked, to sidestep the question of holiday destinations.

'It's mostly digital these days. But if it's a slow news day tomorrow, you might see it in the printed version. Don't be disappointed if it doesn't feature, though. And watch out for yourself – there's a recession on and the vultures might start circling when they find out you've got some money. Trust me.'

'Okay, thanks,' Dot said, genuinely pleased to have received the advice. She hadn't really thought about people wanting to get close to her to access her new wealth, but it made sense.

'At least you don't have two ex-husbands clawing at your bank account, right?' the journalist said, dropping her notepad into her large coat pocket. She shouted to her photographer, who was busy checking through his digital photos. 'Doug, you ready? We've got the baked bean man next.'

Dot really wanted to ask about the baked bean man, but the journalist and photographer were already waving goodbye.

'What about the tea?' Chaha shouted as they walked towards their car.

'Next time!' the journalist shouted back.

Chaha gritted her teeth, staring at the shop door with a look of brimstone and vengeance in her eyes. Dot said a little prayer for the shop owner who, she assumed, was about to get the biggest row this side of Nepal.

*

Home, Dot had to play the waiting game. It was going to take almost two weeks for the money to reach her account. Her purse was practically a breeding ground for moths, but she had just enough left-over lemon drizzle cake to get by, and the anticipation of her massive wealth kept her mind busy.

Dot cleaned Christmas Town and thought about Mini Christmas. It was a small, boutique shop and the people who ran it probably relied on November–December trade to survive for most of the year. She totted up the total of everything she's taken from the shop, which was almost £1,000, and decided it was a small price to pay to set things straight. So, she decided: once the money was safely in her account, she would post an anonymous fat envelope to Mini Christmas to pay off her debt. Rather than having stolen from them for years, it was more like she'd had Christmas Town on loan.

The garden centre could go sit on a large cactus, though – it was huge and had been milking the plant-obsessed community with sub-standard flora and outdoor tat for years. Plus, Dot felt she'd at least paid off some of her thefts in tea and cake purchases over her dozens of visits. She watered her plants without remorse, staring out of her living room window.

She didn't live on the poshest of streets. She didn't have the nicest home. But it belonged to her and Charles, and she felt no great urge to move. It wasn't only a decision based on her emotional link to the raggedy old place – it wasn't just that she had a lifetime of memories drifting between its walls – it was also a decision based on sheer laziness: she couldn't be arsed to relocate. Moving house had been a kerfuffle over fifty years ago when she left her mum's place, so she had almost no desire to do it again now that she was in her seventies. She also liked that the people on her street decorated their homes for Christmas.

Christmas was fast approaching and it was Dot's favourite time of year. When she was younger, she spent Christmas Day with her mum: they cooked and ate the roast dinner together, choosing pork and apples over turkey and sprouts. Nobody actually liked turkey and sprouts, Dot was convinced, they were just part of a blindly followed tradition, possibly started by turkey breeders and sprout farmers. And people were willing to make themselves miserable for tradition, but not Dot or her mum.

Boxing Day was a time to visit friends. She would take little gifts of homemade fudge, excess Christmas crackers and little toys for her friends' children. She would take a bottle of sherry for the grown-ups. But as Dot and her friends got older, and the number of kids increased, Dot and Charles received fewer invitations to join them for Boxing Day. And the visits she did still make became increasingly less drunken, much to her disappointment.

So, once Dot's mum had passed, Dot and Charles stayed at home together for Christmas. They ate until they felt sick, then ate some more. They drank and kissed and watched Christmas TV shows and forgot about everything and everyone else. It was their perfect little Christmas, a world of their own making.

Dot smiled, the memories dancing like sugarplum fairies in her mind.

She stared at the people of Christmas Town, plugging them in so that the town's lights glowed and its train *choo choo*ed on its track, the skaters skated and the candy cane factory churned out its red-white sweet delights. The people looked so happy, singing and holding hands together, and she wished she could join them.

16

Tit for Tat

Dot stared at her bank statement:

Mrs Dorothy Hindley
Current balance: £1,000,154.23

The number was so long that it almost lost all meaning.
But it did mean something: freedom. She'd spent years
scrimping and saving, avoiding expense, worrying what
would happen if her bills rose or her boiler broke down.
Now, all of that worry was gone.

She must have looked at the statement for an hour, at least,
telling herself to wake up from the dream. Eventually she
accepted it as reality even if it felt unreal, made herself a
cheese sandwich, took one bite, wrapped the bitten sandwich
in cling film and put it into the fridge.

What was she doing? Cheese sandwiches were for Poor
Dot, and now she was Rich Dot. Rich Dot didn't eat
cheapest-cheese-per-gram sandwiches; she ate foie gras
and truffles, gold-leafed filet mignon. Poor Dot drank tap
water and sweet tea; Rich Dot drank mountain spring
water and expensive wines from far-away lands. Poor Dot
took the bus or walked to the charity shops to haggle over
second-hand winter coats; Rich Dot took limousines

to the swanky overpriced designer stores.

She reconsidered, because Rich Dot's life sounded a little too far outside her comfort zone. She'd never tasted foie gras and thought it was cruel to force-feed geese until their livers burst.

She didn't much like beef steak, either. And why eat gold? The local tap water was actually quite nice, and her overly sweet builder's brew instantly made her feel warm and cosy, whereas wine sometimes made her feel queasy. And, if she was honest, she quite liked riding the bus – yes, it was usually too hot or too cold, it was smelly and sometimes broke down, but she got to watch some interesting characters along the journey.

She would probably stop shopping at charity shops though, except for the big one in the city centre because that had a great selection of barely worn coats and some brilliant painted plates that she'd been coveting for a long time. Now was her time to become Plate Master Supreme.

Perhaps Rich Dot wouldn't be entirely different to Poor Dot. But she did feel immediately freer and less stressed. She no longer had to worry about money and could easily afford a comfortable lifestyle that would suit her, whatever that might be.

First things first, Dot had debts to pay off with the corner shop owners and the taxi driver. More importantly still, she wanted to thank the woman with the yappy dog who'd found her and probably saved her life. She called the local police station and explained the situation. After some back and forth, Dot received a call from the woman – Bonnie – who had saved her.

'We're glad you're okay,' Bonnie said. 'Clyde, that's my dog, was a little worried.'

'Me too.'

Dot offered to meet up as she wanted to give Bonnie and Clyde a present, but Bonnie declined.

'Maybe we'll just have a chinwag, next time we see each other in the park. What do you think?'

'That sounds lovely,' Dot said, feeling bad for ever having thought of Bonnie as sour-faced. The woman was a pure delight.

And Dot sensed something familiar in Bonnie's voice as they spoke over the phone, something she hoped didn't resonate in her own voice: loneliness. Bonnie didn't want an expensive piece of jewellery or a new TV – she just wanted a smile and a few kind words now and again. Dot could appreciate that. She ended the call feeling happy and a little sad about what had transpired between them.

The taxi driver who took her from the hospital was next on her to-reward list. She managed to get in touch with him and requested his bank details, then logged into her bank account and selected from the appropriate options:

Transfer amount: £500.00

Dot hesitated at first. She still hadn't got used to the idea that such a large amount of money was almost nothing to her now. She told herself that it was like giving away a hard mint from her big bag, that it was just spare change.

She clicked.

A rush of excitement and happiness washed through Dot. She looked at her phone, expecting the taxi driver to call immediately, but he didn't. It was a painful wait, like handing a gift to a friend and waiting for them to open it so she could see their reaction. Thirty minutes later, unable to wait any longer, she called the driver.

'I sent you the money I owe you, and a bit more,' Dot said. 'I just wanted to check you got it safely, that I didn't make a mistake.'

'I'll check, hold on,' the driver said. She could hear the clicking of buttons, then a minute or so later his voice sounded on the phone: 'There's a mistake, you've given me five hundred by accident! I'll send it right back.'

'No, it's not a mistake,' Dot said, her heart racing and palms sweaty with the thrill of it. 'It's a tip. I wanted to say thank you. You were good to me, you looked after me, and I wanted you to have something. Do something nice with it, won't you?'

'Are you sure?'

'Absolutely. I can afford it. Merry Christmas.'

'Wow. Thank you!' He sounded genuinely thrilled, and Dot couldn't be happier.

But the excitement, the joy, quickly faded. She visited the bank and took out wads of cash. She posted her fat envelope of cash through the door of Mini Christmas when nobody was paying attention. She visited the travel agents and bought a £1,000 coupon, returned to the corner shop and paid her outstanding treats bill. She passed the coupon to Chaha, who screamed so loudly that her husband almost dropped his cup of tea.

'You've done it now,' he said. 'I'll never hear the end of this. And I'll have to see my mother-in-law.' Then his brow unfurrowed and he smiled. 'Thank you.'

Dot beamed and continued on her Christmas Miracles Tour. It was only November, but that was close enough to Christmas for Dot to name the tour after the festive season. She walked through the decorated city, enjoying the bustle of people, cheery winter songs and fairy lights. She bought fudge and hot chestnuts, scoffing them as she walked.

She felt the weight of her years evaporate as she took a taxi to the garden centre, its entrance forest-deep with fir trees, its walls decorated with Bumblebee Santas lights displays.

Dot went straight to the café. The two crones she'd framed for shoplifting were at their usual table, sipping tea and muttering that the waiter was taking his sweet time, and maybe he didn't deserve such a cushy job if he couldn't even be bothered to look after them properly.

Dot sat and ordered a pot of tea. The waiter smiled and said hello as he placed the hot pot on Dot's table. Dot drank her tea quietly, smiling at the two crones as they bemoaned the cake for being too dry, and the weather for being too wet. They asked the waiter to give them more hot water so they could refill their teapot to leach a second serving from its already drained leaves.

'Can I get you anything else?' the waiter asked Dot when she had finished her tea.

'No, thank you,' Dot said, nodding at the crones. 'But I'd like to pay for the tea and cake that those two women had, please.'

'I'd better check . . .' The waiter approached the crones' table and spoke to them.

The two old women waved to Dot. 'Thank you!' they said cheerily. 'Do we know you?'

'No,' Dot said. 'But we girls have to stick together, don't we?'

They raised their teacups as a *cheers,* smiling at Dot and the waiter.

'There's a little something for you too, dear,' Dot whispered to the waiter, pointing to an envelope on the table. 'Don't let anyone else take it okay?' She walked away, waving to the newly cheerful crones, and hid among the fir trees.

The waiter screamed happily and ran around the café like

a turkey who'd just found out Christmas had been cancelled.

'Do you know who she is?' the waiter asked the crones, his face red as a robin's breast.

'No. We've no idea. Did she leave you something nice?'

The waiter began to cry, and the crones told him to sit, holding his hand and pouring him some weak tea.

Dot left the garden centre as bright and buzzing as its Bumblebee Santas lights displays.

That buzz, too, didn't last. By the time she was home and her large portion of fish and chips – with extra sauce, a pickled onion, mushy peas, gravy and a suspiciously red saveloy sausage – had arrived, Dot's euphoria had subsided.

Dot ate her dinner slowly, unable to finish it.

What was wrong with her? She had no money concerns, she'd made a bunch of other people ecstatic, so why wasn't she happy?

*

Dot visited the park every day in the hope of meeting Bonnie and Clyde. She was keen to thank them again and be true to her word of a chinwag with Bonnie, and her persistence soon paid off.

'I think you might have saved my life, you know,' Dot said to Bonnie while she gave Clyde belly tickles.

Bonnie blushed and told Dot to hush, and that she was just there at the right time. She really didn't want any fuss and she was glad to see a friendly face in the park, rather than just picking up after Clyde.

'Well, don't be a stranger, will you?' Dot said, when Bonnie told her they'd better get back home because their favourite TV show was starting soon.

'You too,' Bonnie said. 'Say goodbye and thank you, Clyde.'

Clyde licked Dot's hands clean of cheesy treats dust, and they walked away with a brief wave and wag.

Dot walked home again, pleased that she'd made the effort and a couple of new friends, wondering why she'd taken so long to say hello to someone she'd seen probably hundreds of times over the years. She'd make more of an effort from now on, she decided.

Home again, Dot's house was almost uncomfortably hot despite the frost outside. But she liked being able to keep the boiler pumping, making the house roasty toasty. She reclined on her comfy chair and imagined herself on a sunny beach, ignoring the sound of mail falling through her letterbox.

Her post these days consisted of personalised letters from a variety of charities: cancer was the most common appeal, followed by cat and dog rescue centres, then homelessness and help for war veterans. Even donkeys made an appearance.

It was all too much. There were too many mouths to feed, too many outstretched hands and hoofs for Dot to consider. She couldn't help everyone and handing money to people she didn't even know (and probably wouldn't ever meet) didn't feel like it would scratch her itch.

Yes, she wanted to help people less fortunate than her – it was something she'd always striven to do as a nurse and half-decent member of the human race. But she wanted the money to make a big difference, and it had to be for the right cause and not simply the causes that printed the best flyers.

Perhaps that wasn't as altruistic as Dot liked to think she was. But it was how she felt.

The doorbell rang and she answered, taking a small parcel from the delivery man and thanking him. She tore off the brown paper wrapping and opened the long, thin box inside.

A silver locket on a chain.

Online, it had looked remarkably close to the locket her dad had given her. But it felt too new, it weighed less in her hand, the catch was too thin, the hinges opened too smoothly and it didn't contain her dad's picture. It just wasn't the same, it was a fake. She threw it into the bin. Better to have no heart, than a false one.

Dot sat on her comfy seat and gazed at all the new items that overfilled her home:

A big TV – probably her finest purchase, but far too large and overly complex for her basic TV needs. It was seemingly created by an alien intelligence far superior to humankind. She could just about manage to find the old terrestrial channels but was a little worried that she would inadvertently stumble onto some extra-terrestrial ones.

A new mobile phone – to replace the one that had been stolen, although she had no phone numbers to enter into it.

A massaging chair – it seemed like a good idea. It was fine when it was just being a regular chair, but the massages made her feel unwell and slightly fearful for her life.

A coffee machine – it smelled wonderful, but it kept demanding beans and water from her like a particularly farty child. The coffee was also too strong for her tastes, so she went back to using the freeze-dried variety and her kettle.

A tablet computer – how did this thing work? Her regular computer had a mouse and keyboard, but the tablet was more like an expensive chopping board.

Christmas Town expansions – she knew she shouldn't. She *knew* it. But she couldn't resist. She told herself it was to pay back the store for all the confusion she must have caused over missing stock, and to make herself look more innocent. But deep down, deep in her Christmas stockings, she knew that it was because she had a problem. At least Christmas was less than a month away, which meant that nobody would realise the full extent of her problem. Not that she had any visitors.

She wandered about her house, sighing at the other useless items she'd bought: a foot-scrubbing shower mat, a laser hair plucker, a variety of whimsical gnomes, a donut-making machine, a chocolate fountain, the collected records of Pink Floyd on vinyl, a record player that she had yet to set up and, perhaps most confusingly, a four-person table tennis set but no table to play on. She blamed the expensive champagne she'd been drinking recently.

It was all junk, and Dot knew it. The items looked fun or sounded revolutionary but they merely added additional layers of confusion and frustration to her life and not much else beyond requiring her to recycle a never-ending supply of cardboard boxes while hiding the polystyrene under her bed. She would have to give the new items away, creating even more dull administrative work for herself.

Dot came to a couple of conclusions: giving her money to nice people gave her momentary flashes of glee; buying expensive gadgets and gizmos mostly made her grumpy. It felt like she was spending way too much time considering how she ought to spend her money.

When she and Charles were together, she never thought about this kind of thing. She was happy most of the time, or at least comfortable with life, and gained a lot from little things. It wasn't the *stuff* or *big gestures* that made her life happy, it was the feeling that she belonged somewhere, that she had a companion to share her time with.

She wanted that feeling back. She wanted a friend.

17

On Your Bike

'It's top of the range,' the bike shop seller said to Dot, her badge revealing that her name was Chloe and she was apparently *Wheely Happy to Help!*

For once, Dot believed the overly enthusiastic name badge because Chloe was the chirpiest bike seller she'd ever met, especially once Dot had asked to see the best bike in the shop.

'What makes it so good?' Dot asked, running her hand along the smooth frame of the bike. She squeezed its tyre in an attempt to look as though she knew more than zilch about bikes.

'This baby has a chromoly frame, making it lightweight, flexible and strong – it's like riding on a cloud,' Chloe said. 'It has full suspension with high-tech springs and hydraulic dampening, meaning you could ride it through a minefield and not feel the shock, plus it has state-of-the-art electronic shifting for incredibly smooth and quick gear changes, and hydraulic disc brakes that could stop a freight train.'

'Reeeeeally!' Dot said, not entirely listening. Chloe's enthusiasm was enough to convince her that this was the right bike. 'And what colours does it come in?'

'We only have this one in the shop,' Chloe said, rubbing a smudge from the bike's black frame. 'Black looks the coolest, if you ask me. But we could order it in another colour if you prefer. It might take a while, it's a really well-designed bike, so the technicians build it by hand.'

'No, I'll need it today,' Dot said. 'And black looks good with anything.'

'It's for *you*?' Chloe asked.

Dot nodded. It wasn't exactly a lie: she intended to ride the bike at least once, and she wanted to seem like the kind of person who'd ride a really expensive and high-tech bike. She briefly imagined herself on a skateboard, riding it down council railings and flying over unemptied park bins while onlookers cheered.

'That's so cool!' Chloe said.

Dot grinned. She liked this girl's spirit, and that Chloe so readily believed her lies. But she was weaving tangled webs with her words and didn't want to cause any bike-related problems.

'Actually, it's a gift,' Dot corrected. She held her hand up in the air. 'For someone this tall.'

'I see.'

'Do you work on commission?' Dot asked.

'Yes, but I hope you haven't felt pressured.'

'Not at all. But in that case, I'll buy a bunch of accessories, too. I don't know what I need, but can you put a bag of items together for me?'

'Of course! Anything in particular?'

'Do you have a basket and ribbons? Oh and those clickety clack things that you can put on the wheels.'

Chloe smiled awkwardly. 'We do, but I'm not sure a basket and spokester clips really suit this kind of bike.'

'Just the ribbons then,' Dot said. 'The most colourful ones you have.'

'That, I can do,' Chloe said, practically dancing as she picked up a basket and wandered the shop's aisles.

It was a ridiculous amount of money to spend on a bike, but it was worth it – the buzz was back, and stronger than before. She couldn't wait to see Max's face.

★

This bike was a different beast to any other that Dot had ridden before. Admittedly, Dot hadn't ridden a bike in probably twenty years, but the adage was true: she hadn't forgotten how.

After her initial practice wobbles in the shop, as Dot tried to maintain balance with a few worried looks from the staff, she was ready and raring to go.

She rode on the cycle paths, which hadn't existed until relatively recently, or on the pavements when the cycle paths disappeared. There was no way she was going to cycle on the road, even though the cars passed by infrequently – she'd seen too many cycling safety adverts on the TV, back when the authorities were obsessed with making short films showing the public how not to die.

Pushing the terrible images of frazzled children, irradiated suitcases and flaming chip pans from her mind, Dot began to enjoy the ride.

The bike rode smoothly and the wind pushed against her face as she peddled faster and faster. She felt like a kid again and wondered if she should really go through with her plan. Or perhaps she should order another bike in flamingo-pink with plenty of extras – especially the basket, and maybe a comedy horn. But probably not the ribbons because those kept hitting her in the face or threatening to tangle in the bike's wheels.

She'd not seen Max in two weeks and hoped that he'd cooled

down a bit. He'd said that he was doing community service until the new year, so he ought to be at the park unless they had finished all their jobs there. This would prove Dot wasn't lying to him, wouldn't it? He'd feel like a top-notch plonker, and then she'd say, 'Oh, this old thing? It's actually for you!' And he'd gasp and say he couldn't believe it, and then he'd say, 'Oh Dot, you're the best, you know that?'

And then maybe they'd be friends again. Not that they ever were friends, not really, but they had a similar sense of humour, and they spoke to each other like friends. She felt like they were hatched from the same egg, despite their more apparent differences, and she couldn't remember the last time she liked someone as much as she liked Max.

★

Max was alone again, busy painting the fence around the pond with a tiny brush. Had he been in another fight? Had he been gifted some time alone for good behaviour? The reasons for his solitude could go either way, but he looked quite serene as he painted. He took his time; he was precise. He whistled.

He must have been in a good mood, then, because nobody whistles when they're sad or angry.

She rolled the bike along the path, walking beside it.

'Ey up, Picasso!' Dot called out to Max.

Max turned his head slowly to face her. 'Oh, it's you. Hi.' His eyes widened. 'Is that the Rambler 3k, with the hydraulic dampeners?!'

'Oh, this old thing?' Dot said, cackling inside her head. 'Yeah, I just thought I'd go for a ride.'

He placed the tin of paint on the ground, balancing the paint brush on its lid. 'I've read about this – it's pretty much the best bike in the country.'

'Pretty much?' Dot swallowed a momentary glob of frustration. 'Well, I wanted it with clickety clackers and a basket, but the woman at the shop told me not to get them. Shows what she knows.'

'She's right. But I meant it's awesome!'

Dot rolled the bike towards Max. 'And now . . . it's yours.'

Max's fingers shook and he reached towards the bike as though expecting his hands to pass through it, like it wasn't real.

'Huh?' he uttered.

'A gift from me to you. I owe you for that coffee, remember?'

'But, you . . . Huh?'

Yes, this felt wonderful. She loved his mix of confusion and hesitant joy. She wanted to scoop it up and store it in a jar.

Dot grasped one of Max's hands and placed it on the handlebars of the bike. He gripped it and smiled.

'It's yours,' Dot repeated. 'I got it for you. You said that you didn't have a bike but you liked working on them. And I thought it would be useful.'

'It will be,' Max said, inspecting the bike's frame and tyres with a look of surety that suggested he knew much more about bikes than Dot did. Not that knowing more about bikes than Dot was particularly difficult. 'This is amazing. I can do deliveries on this! I can get out of the city and go riding in the hills.' He looked up at Dot. 'What's the catch?'

'No catch,' Dot said.

Although she did want something, but she couldn't really say that she just wanted him to be her friend. It would make her sound like a little kid in school. What was she going to do next, ask him to her birthday party? Tell him to call his mum to check if he could come over to her house for dinner?

'You're just giving me this bike, which must have cost . . . what, about three grand?'

'Three and a half. Yes. You deserve a chance – nobody would give you one, remember? Well, now you've got one.'

Max lowered the kickstand on the bike so that it stood without him holding it. He lurched towards Dot and wrapped his arms around her, squeezing.

'Hey, less squeezy, please!' Dot protested. 'My rib's not fully better yet.'

'Sorry!' Max said, unhugging her and backing off. 'Are you okay?'

'I'm fine. So, are you convinced now?'

'You really are loaded,' Max said. 'Sorry I didn't believe you, but—'

'But I couldn't afford a coffee and my jumper had holes in it. I know, it was hard to believe.'

'Are you like some kind of flamboyant businesswoman who helps random strangers? Do you live a secret life? Are you Batman?'

'No. No. And yes.' Dot lowered her voice. 'I am Batman.'

Max laughed. 'So, what's the deal?'

'I won the lottery. And I don't really know what to spend my money on. But I like you – you seem like one of the good guys – so I thought you deserved something nice.'

'That's it?' Max asked.

'That's it. No strings, no deals, no killer clowns.'

'Well, thanks. Really. This could change everything, and it's so cool!' Max's exuberance suddenly shifted and he sighed. 'But it's worth a fortune. I'll have to hide it.'

'Why?' Dot asked.

'You saw where I lived, right? If I lock this bike up anywhere near my house, it'll be gone within an hour.'

'I'm sure a practical guy like you can work something out,' Dot said. She removed the rucksack on her back and passed it to him. 'There's a bunch of bikey stuff in there, including a strong lock. The girl who sold it to me thought the same thing as you, so she included a lock which she said was unbreakable.'

Max peered into the bag, rummaging through its contents. 'This is insane. Dot, thanks.' He looked like he might tear up, and Dot willed the tears to fall – she loved a good old happy cry. But Max remained composed. He dipped his hand into his jeans pocket and took out his phone. 'What's your mobile number?'

'I recently got a new one, so I've no idea,' Dot said. 'I can give you my landline, but why?'

'I'm going to repay you. Not in money, I'm not a millionaire like you. But I can do stuff, you know. Like, if you need some groceries delivered, or you want me to drop some weed off at your place.'

'Weed!' She tried to sound appalled, but a sudden urge to try it erupted within her. 'We'll see. I mean, that's really nice but not necessary.'

'I'm your genie,' Max said. 'At least, until you get too demanding, or this becomes weird. This isn't *Harold and Maude* territory, is it? This isn't . . . weird, is it?'

'One hundred per cent not weird,' Dot said, smiling.

She told him her landline number and he entered it into his phone. She retrieved her new mobile phone from her coat pocket and Max dialled his phone with it to store her mobile number.

'This is the best thing ever!' Max said, beaming. He hopped

onto the bike and cycled it around Dot. 'It's so smooth; the suspension is amazing. Let's go on a ride some time, you and me!'

He looked almost impossibly happy. She imagined herself riding alongside Max on her pink bike, both of them laughing and singing and smiling. If she really had a chance at fulfilling her dreams, at trying to make and complete her bucket list, then she thought she might like to do it with someone like Max.

Dot felt the buzz grow inside her, stronger than ever. And this time, it didn't fade.

18

Out with the Old

Boxes and drawers, cupboards and closets. Why did people hide everything away? Tidying up was about as enjoyable to Dot as shaving her legs with a rusty razor, but on occasion it was a necessity. And this was one of those occasions, because her house was becoming cluttered with new knick-knacks and old keepsakes. The cardboard boxes from her tipsy midnight purchases were also mounting and Dot wondered whether it was easier to abandon her home completely in favour of building a cardboard box castle.

She'd considered hiring a cleaner, but was too embarrassed about her mess and didn't really want a stranger going through her things. Plus, her mum's voice sounded in her ear: 'Paying someone else to clean *your* house! Ridiculous!'

Dot tried to convince herself that hiring a cleaner would not only provide someone with paid work, but that the knock-on effects to the economy could be exponential. The cleaner would pay taxes and spend money, which would go into funding libraries and parks and social services. Or, possibly more likely, the money would find its way into the pockets of corrupt politicians. Which was to say, the pockets of pretty much any politician.

Dot's mum's distaste for hiring a cleaner won out from beyond the grave. She really did shout quite loudly to Dot from beneath the soil, and so Dot hoped her mum's yelling wasn't keeping her dad awake, down there. Or, hopefully, *up* there.

Dot flattened an unholy number of cardboard boxes and barely remembered objects (faded *Simpsons* mugs, a headless dog statuette, musty library books she'd not returned in twenty years – oops, calculating the fines made her head spin – mismatching shoes, four lidless and chipped casserole dishes, and plenty more besides) into the big communal bins on the street. She tossed old clothes into black bin bags, to re-donate them to the charity shops they'd originally come from, like old friends returning home a little worse for wear.

Dot felt a little remorse at decluttering, more so than she had with previous declutters. Her home had a lot of new items in it, and it felt as though she was pushing out the old to make way for the new, like she was exchanging parts of her past for parts of someone else's future.

'Sentimental fool,' Dot said aloud to herself to prevent her from returning the chipped *D'oh-Nuts! Simpsons* mug into a kitchen cupboard. 'Why cling onto things I forgot that I owned?' she said, feeling silly for talking aloud to nobody.

After decluttering, she cleaned (which she hated even more than decluttering). To help the time pass as cheerily as possible, she plugged in her record player and let The Clash sing about fighting the cops, boogaloos and bankers. And, to her surprise, cleaning up wasn't quite as bad as she had expected.

Why hadn't she done this years ago? The place felt so much bigger, so much airier and freer than it ever had. Except for Christmas Town and the Amazin' Rainforest, which still dominated the lounge.

She looked over Christmas Town, all of its Christmassy

people and other magical inhabitants, and thought about getting rid of it. But she couldn't do it; she'd spent so long stealing them and putting them all together that she couldn't bear to tear them apart. And they didn't really demand much of Dot – if she left them for a few days, a month, even years, they would remain unchanged, for ever enjoying the festivities.

But the plants of the Amazin' Rainforest were another matter. They required watering and repotting, and some of the less fortunate specimens had taken several turns for the worse. She separated the sick and dying plants from the jungle, placing them on her coffee table, then penned a sign on a particularly thick piece of rogue cardboard that had evaded her recent cardboard massacre:

FREE PLANTS
Take good care of us

She drew a happy plant on the sign and placed it beside her front door. Then she moved all of the healthy plants next to the sign (ignoring the fact that she'd created a serious botanical tripping hazard) and returned indoors to drink mugs of hot, sweet tea while hoping that passers-by would take her kidnapped children home with them.

While Dot was busy straining her teabag for a second use, a little *tippity tap tap* sounded on her front door. She opened it to a couple of small runny-nosed kids who were wrapped up in thick coats.

'Hello,' the eldest of the kids, approximately seven years old, said.

'Hello,' Dot replied.

'Can we have your plants, please? The sign says it's okay.'

Dot peered out to see that a few of the plants had been taken, but many still remained.

'What for?' Dot asked, unsure why two kids would want so many houseplants.

'We're making special boxes to give to people who don't have many things,' the older kid said. 'People like plants, don't they?'

'Yes, they do. That's a great idea,' Dot said. 'So, sure, take as many as you like!'

'Thaaaank youuuu,' the kids said in unison.

Dot watched them run back and forth between her plants and their house. Their dad stood in the doorway of their home, observing his kids. He waved to Dot from across the street and shouted: 'Thank you.'

Dot waved back, shouting: 'No problem!'

Between the eager kids and a few more interested neighbours, soon enough all the plants had found new homes.

Purged – that's the word that came to Dot's mind. She had purged the house of the baggage she had been gathering over the years, and despite the missing oxygen that her plants had provided, Dot felt that the air seemed cleaner and she could breathe more deeply.

But some parts of her past absolutely could not leave, especially her photo albums. She had dozens of them and she flipped through them now with hesitation because she knew the past had the power to upset her. And she was right: her heart broke a little when she saw pictures of Charles, all handsome and happy. But they also reminded her that she'd done something worthwhile with her life – she'd spent the best parts of her life with a man she loved, and who loved her.

There were so many people in her past that she didn't even recognise them all. Many were on the verge of being remembered. How many people had she forgotten, and how many had forgotten her?

It felt uncomfortable to think of herself as a background character in someone else's life, but she must be exactly that to dozens, hundreds, or even thousands of people – a forgotten face in a photograph, barely even noticed. Dot had thought of herself and her life as the main story, but there were so many others going on, so many sadder stories, so many better ones too.

She looked at herself through the decades and thought that she was beautiful back then, elegant and smiley. Was that arrogant? Vain? She didn't care. She and Charles were a cute couple, narcissism be damned.

But visiting the past made Dot miss Charles and her parents and her friends. It made her realise how much her life had changed. Still, it was nice to see them again, to remember that they had lives together once upon a time. She picked out some of her favourite photos so she could frame them later: Dot and Grace bowling with the nurses. Dot and Charles at the beach, trying to out-eat each other at the ice cream van. Dot and her mum in the garden, cutting flowers for her cousin's wedding. They were good memories, and she wanted to keep making them.

Perhaps she'd been handling her lottery win wrong all along! Her newfound wealth wasn't just able to buy *stuff*; it was able to buy *experiences*. It could help her to forge new memories, to enjoy her time rather than simply surrounding her with mod cons and Christmas ornaments. She ought to break out of the cocoon of her home and *do* something with her time and money.

Dot had hoped Max would call, but she didn't expect him to. He was just nineteen, after all, so calling an older *weird woman* (as he termed her) was unlikely to be high on his agenda. But she hoped he would.

And then, as if answering a prayer, her mobile phone rang. She answered.

'Dot?' Max's voice sounded.

'Yes, who is this?' Dot asked coolly, not wanting to scare him with her enthusiasm.

'It's Max. You remember, from the park. You gave me the bike. Remember?'

'Of course I remember, I'm not senile.'

Max cleared his throat. 'I know, sorry. I was just calling because I was wondering . . . do you need anything? I've got the bike, so I can run some errands.'

'No need, but thanks,' Dot said. She was a little disappointed that he was only calling to offer support, though she appreciated his kindness. If she wanted to make friends, Dot told herself, she ought to take some initiative. 'But how about a little trip out? You and me.'

'We could, but . . . I can't give you a backie. I mean, I could, but it's kinda dangerous. And the bike's not got a spare seat.'

'I'll meet you there. I'll take a taxi.'

He hesitated. 'Well, okay then. When?'

'Tomorrow?'

'Okay, I'm free. Where?'

'You decide. I want to do something fun.'

Max hummed. 'The zoo? Is that a stupid idea?'

'I love it!' Dot practically yelped. 'Meet you outside the zoo at 10 a.m.? I'll pay.'

'All right, Dot.' He sounded surprisingly chipper, so maybe he was as excited as she was! 'They've got pandas. Awesome.'

'Awesome, indeed.' She hung up and smiled happily.

19

Tigers May Bend Their Bars

Dot's taxi stopped outside the zoo, where Max was already waiting, his breath clouding in the cold air. She had imagined he would be on his bike, figuring that he was enjoying it so much that it would need to be surgically removed from his buttocks, but he was hopping on the spot with his hands buried in his trouser pockets.

Dot waved to Max and he waved back.

'Your grandson?' the taxi driver asked, adjusting her car's mirrors for a better look.

Dot wasn't keen on the assumption. 'A friend.'

She paid the taxi driver, tipping slightly less generously than she would have if the driver hadn't made that remark, and joined Max outside.

'Ready to check out those pandas?' Dot asked.

'Yes, but they're pretty rowdy. I heard they've been causing panda-monium.' Max chuckled at his own joke and looked at Dot expectantly.

'Why do men love puns so much?'

'I dunno, they're infectious. It's a panda-emic.' He chuckled again.

Dot sighed. 'There are a lot of animals in there, and I'm guessing you've got a lot of animal puns lined up, right?'

He blushed. 'Yeah.'

'Do you want to get them out of your system now, and we'll call a ceasefire on the puns while we're inside? Come on, tell me your best ones now, and I'll pretend they're amusing.'

'Jeez, Dot, lighten up! I've bear-ly started.'

'I'll not panda to your whims, Max.' She felt a little disgusted with herself. 'Now that's over with, let's go inside and you can tell me some of the animal facts you've memorised.'

'Have I?'

'Of course you have. You love to share movie quotes, so you almost certainly love to tell people facts.'

Max raised his hands, as if at gunpoint. 'Okay, you caught me. But is it going to be like this the whole time we're here, you telling me what I can't say? That's not cool, Dot. I thought you were cool.'

'I *am* cool!' Dot said. She shivered. 'Cold, actually.'

'Let's head inside, then. The monkey house is heated, and the monkeys are my favourites.'

★

'Queen, your people await,' Max said, saluting to Dot outside the monkey house.

'The cheek!' Dot said. She smiled and waved a hand in circles as she entered, like royalty waving to her subjects. 'Thank you.'

Inside, Max watched the monkeys with wide eyes and an even wider grin. The animals leapt between food bowls and branches, hung on their tails and chased each other around their glass enclosure.

'Go on, then,' Dot said. 'What are your monkey facts? Educate me.'

'Capuchins can use tools,' Max said, pointing to a capuchin. 'They've been doing it for more than three thousand years!'

'They live for three thousand years? I never knew! They must have seen an awful lot. It seems a shame to trap them in this glass box.'

Max rolled his eyes. 'Sarcasm's the lowest form, Dot.' He pointed to a finger-sized monkey. 'That's a pygmy marmoset, the smallest monkey in the world. The babies weigh as little as three grams.'

'Okay, that's quite impressive,' Dot said, feeling a little bad for her snarky comment about the capuchins. 'How do you know all this?'

'The internet,' Max said. 'You should try it some time.'

'Actually, I use the internet all the time. Less of the stereotyping, thank you very much.'

'Less of the bossing me about, thank you very much.'

Dot held out her hand. 'Deal.'

Max shook it. 'So, what do you do on the internet? The same as everyone else?'

'What does everyone else do?'

'Watch . . . *extreme romance.*'

'No!' Dot's voice squeaked with alarm. She wanted to get his mind out of the gutter. 'I look up monkey facts as well. Like, did you know there are more than two hundred and sixty kinds of monkeys in the world?'

'So, you're a geek.' Max laughed.

'No, I'm just interested. And I do some online shopping.'

'Like what?'

Dot thought of Christmas Town. 'Bits and bobs. Rolling pins, mainly, to hit men with.'

'Have you decided what you're going to spend the rest of your money on?' Max asked, placing his hand against the glass to allow a monkey to inspect his palm. 'You can't spend it all on bikes, even though that'd be amazing.'

'I've no clue,' Dot said. 'I'm open to suggestions.'

Max led them out of the monkey house and towards the pandas. Dot stopped to buy ice cream panda faces on sticks. Max questioned the logic of eating ice cream when it was so cold outside, but Dot assured him that ice cream didn't follow the rules of conventional logic, and he was satisfied.

The pandas were asleep, so Dot and Max watched a brief video about the zoo's attempts to breed the bears to raise their numbers. The video informed them that pandas were shown videos of other pandas *being intimate*, to encourage them to mate.

'They're just like you, Max,' Dot said.

'Sleepy?'

'No, they're into their *extreme romance* movies.'

Max glanced around at the other zoo visitors, his face reddening. He didn't laugh, and Dot wondered if her jibe had been too public. She'd try not to embarrass the poor lad in public again – until his hairline-fractured ego had mended, at least.

'Do you think you'd want to live in a zoo?' Max eventually asked. 'If you were an endangered animal, I mean.'

'Probably not. It seems quite boring,' Dot said.

'But nature's scary. Most wild animals are either killed by another animal, or they die of some horrible disease. And they're always looking for food and trying to avoid danger.'

'So you'd rather be in a cage, where it's comfortable?'

'I dunno. Maybe. I was reading about zoo animals and got to tigers, then I dived down this Wiki-rabbit-hole and read this poem about a tiger. It was questioning how a good God could make something as fearsome as a tiger. I can't remember that much of it, it was old. But it was decent. It started like this: "Tyger Tyger, burning bright / In the forests of the night / What immortal hand or eye / Could frame your fearful symmetry?"'

'Is it by William Blake?' Dot asked.

'Yeah, that's him! Do you know him personally?'

Dot felt like slapping Max. 'He was around hundreds of years ago!'

'Exactly. So, did you know him?' Max winked.

Dot cuffed his shoulder gently. 'Cheeky sod. We read him at school.'

'I didn't like poetry at school, but this was pretty interesting. It made me think about how we think we're meant to be one thing, but maybe deep down we're something completely different. Then I got this voice in my head, like this little fire crackling. It made me want to write, so I wrote my own poem about a caged tiger and how we're all trapped behind invisible bars.'

Dot hadn't expected an existential crisis from their zoo visit, and she was taken aback by Max's sudden philosophical musings.

'You're a poet?' Dot asked. 'You're full of surprises, aren't you! Can I read it?'

Max shook his head. 'It's the first one I've ever written. I sent it to my dad, as part of his letter. I thought he might get what I was trying to say because he's literally pacing behind bars, desperate to get out. But we're all a bit like that, too, aren't we? We're just animals that want to break out, but we're held back.' He bit his lip. 'But you're not. I mean, you're not held back anymore. You can do whatever you like.'

'Can I? I feel like I've got my own cages, too. My knee keeps giving me gyp, for example.'

'Sure, but you don't have to work and you don't have to worry about money. Why aren't you out there, just doing whatever the hell you want?'

It was a sharp question, it cut.

'You might be right,' Dot said. 'I was thinking the same thing, recently – what would make me happy?'

'What did you decide?'

'I'm not sure. But . . .' She wasn't sure whether she should be so candid – it could scare Max away. But then again, he'd proven himself to be much deeper than she'd expected. He'd surprised her several times in the short time she'd known him. 'Maybe having a friend to do things with. Fun things.'

His voice softened, as though he didn't want the people around them to hear. 'You don't have any friends?' he asked.

Dot felt her eyes well. Her loneliness had seemed like a whisper, and she didn't want to admit it aloud.

'No,' she finally said. 'Not really.'

They watched the pandas sleep.

'Me neither,' Max said. 'Not really any proper friends since I left school. They're all busy at work, or looking after their kids, or in jail, or somewhere else.'

They continued to watch the pandas sleeping, their fat bellies slowly rising and falling. Dot's sadness and concern began to fade. She wasn't the only lonely person, then. Max was like her.

'I'll be your friend,' Max said, not taking his eyes off the sleeping pandas. 'If you want to be friends. We could do a lot of things.'

'Really?' Dot asked.

'Yeah. You seem nice, I think we could have fun. Plus, you're loaded.'

Was he just joking? No, he wouldn't be cruel enough to joke about this.

'Okay, then.' She smiled. 'I'd like that.'

Max adopted a husky, old-fashioned New York accent. 'Louis, I think this is the beginning of a beautiful friendship.'

'*Casablanca*?' Dot asked.

'Correct.'

'Okay, then,' Dot said. 'We can meet up whenever you're free. My diary's pretty much empty, in between doing nothing and zilch.'

'I've still got community service and I have to keep looking for work, but otherwise I'm the same.' Max's capuchin-like smile reflected in the glass of the panda enclosure.

'How about we try a bucket list?' Dot asked, the idea swiftly becoming more enticing to her with the promise of Max's company.

Max raised an eyebrow. 'Isn't that a list of things to do before you die? Are you planning on killing me, after all? Where's your rolling pin?'

Dot laughed. 'Not murder, not this time. But we're all dying, aren't we? I want to get a head start on my list. I don't have a lot of time to waste, you know.'

'Yeah, all right then!' Max beamed, holding out his hand. 'You think up some ideas, since it's your list.'

Dot was unable to contain her excitement. 'I hope you're ready!' She shook his hand so hard and fast that she worried it might tear off.

'Bring it on.'

20

The Bucket List

It had been snowing. Snow was Dot's favourite form of precipitation – it painted everything a comforting, blankety white. She liked that snowfall made the world look like television static. She loved that layered snow seemed to mute the city noise, that your foot left imprints on the snowy ground. It changed her sense of the city, made it feel gentler to her.

Sipping sweet tea, she watched it fall from behind her lounge window. It reminded her of walking through the Baltic cold in a miniskirt to meet her girlfriends, and the winter morning that Charles woke her up extra early to build a snowman.

Dot sang a rock ballad medley to herself as she retrieved a pen and notepad from her newly tidied desk drawer. She sat at the coffee table beside her sickly-but-improving ward of plant patients. She gave them a quick dousing with her miniature watering can and considered what she ought to add to her bucket list.

She wanted to choose a mixture: some things that she'd never done before, but maybe also a few that she'd not done in a long time and used to enjoy. While it was *her* list, she wanted to have fun with Max so didn't want too many activities that he might find boring or hate. One or two, perhaps, but not too many. And she shouldn't choose anything that would span a lot of time, like a holiday, because she couldn't expect Max to sacrifice days or weeks on end. Any lengthy activities would have to be done on her own, if at all. So, Dot decided to start small.

She stared at the paper, waiting for inspiration. She tried to think about the times she was happiest and what kinds of things she was doing, and the ideas started to arrive all at once, like buses. She began to write:

> *The Bucket List*
> *1 Build a snowman*
> *2 Afternoon tea*
> *3 Go dancing*
> *4 Day at the fair*
> *5 Movie marathon*
> *6 Ride a horse*
> *7 Fire a gun*

Had she really got the hang of this? Aside from firing a gun (where had that come from?), each of the items on her list felt pretty tame, albeit enjoyable. The movie marathon wasn't even that appealing to Dot, but she thought Max would like it.

Still, the first item on her list was easy to achieve.

She picked up the phone and called Max.

★

'This weather's a nightmare to cycle in,' Max said, his face covered in a mask of melting snow. 'And what's this?' He picked up a plastic box from beside her front door and lifted its lid.

Dot peered inside the box, which was filled with a few fairy cakes, teabags, a scarf and gloves, two Mills & Boon novels, a familiar-looking houseplant and a note written in colourful crayons. The note read:

Enjoy this winter box, from the kids at
Craigmillar Primary School!

'It's from some of the local kids,' Dot said. Those little sweethearts, they'd really done it! 'Bring it inside, will you?'

Max stepped through the door and placed the box on the hallway floor. Dot noticed that there were similar boxes on the doorsteps of several houses around the estate.

'So, you've finished writing the list?' Max asked.

'Not exactly,' Dot said. She ushered Max into her house, where the boiler had been put into overdrive to keep the rooms roasty toasty.

'Nice place,' Max said, his eyes zipping frantically around the room as if following the trajectory of a trapped fly. 'You like Christmas, huh?'

Dot stepped between Max and Christmas Town. 'Yes. But back to my list . . .' The more she thought about her bucket list, the more mundane it seemed. 'I was hoping you might be able to help. But we can at least do the first thing on it right now.' She took the list from her pocket and showed it to him.

'Build a snowman? Dot, calm down! You'll give us both heart attacks at this pace.'

Dot crinkled her nose with false disgust. 'I know it's not exactly skydiving, but—'

'You want to go skydiving? That sounds awesome. Let's do it!'

140

'No, I definitely don't want to go skydiving. I want to build a snowman, and then maybe warm my hands on a mug of hot chocolate.'

'Snowmen, hot chocolate . . . I cycled across town for this!'

'It's what I want to do, okay? Next time we can do something a bit more exciting.'

Max brushed snow from his hair. 'Like watching paint dry?' He sighed. 'Okay, let's build you a snowman.' He pointed to the front and back doors. 'Front or back?'

'Front!' Dot exclaimed. 'Then the neighbours can enjoy it, too. They can wave to him when they walk past.'

'Good, I can keep an eye on my bike as well – it's chained to your gate and I don't know how sketchy your neighbours are.'

'Most of them have one foot in the grave,' Dot said, 'and their other foot in a thermal sock and slipper. They're not going to steal your super bike, don't worry.'

She liked that he was so protective of his bike – it clearly meant a lot to him.

'Wait a second,' Dot said, noticing that Max was ill-dressed for snowman building, as he was wearing a thin, almost transparent, waterproof coat.

She left him in the lounge and went into the kitchen to rummage through one of her big black bin bags containing to-be-donated clothes. She pulled out a thick winter coat and returned to Max, who was staring at Christmas Town.

'This thing's mental,' Max said, turning the Ferris wheel carefully with his fingertips.

'It got a bit out of hand,' Dot said, cradling the winter coat in her arms.

'No shit!' He scrunched his lips. 'Sorry.' He stared at the winter coat in Dot's arms. 'What's that for?'

'You. It's cold out – you'll freeze in what you're wearing.'

'I'm not wearing *that*!' He took it from Dot and held it up, aghast. 'It's for women. I'm fine as I am.'

'It's your funeral.' Dot took the coat back, flung on her own heaviest winter coat, gloves and scarf and opened the front door to a thick flurry of snowflakes. 'Shall we?'

She went outside and began rolling snow along the ground to form a ball.

Max watched her.

'Well, are you going to help?' Dot asked. 'I'll do the hard bit, the base. You roll the middle bit of his body.'

'Are you sure you understand a bucket list?' Max asked. He pulled the front door closed behind him and breathed into his gloveless hands. 'It's not just a list of things you want to do, it's not just normal everyday stuff you find fun. And PS: this isn't fun.'

'Yes, it is,' Dot snapped, continuing to roll the ball of snow in a widening circle so that it fattened.

'Tell me some of the things on your list again,' Max said.

'Roll,' Dot replied, gesturing to the snow.

Max bent down and began to form a snowball, copying Dot's technique of rolling it in the untouched snow.

'Remember our pact about you being bossy?' Max asked. 'You OAPs can be forgetful.'

OAP?! Dot hated that term, especially when anyone used it to refer to her.

She straightened. 'And remember our pact not to stereotype me as some useless, frail old woman who doesn't know her antique arse from her ancient elbows?'

'All right, sorry,' Max said, pushing his ball along the ground. 'What else was on your list?'

'Dancing.'

Max groaned. 'I hate dancing. Won't do it, never. Never ever.'

Dot returned to rolling. 'Well, what about afternoon tea?'

'See, that's nice, but it's not really *bucket list* material. That's just something you'd do on a Saturday afternoon. Any Saturday afternoon. A bucket list is meant to be full of things you want to do before you die. You have to think *bigger*!'

'I couldn't think of much,' Dot said. 'I have simple tastes.'

'Well, let's buff it up, add some muscle – let's Schwarzenegger it. Afternoon tea . . .' He hummed. 'How about we eat the most expensive meal in the most expensive restaurant?'

'But I want cake!'

'Fair point. All right, so let's get some incredible cake made especially for you. Like, let's have a cake made that looks just like you. A Dot Cake Clone!'

Dot laughed. Bizarre as Max's suggestion was, it also sounded like fun.

'All right, I think I understand.' She rolled her snowman's body into position beside her door. 'The lower part of the body's ready. How are you getting on?'

'Almost there,' Max said, rubbing his hands together. 'I'm freezing.'

'I bet my old winter coat's looking pretty cosy right now, aye Maxy?' Dot winked. 'Shall I fetch it for you?'

Max looked at the surrounding windows. 'I dunno.'

'Nobody here cares what you look like. You could walk down the street in a leotard with pink feathers on your head, and nobody would bat an eyelid. They don't care, Max. And even if they did care, you shouldn't give a hoot what they think.'

'Okay. Get the coat.'

Dot stopped herself from giggling like a schoolgirl as she ran inside to fetch her old winter coat and a tasselled scarf. She passed them to Max and he put them on.

'Wrap that scarf nice and tight – we don't want you to catch a cold!' Dot said.

'You're loving this, aren't you?' Max said, looking ridiculous and adorable in the oversized, unflattering tartan coat and matching scarf.

'Admit it, you're warmer,' Dot said.

'Yes. I am warmer now. Thank you, Devious Dot.'

Dot cackled. 'Okay, let's join his body parts together.' They lifted the middle section of the snowman, then placed it onto the bottom section. 'Now the fun part, the head!'

'He'll need eyes,' Max said.

'And a scarf.'

Dot's eye caught a movement across the street. An old woman was standing at her open front door, watching them with interest.

'And arms,' Max said, looking at a nearby tree. He ran to the tree and dug in the snow like a squirrel searching for its buried nuts and retrieved a stick from the ground. He held the stick above his head like a sports trophy. 'One arm down, one to go!'

Dot returned to the house and searched for another scarf from her charity bags. She pulled two loose buttons from old coats, then grabbed a parsnip from the fridge. By the time she returned to the snowman, he had gained two arms and a featureless head.

More doors on the street had also opened: at number thirty-six, two kids ran outside and started throwing snowballs at each other. Outside number forty-four, an old man wearing a smart Paddington Bear duffel coat and journalist's trilby hat was rolling snow with a young boy in frog wellies. They looked towards Dot's house, and she waved at them. They all waved back.

'Here.' Dot handed a pulled-off coat button to Max. She pushed another button onto the snowman's face, and Max followed suit. Dot dug a little hole into the middle of the snowman's face and inserted the parsnip, holding it in place while Max cemented it into position with additional snow.

The duffle-coated neighbour approached, smiling and a little out of breath.

'My grandson saw you, he dragged me outside,' the old man said. 'I'm Jacob.' He smiled again, expectantly, and raised his hat in a *how do you do* old-fashioned genteel kind of way that made Dot giggle. 'Are you new to the area?'

'Oh no!' Dot uttered, surprised at the question. Then again, she'd never really noticed him much, either, and they'd not spoken until now. 'I've been here for a long time, years and years. What about you?'

'Since 1987,' he said. 'You'd think we'd have met before now, wouldn't you?'

'I know. Well, it's nice to meet you at long last, Jacob.' Dot held out her hand. 'I'm Dot.'

Jacob shook it gently, and Dot thought she could see a little twinkle in his eye – perhaps the kind of twinkle that guys used to get when they found out Dot was single, though she didn't want to assume too much.

'And I'm Max,' Max said.

'Nice to meet you, son,' Jacob replied, shaking Max's hand firmly. 'Well, you two have brought a bit of cheer to a chilly day, and your snowy fella here looks like he's not fully dressed, so . . .' He removed his hat and placed it carefully on the snowman's head. 'There, that's better.'

'Your hat!' Dot protested. 'Are you sure?'

'I'll pick it back up again when the sun's back,' Jacob said, turning abruptly when his grandson called out for him. 'It'll give us a chance to say hello again, won't it?'

'Yes, see you soon!' Dot smiled. Jacob seemed like a pleasant enough chap, and it would be nice to see a friendly, familiar face around the street sometimes.

Jacob walked back to his grandson, looking back briefly at Dot.

Max chuckled. 'Well, someone's keen.'

'What do you mean?' Dot asked.

'I think Jacob might have a little crush. It's cute.'

'It is *not* cute.' She did a little curtsy and fluttered her eyelashes at Max. 'But I can't really blame him, can I?'

'I'm saying nothing.'

'Well . . .' Dot turned her attentions back to their snowman. 'Ta-da! He's done!'

'It's aliiiive!' Max screeched like a mad scientist. 'That was actually more fun than I expected. And more of your neighbours have come out, too. Imagine every house with a snowman outside – it'll look like something from a horror movie.'

'*Night of the Living Snowmen*,' Dot said.

'Terrifying,' Max said unconvincingly.

The cold air was beginning to ache in Dot's lungs and her knee throbbed with pain, but she was glad they'd done this together.

'That's the first item on my bucket list done,' Dot said. 'Shall we warm up with some hot chocolate, now? I might not like the OAP stereotypes, but my knee hurts like heck in this cold.'

They returned to the house and Dot put the kettle on. She made hot chocolate and returned to the lounge, where she caught Max exploring Christmas Town again. She handed him a hot mug.

'Thanks.' He took a sip and grimaced. 'It's hotter than Venus!'

'It's hot chocolate. The clue's in the name.'

He blew steam from his mug with a faux-angry expression. 'Your snowman idea was better than I expected. But I still think you ought to go bigger with the others. So, how about you give me the list and I'll turn the volume up to eleven?'

'You mean you'll turn my everyday stuff into something more special? Something a bit more bucket-listy?'

'Exactly. We'll have to do a bit more planning for some of them. I can do that, since you're paying.'

'Am I?' She faked surprise. 'Okay, I suppose that's appropriate. Since you're doing the admin, I'll pay the bill.'

'And I have community service until the new year, so we'll have to do the bucket list on my days off – Wednesdays and the weekends. How about it?'

Dot had that buzzing feeling again. She glanced out of her window and smiled at the snowman they had made together, and at the people who'd come out of their houses to enjoy the snow.

Yes, this is what she had wanted. *This* is what she had been missing.

'Let's do it,' she said. 'I'll set up a special Bucket List bank account, and you can have the card to pay for whatever we need!' She raised her mug into the air and clinked it against Max's.

Max grinned. 'Next stop: cake.'

21

Let Them Eat Cake

Dot didn't eat breakfast – she didn't want to waste stomach room on such mediocrities as cereal or toast. Eggs could get in the bin and stay there, as far as her bulging sweet tooth was concerned. Today was about one thing: cake. Lots of cake.

Cake was in Dot's *top ten best things to exist* list. Much like hot sweet tea, cake had the ability to calm nerves, to dispel grave concerns, to repay debts and settle conflicts. Perhaps, Dot considered, the right kind of cake might even be able to prevent war. The right kind of cake might bring about world peace.

And so the wave of hungry nausea that Dot was experiencing was worth it, because cake would make everything better.

She had dressed in her new suit – a sharp aubergine-coloured number, supermodel-slim at the waist and over-wide at the shoulders with ski-slope lapels. She'd had it cut to her precise measurements, and the snooty seamstress in the *boutique* (the seamstress's word for her shop) had said the suit was a popular design with some of her more *travelled* (Dot read between the lines – the seamstress meant *aged*) clientele, so Dot felt assured that she wouldn't look like a complete tool, even though she'd only really worn suits at weddings and funerals before.

Max had called in advance and told Dot that she would be

picked up and delivered to a mystery location, which she loved. The mystery made her feel like a kid again.

The doorbell rang and Dot answered. A black-suited driver with a black flat cap smiled at her and said that her limo was waiting, when she was ready.

Dot exited and locked her front door, spotting several neighbours peering through their net curtains at the long black car in front of her house. Dot waved to Jacob, but his attention was superglued to the limo. The long black cars that usually came to her street tended to be hearses.

The inside of the limo was leather, and a bottle of champagne sat in a bucket of ice. The driver told Dot to sit back and relax, that their drive wasn't long. Dot popped the champagne and poured herself a glass, letting the bubbles tickle her nose when she sniffed the drink. She took a sip and it tasted like almonds and peaches.

Perhaps Max had the right idea about Schwarzeneggering her list, after all.

A seed of the past began to sprout within Dot, because – despite her best efforts to quash the thoughts with champagne and mental blocking tricks she'd learned as a nurse – she couldn't help but think of riding in hearses to funeral homes: her dad's funeral, her mum's and Charles's in particular. Each of their deaths had felt unreal, until she saw their coffins disappear behind the curtains and heard the prayers.

And then they were gone. They had each left her behind, one by one. At least she'd had Charles to hold and comfort her when her parents died, but then he passed away too. Her best friend, Grace, had been her rock at that time, but even she left Dot for a new life in the USA. And then Dot really was alone.

Dot took a deep breath and dried her eyes. She was being

stupid, thinking of such sad things at such a happy time, but she couldn't control it. It was still strange to her, how suddenly and unexpectedly grief could arrive. The smallest thing – a certain smell, a particular noise, just the wisp of a reminder – could set her memories racing, and it could be hard to stop them.

She needed a distraction, so she watched the world pass by the limo window. Children played in the snow; cars drove slowly through the slush; a flock of geese cut through the winter sky. The posh parts of the city were bright with festive lights, which looked a little out of place on the gothic spires and Georgian shop fronts. Before Dot realised it, her memories had subsided and the limo had arrived at its destination.

Dot looked up at the grand hotel's pillars, that were wrapped in green and red garlands. Large fir trees, decorated in baubles and fairy lights, guarded each side of the reception door. Gold and white snowflakes were projected onto the clean sandstone walls of the hotel, and Dot felt the last of her grief return to its hiding places, knowing that it would be back to see her again.

★

Dot slipped a twenty-pound note into the limo driver's pocket as she got out of the car. He tipped his hat and thanked her.

The hotel's doorman, also dressed in a smart black suit, met Dot at the bottom of the hotel steps and lent her the crook of his arm. He welcomed her to the hotel as they ascended, and then he directed her towards the hotel's restaurant.

Oversized silver snowflakes hung above the thick red carpets and mahogany furniture of the vast reception room. Huge chandeliers dangled from the tall ceilings, their magical lights glittering through their crystal tears. It was the grandest room Dot had ever been inside, and she felt out of place until she saw Max, who looked even more out of place than she felt.

'Max!' Dot rushed towards him.

Max smiled weakly. 'Hey, Dot. Did you like the limo?'

'It was wonderful, thank you,' Dot said, feeling her head swim a little. 'Although I had a glass of champagne so . . .'

'Are you drunk?' Max asked, smirking.

'No! Well, not *drunk* drunk. And look at you, don't you brush up nicely?'

Max wore an ironed black shirt, dark jeans and black shoes. He'd clearly made an effort.

'I tried to iron a crease into the trousers, but it didn't work,' Max said. 'I think our table's ready.'

He signalled to a waiter and they were shown to their table, which was topped with a white tablecloth that reminded Dot of crisp white snow. A log fire burned nearby, sending out waves of warm, wood-scented air.

'This cutlery's silver!' Dot said, checking for the maker's imprint.

'Well, don't pinch it, or we'll get chucked out.'

'Like I would!' Dot exclaimed, thinking that maybe she should steal it because the staff probably wouldn't notice and she liked the weight of the knives. She'd like to eat with posh cutlery at home, and maybe it would impress Max to know that she had a dark edge, that they had theft in common, too. But she refrained, not wanting to risk a bust-up and also worrying that Max might judge her. After all, she had escaped capture completely so far in her criminal life, and he hadn't been so fortunate. It was hardly fair. She placed the cutlery back onto the snowy tabletop.

Soft music sounded from nearby as a pianist massaged the

keys of an upright piano. Though the tune wasn't entirely distinct, Dot was convinced she could hear shades of 'Driving Home for Christmas' among the flurry of notes.

'I love this song. Do you know it?' Dot said, tapping her leg.

'I recognise it,' Max said, squinting as he listened, as though squeezing his eyes shut would improve his musical memory. 'But I'm not the biggest Christmas music fan, to be honest. And it's not even December. My mum's only just taken down the Halloween decorations.'

They continued to listen until the notes morphed into another non-distinct festive song.

'Play it again, Sam,' Dot said, wondering if Max would catch her movie reference.

'That's not quite right,' Max said. 'He says: *Play it, Sam. Play "As Time Goes By".*'

The pianist nodded to Max, and his tune shifted to 'As Time Goes By', with the musician's own sprinklings of interpretation.

'I didn't think you'd get that one,' Dot said. 'It's old.'

'I like the old movies, too,' Max said. 'And that one's a classic.'

The waiter arrived to fill their glasses with water and hand them the menus.

'We're here for the special order,' Max said. 'I spoke to someone called Jean-Pierre.'

'Ah, of course, sir.' The waiter took the menus back. 'All at once, is that correct?'

'Yes, please,' Max said.

Dot's heart pounded. Her stomach churned in anticipation. At long last: cake. Cake was coming!

Six waiters appeared from the kitchen, each carrying a tray laden with desserts on multi-tiered stands: trifles and tray bakes, meringues and mousses, muffins and marshmallows, scones, jams, creams and jellies, truffles and chocolates. The waiters placed the desserts on the table, filling it so that Dot could barely see Max over them.

'The pastry chef hopes you enjoy,' the main waiter said. 'And asks if you're sure you'd not like some savoury items? Perhaps a sandwich or two?'

'Just tea,' Dot said. 'Sweet. Thank you.'

The waiter nodded and returned to the kitchen.

There were more desserts on their table than Dot had ever seen.

'Should we start?' Dot asked Max, feeling like a little girl who was asking her dad for permission.

'You better had, or you'll regret it. Maybe not today, maybe not tomorrow, but soon and for the rest of your life.'

Dot didn't hesitate any longer. She dug her spoon into a chocolate mousse and opened wide, fizzing with joy as the chocolate melted on her tongue. She gobbled a corner of lemon tart, followed by a meringue with cream and strawberries, then tossed a boozy truffle into her mouth.

Max watched her with a look of admiration and disgust, his hands at his sides.

'Why aren't you eating?' Dot asked. 'Don't tell me you're on a diet, or you're diabetic? I don't think we can be friends if you don't like sweets.'

'I love them,' Max said sheepishly. 'I was just waiting for you.'

'Well, I've started. So start! The mousse is amazing.'

Max nodded. He picked up his spoon slowly, eyeing the feast, then dived in as eagerly as Dot had.

A china pot of sweet tea arrived, and they gulped it down while listening to the piano, barely a grunt passing between them as they shovelled sweet treats into their mouths.

'I think I'm starting to fill up,' Max eventually said.

'You'll get a second wind. Drink more tea!' Dot refilled his cup from the pot. 'And surely you've not even begun on your dessert stomach.'

Max picked up a miniature glazed fruit flan. 'I guess not!' He took a monstrous bite. 'Surely this counts as one of my five a day.'

'Surely.'

By the time they had slowed to a stop, Dot's belly was bulging. She wanted to eat more but was concerned that she'd throw up in the posh restaurant and gain a lifelong ban. That wouldn't do, because she loved her afternoon tea with Max so much that she definitely wanted to repeat it once her blood no longer felt like syrup.

'I'll take the rest home,' Dot said to the waiter as he passed. 'Do you have a doggy bag?'

The waiter's smile turned to a frown as he surveyed the destruction they had wrought.

'Yes, ma'am. Of course,' he said. 'We'll take these away and box them for you. What would you like to take?'

'All of it,' Dot said. 'We barely managed a quarter. But it was lovely, please tell the cooks *thank you*.'

'I will.' The waiter filled several plates with cake remains and returned to the kitchen.

'Have you had enough?' Dot asked Max. 'I don't know what I'll do with all the leftovers. I don't want to waste them.'

'I'm stuffed,' Max said, rubbing his swollen belly and loosening his belt. He lowered his voice, as if not wanting people to overhear him. 'Do you feel different, now you're rich?'

'A bit. I used to worry about money, or not having any. I would never have spent so much on cake before now, but now I needn't worry. It's been easy going from poor to rich.'

'Better than the other way around.' Max licked chocolate ganache off his spoon. 'I wonder how I'd feel, having so much when other people can't pay the gas bill or buy enough food.' A sudden look of panic spread over his face. 'Sorry, I didn't mean you should feel bad or anything. I've just been thinking about it since you gave me the bike. I could have sold it and helped pay my mum's bills, and I felt guilty that I didn't.'

Dot didn't know what to say, so she said nothing in the hope that Max would fill the silence with reassurance that she wasn't a bad or greedy person.

'I was worried about telling my mum about the bike,' Max continued. 'She doesn't know how much it's really worth, and I kept it a secret. She doesn't have much, and I thought she'd be angry. But when I wheeled it out from behind the bins, where I keep it chained up under a plastic sheet, she saw me and asked about it. She thought I'd stolen it, and I was getting into trouble again. So, I told her where I got it from.'

'What did she say?' Dot asked.

'She said *good for you* and that I seemed happier lately. I told her the bike had cheered me up, but I'd sell it if we needed the money.'

'Does she want you to sell it?'

'No. She told me I'd better not sell the bike because it'd turned me around. She said what's the point in having more money if we're miserable?'

'She sounds like a good mum.'

Max smiled. 'She is, most of the time. So, I promised I wouldn't sell it unless we were absolutely desperate. And I promised I'd try to keep my anger under control because it was causing me problems. And that was it. She turned the TV volume back up and watched her shows. She's not mentioned it again.'

'So, you're not selling it?'

'No.'

Dot subtly unbuttoned her trousers to ease an oncoming tummy ache. 'Good.'

'So, I guess I told you all that because I didn't want you to feel bad. You're a nice person, and you've tried to help people. You were a nurse, right?'

Dot nodded. 'Yes. Intensive care, mostly.'

'So, you've done a lot of good things for other people. I'm not saying you shouldn't keep helping people, but I think you deserve to be happy, too. I don't think you should feel guilty for treating yourself. This bucket list could be great.'

It was hard for Dot to hear that, because a part of her had been feeling rotten for being rich. She'd slept poorly some nights, worrying about the people who were struggling when she had so much excess.

'Thank you,' Dot said.

She turned her attention to two waiters positioning a fir tree beside the pianist – the hotel was still obviously putting up its festive decorations. The tree reminded Dot that she'd been remiss. Since Charles passed, she'd not put a tree up in December, partly because she had Christmas Town anyway, and partly because it felt like an unnecessary expense (and not even she would dare to steal a tree). Maybe now was a good time to resurrect the tradition.

'Are you in a hurry?' Dot asked Max.

'No, why?'

'I wonder if you can help me with a little errand.'

22

How Lovely Are Your Branches?

Max stared up at the tip of the towering fir tree. 'This will never fit on my bike – it's the biggest one here!'

'We deliver,' the tree seller said, puffing on his vape.

'Also, it won't fit in your house,' Max said to Dot.

'Yes, I know, but it's not going in my house.' She turned to the seller. 'I'll take it. Is cash okay?'

'Perfect,' the tree seller said. He took her address and cash, checking his watch. 'We can deliver and install it – so it's safe – in two hours, if that suits you?'

'Perfect,' Dot echoed him.

The seller returned to his festive forest.

'Next stop, Mini Christmas,' Dot said. 'We can walk. It's not far.'

'Fine by me,' Max said. 'I'm guessing you're putting this monster in your garden, so if you want to light it up—'

'Of course it will need lights,' Dot interrupted. 'It's not a Christmas tree without lights. The magic won't work properly.'

'Okay, whatever you say . . .'

★

Max walked next to Dot, rolling his bike beside him. The short walk through the snow to Mini Christmas was just what Dot needed to get her in the mood for decoration buying.

Max checked his phone as they walked, tutting and sighing before shoving it back into his pocket.

'Problems?' Dot asked.

'Some of my old acquaintances. They have some things they want me to sell on. I keep telling them I'm not doing that anymore, but they keep asking.'

'Best to stay out of it.'

'Exactly. Things are going okay for me right now, and I don't want to mess it up. The money's tempting, but it's not worth the risk.'

'You need some cash to help you get by?' Dot asked.

'No,' Max said somewhat solemnly. 'But thanks.'

'Christmas is coming, so just let me know. It's an expensive time of year.'

Max stared at his bike in contemplation, and Dot wondered whether he was still thinking about selling it.

'You asked me whether I felt guilty about being rich, and—'

'I didn't mean it like that,' Max said. 'I just meant—'

'I know. It's fine, really,' Dot said, trying to put him at ease. She anticipated that her follow-up question could put him on the back foot. 'But I wanted to ask you something similar.'

'Go for it.'

'Do you ever feel guilty, thinking about the people whose things you stole?'

She tried not to remember her muggers' faces, their voices, the chill of lying on the cemetery ground as they tore her locket from her neck and ripped her bag from her shoulder. Her rib ached.

Max's voice shivered. 'At the time, no, I didn't. I didn't

actually take them myself – other people brought them to me. I bought them cheap, then fixed them up and sold them on. I never actually stole them.'

'But you did, sort of,' Dot said, realising that she was sounding quite accusatory. But Max's questioning of her feelings of guilt at the restaurant had touched a nerve. She'd stolen, too – should she feel more guilt about that than she did? At least Max stole to make money to support himself.

'Now, I feel worse about it,' Max said. 'People with bikes probably aren't rolling in cash, especially some of the crap bikes they brought to me. Sometimes I'd find little things, like a notepad or something, and that felt worse than taking their bike because they were personal. Once I found an empty baby's bottle and a purse – the purse only had a fiver inside, and the baby's birth certificate folded up. I wished I could give it all back.' He cleared his throat and took a deep breath. 'Do you think I'm a bad guy?'

'No,' Dot said. She meant it. 'You did some bad things, that's all. And nobody's a saint – we've all done things we aren't proud of.' She wasn't sure she should admit her own crimes, but Max had been honest with her and she wanted him to feel better about himself and his past. 'This shop we're going to, Mini Christmas, is one of the places I used to steal from.'

'*You* stole?' Max asked, his voice shrill with surprise before returning to normal. 'What did you steal?'

'You saw it: Christmas Town. The little people and the rides. I bought some of it but stole most of it. And a bunch of plants from a garden centre.'

'Why?'

It was a damn good question. Dot had thought about it more and more recently.

'I'm not sure, really,' she said. 'I liked the buzz I got from

159

stealing, like I'd managed to break the rules. It felt like I had some kind of power, because nobody was able to catch me.'

'That's what some of the guys who sold to me said.'

'Really?' She liked that other people had felt the same as her – it made her feel less of a villain to know that she wasn't the only one who got a thrill from stealing. It was just a normal reaction, after all. 'It made me feel like I was in control of my own life.'

'Did you feel different, then?'

'For a little while, but the buzz went away quickly. And now I'm not even sure I like Christmas Town. Sometimes it feels like I have to keep it or all that effort was pointless, and then I've wasted years of my life building this miniature town for no good reason.'

'I did something like that, too,' Max said, walking a little closer to Dot, so she could almost feel the heat radiate from his body. 'I like movies, you know that.'

'I had put the pieces of that puzzle together, yes.'

'Well, I had this collection. Hundreds, maybe even a thousand movies on DVD. I had posters and books. I even had a couple of random props and statuettes, a bit like your Christmas people but of aliens and cowboys, those kinds of things. My dad got a lot of them for me, when I said I liked them, which meant they were probably stolen, too. Anyway, I had so much stuff in my room that I could barely move. I couldn't bring anyone back to see it because I was a bit embarrassed, and I realised I was keeping all this stuff but never really enjoying it. I watched quite a few of the movies, but I didn't need all the boxes and other things. I was just keeping them because I thought I should, like they were part of who I was.'

'What did you do?' Dot asked.

'One day, I got angry about something. I can't even remember what. I smashed my shelves and hurled a statue out of the window. And I felt no different. I'd destroyed some of my collection, and it made me realise I didn't need any of it. I started getting rid of it, selling items or giving them away, until I only had my favourite movies and my room was back to being normal. I was still me, and I was okay without it all. I wished I'd done it sooner, but I was glad I did it.'

'You think I should get rid of Christmas Town?'

'No, not if you don't want to. But if you feel like it's trapping you somehow, then yeah, I'd think about getting rid of it.'

'It's mostly stolen,' Dot said. 'If I threw it away, maybe it could be traced back to me.'

'I really don't think anyone will care about some Christmas ornaments, to be honest. Maybe when people stop selling drugs, knifing each other and robbing cars. But until then, I think you're probably safe.'

'But I also like some of it. I mean, there's—'

'Dot,' Max said quietly. 'You don't have to. It was just an idea. I'm just telling you what I did. You're not me. I just think it can be good to get rid of things that don't make you happy, and find things that do.' He looked across the street and pointed. 'Is that the place?'

Mini Christmas shone with warm twinkling lights, the moving figurines in its window bringing it to life. Dot wasn't sure she was ready to let go of her town just yet, because it had brought her comfort over the years, it had reminded her of happier times and happier places than where she was. And it was her inspiration for what she was about to do next.

★

Dot and Max unwrapped dozens of baubles and strings of fairy lights while they waited for the tree to be delivered. As the truck pulled up to Dot's house, she ran outside to meet the delivery men.

'Not in my little garden!' Dot shouted. 'Over there, on the common!'

She pointed towards the circular patch of snow-covered grass that sat between the various streets, where many years ago there had been public parties to celebrate the royal wedding.

'Do you need permission?' one of the delivery men asked.

'Oh, I have it. No problem, just secure it over there, please.'

The driver shrugged to his partner and they began positioning the twenty-five-foot tree on the common.

Max came out of Dot's house carrying a large box of decorations. 'What are you doing?' he asked Dot. 'Isn't the tree coming inside?'

'It's not just for me – it's for all of us.' Dot smiled. 'There are some ladders in the back garden, can you fetch them?'

Max placed the box of decorations on the ground and ran back inside Dot's house. By the time he'd returned with the ladders, the tree was in position, secured with ropes that were tied to stakes in the ground.

'I'll do the low branches, you do the high ones,' Dot said, placing a bauble on the tree.

She thanked the delivery drivers and tipped them, wishing them a merry Christmas, and they drove away happily.

Max opened the ladders beside the tree. 'Why do I have to climb up?' he asked.

'I'm in my seventies, you're nineteen.'

'Funny how you don't mind the OAP stuff when it gets you out of climbing a ladder, isn't it?' Max said in a huff as he began climbing.

Dot chuckled. 'It has its uses. Also, I have a bad knee and I don't care for heights. When I was a nurse, I saw some awful accidents when people fell from ladders. Mostly men fixing roof aerials, mind you.'

'Oh, great. If I fall, I'm suing.' He was almost at the top and looked down at Dot with gritted teeth.

'Let's see who can make their part the prettiest. The loser has to work out how we'll get the lights up here with electricity running.'

'You didn't work that out?' Max shouted down.

'No.' Dot hung another bauble, making sure that it was secure enough on the branch so that it wouldn't blow off in the wind. She caught her reflection in its mirrored surface and noticed someone else's reflection as they approached from behind her.

'I hope you don't mind . . .' a woman's voice sounded.

Dot turned to see the young couple with the noisy baby who lived opposite her. The woman carried a box of decorations and the man carried the baby who, for once, wasn't creating an unholy caterwaul.

'We saw you out here,' the man said. 'We thought maybe we could help out. We have some decorations to add.'

'Of course!' Dot said, beaming. 'The more, the merrier. We've only one ladder, so we may all have to work on the bottom section.' She grinned up at Max.

'Hey, no fair! That's three against one!' Max yelped.

'I have another ladder, from my window cleaning days,' Jacob said as he approached with a tray of steaming mugs, his Paddington Bear coat buttoned up tight. 'I thought you might like to stay warm with a cuppa.'

A couple more neighbours came out and joined them, chatting to one another about the tree and their plans for

163

Christmas. Dot was glad to see them getting along so well – it felt very much in the spirit of Christmas.

More people left their houses, bringing baubles and snacks, ladders and tinsel, until a dozen or so people were around the tree. Not wanting to be outdone by Jacob's tea tray, Dot raced back into the house and loaded a tray with her posh desserts from the restaurant, quickly returning to the common and passing them around so that everyone had a bite to eat. She basked in their *ooohs* and *aaaahs* as they complimented the expensive treats. She was tempted to say she'd made them herself, but didn't want to get tangled in a web of dessert-based lies.

With the tree decorated, it still needed lights to make the magic happen. They all talked through their ideas and the logistics before deciding to feed a thick electrical cable out of a nearby kitchen window. With the flick of a switch, the tree lit up, and they all cheered and clapped. Dot looked up at the tree and couldn't stop herself from crying.

Max descended the ladder and handed Dot a tissue. 'It looks good. You okay?'

'I'm fine,' Dot said, feeling a little silly for crying. She glanced at all her neighbours, their happy faces brightly lit by the tree's lights, and smiled.

Jacob's grandson climbed the ladder in his frog wellies and placed an angel on top of the tree, and everybody cheered again. It reminded Dot of Christmas time on her ward, when people who were usually in a bad way would, for a moment, forget their worries and pains.

'I'm better than fine,' Dot said.

23

A Ward

Lottery number 5

(Dot is twenty-five years old)

'Ladies and gentlemen, I present to you . . . the nurse of the year!' Charles opened the door to the social club and 'Bye, Bye, Baby' by the Bay City Rollers filled the beery, smoke-clogged air.

'Not quite.' Dot smiled awkwardly to a colleague as she entered the bar, where an Angel of the Ward *Awards* banner hung over the door.

She'd worked hard on Ward 5, and appreciated the gratitude for her efforts, but felt a little guilty for her accolade. And she was anything but an angel. There were plenty of other nurses in the hospital, even one or two on Ward 5, who were just as deserving as she was.

She whispered into Charles's ear: 'Don't make a fuss, please. It's awkward enough as it is.'

'Okay, but I have to ask . . .' He raised his voice as Dr McLaughlin shuffled past her to reach the men's toilets. 'What does the hospital's best nurse like to drink on such an auspicious occasion as this?'

Dot wanted lager, but noticed the other nurses were sipping orange juices. She hoped they at least contained vodka, although Matron was sat stoically among them like a hawk scanning a field for prey. The nurses' husbands clutched pints, chatting and laughing with one another.

'Piña colada, please,' Dot said, waving to Grace from across the room. 'Then at least I can pretend I'm on a tropical beach somewhere.'

Charles approached the bar and Dot trundled to Grace's side. Grace looked gorgeous, as usual, and she planted a kiss on Dot's cheek, leaving a red imprint of her lips behind.

'Oh, it's the Angel of the Ward herself!' Grace smiled at Dot like a movie star. 'Hello, Dotty.'

'Don't,' Dot said flatly.

'The others are furious,' Grace said, side-glancing a table of nurses. 'There's a cash prize, you know. It's not a lot, but it's money. What will you do with it? Maybe treat your best friend?'

'The house needs work.' Dot held in a groan. 'It feels like such a boring way to spend money.'

'Is Charlie-boy holding out on you? Is he a cheapskate?'

'Well, he bought me Brussels sprouts for Christmas so that I could have a bubble bath on Boxing Day.'

Grace snorted, choking on her drink. 'Don't do that!'

Dot smirked. She always enjoyed it when Grace was scandalised by her jokes. 'He's not stingy. I just wish we could go away somewhere sunny rather than fixing the leaky roof and sink. Everything's leaking lately, our bank account included. You know?'

Grace's eyes widened and she smiled as Charles approached. 'Well, hello, big spender.'

Charles passed Dot her piña colada. 'The barman apologised

– they've run out of sparklers and little umbrellas.'

Dot took a sip and felt the tropical alcohol burn the back of her throat. 'That's okay, I just wanted the booze, anyway.' She looked up to the stage, where one of the hospital's VIPs was approaching the microphone.

'Do you have to make a speech?' Charles asked.

'God, I hope not,' Dot said, taking a much bigger sip of her cocktail.

'Dotty, did you tell him about the prize money?' Grace asked.

Charles raised an inquisitive eyebrow and took a gulp of his pint. 'No, how much?'

'Not enough to retire on, unfortunately,' Dot said.

'Tell her to spend it on something nice,' Grace said. 'She wants to fly off to a romantic beach in the sun, don't you?'

'Yes, please,' Dot said, taking another sip.

'That'll really make the other girls seethe.' Grace clinked her glass against Dot's.

Grace scowled at the table of nurses who were whispering to one another while giving Dot and Charles pitying looks. Dot and Grace had never really felt part of the nurses' collective; they were all younger and were broody as rabbits.

'Don't take it personally,' Grace said. 'I don't. At least you're married; they think I don't know that they call me a spinster. We either pop a few kids out, or we're selfish, or barren. The alternatives don't even register with those clucking hens.'

The VIP tapped the microphone, sending a wave of feedback across the bar. The banter died down, and everyone turned their attention to the stage.

The VIP droned on about the hospital and its services, how well it had been doing in a difficult time, and how it wanted to reward its employees who were, on occasion (Dot tried not to laugh at the use of 'on occasion'), under-appreciated.

'And so it's my pleasure . . .' the VIP started, taking an envelope from his pocket. 'The Angel of the Ward Award goes to Nurse Dorothy Hindley, for her outstanding work on Ward 5. Nurse Hindley's quick reactions helped save the life of a member of the hospital board of directors and, though he couldn't be here tonight, we all want to extend our thanks to her.'

The social club filled with applause. Dot passed her empty cocktail glass to Charles and walked onto the stage. The VIP extended his hand and she shook it. He handed her the envelope and a small angel-shaped trophy, then Dot turned towards the photographer from the local newspaper to be blinded by his camera flash.

'Speech! Speech!' Grace yelled out.

The VIP gestured to the microphone and – against her better judgement but bolstered by the coconutty booze conga-dancing through her veins – Dot approached the mic. She shot a glare at Grace and cleared her throat before catching brief admonishing looks from the nurses' table.

Dot took a deep breath. 'Thank you.'

She walked away from the microphone, re-joining Grace and Charles as the social club attendees applauded once more. Dot placed the angel-shaped trophy into her handbag, so as not to be on show.

'Quite the speech,' Charles said.

'I'm a woman of few words.'

'Let's see the fortune, then!' Grace said, reaching for the prize envelope.

Dot snatched her envelope away and peered inside. She

folded the envelope and placed it into Charles's inside jacket pocket.

'I have to keep him sweet,' Dot said. 'The poor boy's at a loss without me bringing home the bacon.'

'Well done, love,' Charles said, leaning in to kiss her cheek. He whispered into her ear: 'About the house, this money—'

'It's okay.' She smelled beer on his warm breath, noticing his and Grace's glasses were nearly empty. 'It's my round. Vodka and orange for Grace?'

'Yes, please,' Grace said, blowing a kiss. 'You spoil me!'

'And Charles?'

'Lager, please. Shall I get them?'

'No.' Dot reached into Charles's jacket and took a note from her prize envelope. 'I want to stretch my legs and bask in the glory of my award, thank you very much.' She approached the bar, smiling to her nicest colleagues and avoiding Matron's death glare.

Several men stood at the bar, watching Dot approach.

The barman sighed before turning to Dot. 'We don't serve women, not even angels. Maybe ask your husband to come over and I'll explain it to him.'

Dot gritted her teeth and signalled for Charles to join her at the bar.

'They won't serve me,' she said, fuming.

'Why not?' Charles asked the barman.

'Policy,' the barman said. 'It's not right, especially all these nurses. It sets a bad impression. She can have a soft drink or a cocktail, no beer.'

'Great place you have here,' Charles said, his knuckles white as he rapped his fingertips on the bar.

Dot sighed. 'Just order the drinks.'

Charles ordered two vodka and oranges and a pint of lager.

Dot took long, slow breaths as she waited for the drinks to be poured. She passed her money to Charles, who paid for them and collected her change.

'Sorry, honey,' Dot said to Charles, picking up his fresh pint in both hands.

'Hey, what are you doing? I said no beer!' the barman snapped.

Dot smiled sweetly and downed the pint in one, barely spilling a drop. The men at the bar stared at her in shock and awe. She picked up the two vodka and oranges and returned to Grace, followed by Charles.

'Sorry, Charles,' Dot said, feeling giddy with the booze and adrenaline. 'He riled me the wrong way.'

'Don't poke this tiger, she bites!' Grace said, sipping her drink happily. 'God, I love you.'

Dot held her vodka and orange out to Charles, but he shook his head.

'I'll get my own pint, if the caveman behind the bar will let me. But' – he held Dot's elbow and gently pulled her aside – 'I've been thinking. The house can wait, it won't fall apart any time soon. How about we do something else with our savings?'

'Like what?' Dot asked, her heart beginning to race.

'A holiday. Let's go somewhere.'

'Where? Somewhere warm and sandy?'

'Exactly. Spain? Italy?'

'Yes!' Dot screeched, wrapping her arms around Charles and squeezing him as tightly as she could. 'Are you sure?'

'Absolutely. We can let the pipes leak a few more years. We've plenty of leftover wedding casserole dishes to catch the water.'

24

A Day at the Races

Dot spent the next two days eating leftover desserts. It was a tough job, but someone had to do it, and she was the perfect woman for the task. But she hadn't sent Max home empty-handed, either, and figured his mum might like a few sweet treats as well. It couldn't hurt to ingratiate herself with Max's mum, as she must have thought it peculiar that her son was spending so much time with a relative stranger.

She watched people admire the neighbourhood Christmas tree in the common, enjoying how happy it had made her neighbours. Dot was still exhilarated by the fact that it had brought a sense of community back to the area. She was powering through the last of the cake supplies with an extra-large mug of sweet tea, when a golden envelope slipped through her letterbox. Inside was an invitation printed on pink paper:

> *You are formally invited to a day at the races.*
> *Wear comfortable clothes and shoes.*
> *The car will pick you up on Saturday morning at 9 a.m.*
> *— Bucket Master*

A day at the races! Dot had seen Royal Ascot on the telly several times and would occasionally have a little flutter.

Nothing big – she knew that gambling was generally a fool's errand – but enough to make her excited to see the results. She always chose her horse based on its name, rather than the odds, of course. And she enjoyed laughing at the ridiculous hats the women wore, some of which must have cost more than her monthly food and gas bills.

Dot wasn't fussed about wearing a massive gaudy hat, particularly because her hair was looking great as she'd now been to the posh salon a few times since winning the lottery. She considered wearing her aubergine suit but reconsidered because Max (a.k.a. the self-appointed Bucket Master, apparently) had clearly instructed her to dress comfortably. So, she wore her loose semi-smart trousers and jacket.

The snow had unfortunately melted since the raising of the Christmas tree. However, despite the winter sun, it was still cold out. It was hardly ideal horse racing weather, but Dot trusted that Max had thought the day through. When Saturday arrived, she waited for her limo, but was collected by a regular black cab.

Dot had never been to the racetrack but knew where it was – not in the direction the taxi was headed.

'Where are we going?' Dot asked the driver.

'Apparently, I'm not to say. It's a surprise,' the driver replied. 'But I have to tell you if you want to know. Health and safety. We don't want to be involved in dropping you off to be assassinated or something!' He laughed, eyeing Dot through his rear-view mirror.

'No, it's okay,' Dot said. 'Thank you. I'm not worried.'

The driver nodded and continued to drive until they arrived at Full Throttle Test Track.

'This is your stop, have fun!' the driver said.

Dot got out of the taxi and was met by Max.

'I thought we were going to go horse riding, oh great and powerful Bucket Master,' Dot said. 'Or at least to watch a horse race.'

'It's a bit cold for that,' Max said. 'And I thought this would be more fun. You wanted horses; I've given you hundreds of them in horsepower. A whole stampede!'

Engines sounded from behind the tall metal fence. Dot looked through the fence at the grey asphalt track.

'We're watching the cars race?' Dot asked.

'No, much better than that,' Max said, hopping on the spot with excitement. 'We're going to race them!' As Max watched several shiny racing cars speed around the track, their engines humming like hornets, a look of concern spread across his face. 'Is this okay? I thought it sounded fun, but maybe it's not your kind of thing.'

'It's *exactly* my kind of thing!' Dot grinned.

'So, you're game?' Max's concern seemed to falter and fade.

'Absolutely!'

He smiled. 'Great! And I thought we could make this one a little more interesting.' Max stretched his arms as if preparing for a boxing match. 'How about a wager?'

Dot raised an interested eyebrow. 'What kind of wager?'

'If I win, I can add my own item to the bucket list.'

'And if you lose?'

Max guffawed. 'I won't lose. I've driven a lot of cars. I started when I was a kid.'

'Illegally, then?' Dot asked.

Max nodded. 'Maybe.'

'Well, entertain an old girl. What's your forfeit if you *do* lose? What will I win?'

'What do you want? You already have money and a manservant who plans your activities.'

Dot thought about potential prizes. There was only one thing she could really think of.

'Your poem,' Dot said. 'If you lose, I want to hear the poem you wrote about tigers and invisible cages.'

Max held out his hand. 'You've got yourself a deal.'

Dot shook his hand, trying not to let a smile break too widely across her face. She didn't really care about the wager all that much, but she really wanted to thrash Max on the racecourse.

'All right, then,' Max said, turning towards the track entrance. 'Fasten your seat belts. It's going to be a bumpy ride.'

★

'I'll take the blue one,' Max said, having won the coin toss for first choice of cars. He marched in front of the five available cars like an admiral inspecting his troops. 'It's the sports model, it looks the fastest. You won't catch me on the straights.' His chest buffed out like a penguin who'd caught the biggest fish.

'How many laps are we doing?' Dot asked the race coordinator.

'Thirty,' he said.

Dot checked the map of the course; there were eight main curves and turns that would require any car to slow down to take them safely.

'This one's tyres aren't worn down,' Dot said as she inspected the custard-coloured car. 'It ought to give good grip on the tight corners.' She peered through the window at the interior. 'Smaller seats and no extras, no wasted weight.' She winked at Max. 'Oh, and it's yellow, since you based your decision on your car's colour, like a total layman.'

The race coordinator nodded. 'It's just been tested, and it's in top condition.' He rubbed his neck and looked at Max. 'They're all safe, though, checked regularly.' He nodded to Max's car. 'That one has a slightly higher top speed.' He pointed to Dot's car. 'But this one has better handling.'

'Then I'll take it.' Dot turned to Max. 'Speed isn't everything. I learned that when I rode with the delivery drivers between the hospitals. They even let me take the wheel a few times, though we weren't exactly following protocol. We had to move those organs quickly with our blues and twos flashing. It got me interested in Formula 1 – I was a bit obsessed for a few years. But I'm better now; I weaned myself off.'

'Looks like you're in trouble, mate,' the race coordinator said to Max.

'Whatever, she's all talk,' Max said, cracking his fingers. 'Age before beauty . . .' He gestured to Dot's car and opened the driver-side door for her.

'I'd say brains before brawn' – Dot put her helmet on – 'but I'm about to flex this baby's muscles and leave you in my dust, crying.'

'I like your enthusiasm,' the race coordinator said, perhaps with a hint of nerves. 'But let's be safe. Watch your speed, slow down on the corners. And, obviously, no dangerous overtaking. Keep a safe distance from one another, or I'll pull the plug. Got it?'

'Got it,' Dot and Max said in unison.

They got into their cars and the race coordinator checked their helmets and seatbelts before giving them the all-clear.

Dot started her engine, staring down Max through the car window. She ran her finger across her throat, then pointed at him to complete her *You're Dead* gesture.

Max placed both hands on his steering wheel, watching the starting lights above the track. He revved his engine.

Dot revved her engine back at him.

The lights changed and a horn sounded.

Dot put the pedal to the metal and the car flew forward, forcing her spine against the seat with alarming power. She settled her breath, concentrating as Max's car edged in front of hers. He was right, on the straights her car couldn't outspeed his, but the corners were where she hoped to make back her losses.

Dot moved her car to take the corner tightly, getting her close behind Max. She pushed her palm on the middle of the steering wheel to honk the horn, but the car didn't have one so she made the noise in her head.

They sped around once, and the practice of one lap was all she needed. She could feel her heart pounding hard, but the adrenaline in her body kept her sharp – she felt like she'd drunk six double espressos. Her entire attention was on the track, her steering, her speed and Max's position.

She could win this.

Dot stayed tight on Max's rear bumper, and it was neck and neck by the final lap, with just one more corner to go and one straight to finish. She knew Max wouldn't miss this chance, but neither would she.

Dot sped up as she took the final corner, but she was going too fast. Her car screeched as it tried to turn, spinning out of her control. Dot's head whipped to the side, her helmet colliding with the frame of the car door.

★

An eternity seemed to pass until the car came to a full halt and Dot's door opened.

'Are you okay? Shit, Dot!' Max said.

'Stand aside!' the race coordinator yelled, pushing Max away from the door. 'Are you hurt?'

Dot's head was a little cloudy, but she was fine. 'I'm all right. Nothing's hurt.' She removed her helmet. 'Thanks to this thing.'

'Take your time,' the race coordinator advised. 'Breathe. Don't hurry or turn quickly.'

A few minutes of calming down passed, but Dot felt that the two men were much more concerned and frantic than she was. More than anything else, she was annoyed that she'd lost the race to Max, though his car actually hadn't quite passed the finishing line.

She got out of the car and Max held her arm, unnecessarily, to keep her steady.

'Careful,' Max said.

'I told you to take the corners slowly!' the race coordinator snapped, quickly checking Dot's car before turning back to her. 'Are you sure you're okay? We'll have our first aider check you over.'

Dot waved her hand dismissively. 'I'm fine. Honestly, you two.' She nudged Max's hands away from her arm and walked around her car. 'I can't see any damage. Can you?'

The race coordinator released a long-held breath. 'No, the car's fine. But I want you to see our first aider before you leave, and you may need to go to the hospital.'

She nodded. A dull, aching pain had begun to spread through Dot's neck. She held it and Max returned to her side.

'It's just a bit of whiplash,' Dot said. 'I've had it before. All right, I'll meet your first aider if it keeps you boys happy.'

'I'll go fetch them, wait here,' the race coordinator said and ran off in the direction of a small building situated just past the finish line.

'That was stupid,' Max said.

'I know. I shouldn't have taken the corner so fast,' Dot said. 'But I couldn't let you win!'

'Not that. I meant it was stupid of me to do this. I shouldn't have put you in danger. You're an o—'

Dot's nostrils flared. 'Let me stop you there!'

Max dropped silent.

'I knew the risks. I make my own decisions, okay?'

'Yeah, but—'

'No buts,' Dot said. 'I'm not going to be told what I can't do. I won't be bossed about. I'm fine, we're both fine. And I'm glad we came – it was really fun, wasn't it?'

'Until you crashed? Yeah.'

'If we're going to do this bucket list properly, we have to go for it. You were right, my old bucket list was too tame, and you've made it a hundred times better. So far. So don't go changing things. I don't want to give up on it, and neither should you.'

'Now who's being bossy?' Max said. He wiped his forehead and took a breath. 'Okay. I'll still do my bit.'

'And you're not going to try to make it OAP-appropriate, are you?' She grabbed his arm and began walking in the direction the race coordinator had run, past Max's car. 'I want the full sugar version, not the diet version.'

'Okay, I'll not hold back.'

'Promise you won't take it easy on me,' Dot said, picking up her pace a little.

'I promise.'

'Good.' She loosened her grip on his arm. 'Then you won't mind me doing this.' She ran forward, leaving Max behind her, and stepped over the finishing line. She raised her hands into the air and yelled triumphantly: 'I wiiiiiin!'

25

Under Construction

Sunday was, mostly, a day of rest. Dot's neck thanked her for it, because – between dodgy knees, fractured ribs, hardcore cleaning, cake overloads and car accidents – she'd been putting her body through the proverbial meat grinder. Her neck throbbed from the whiplash of her crash, and she ventured into her drugs drawer to find an appropriately strong painkiller.

As Dot washed back her medicine with a mug of sweet tea, she remembered being a girl and chasing a cat down a hill. She had taken a tumble and bounced like a rag doll on her way down before smashing into a thick drystone wall at the bottom. But she stood right up without a single break, bruise or ache, then carried on chasing the justly frightened cat.

Her fortitude had begun to wane noticeably in her thirties. She recalled waking up one morning and stretching too vigorously, trapping a nerve in her shoulder. Her knees had started to weaken in her forties, as though they'd grown tired of her shenanigans and just wanted her to sit down. Then things only continued to degenerate, and she felt a bit like a jelly that had been left out in the sun.

But, all things considered, she was in good health. And a little pain wasn't going to prevent her from doing anything. She'd seen what chronic pain really looked like, how debilitating it could be, and hers was nothing so bad as that.

The Christmas market along Princes Street was opening to the public, and Dot didn't want to miss the Ferris wheel being switched on. Determined not to let a literal pain in the neck become a figurative pain in the neck, she wrapped up warm and headed into the cold, where the sky threatened to snow with grumbly blue-grey clouds.

Dot's rib panged as she walked. She thought there was a good chance that her crash had caused some damage to the already-weak bone, but she tried to ignore it. The race had been worth it, and she felt like she'd completed something from her bucket list that a lot of other people would have been jealous of.

Halfway, her knee demanded that she stop for a rest, so Dot slowed alongside the half-completed skate park, which the council abandoned when their budget was cut. The park was surrounded by a tall metal fence covered in signs warning people not to enter. Through the fence, Dot could see an array of slopes, rails and tunnels, as well as a large space that was littered with broken glass bottles and makeshift fire pits.

Shame, she thought, that the city had abandoned the skate park. It was a waste of public space and it could have been an outlet for a lot of the kids that hung around on the streets, like those she'd seen drinking at her old school playground just before she was mugged.

Dot moved on with a sigh, keen not to let the council's birdbrained management style interrupt her flight towards the Christmas market.

The pavements grew busier with scarfed, coated and booted pedestrians. The unlit tip of the Ferris wheel dominated the skyline, and Dot caught the smell of mulled wine and spiced hot chocolate before finally reaching the market entrance.

Happy children cheered and screeched as they ran between

the market's wooden stalls. Parents perused nutcrackers shaped like crazed kings, inspecting turtle dove tree decorations and underdressed gingerbread men. The biscuits' fiery legs and necks were kinked as if spasming in pain, so they looked like gingerbread Dots. Feeling sorry for the misshapen treats, she bought a dozen and placed them into her handbag.

Someone off the telly, who Dot recognised but couldn't put a name to, said a few generic words about Christmas and having a great time, then switched on the Ferris wheel lights to great applause. The wheel turned and a queue formed to ride the attraction. Dot considered lining up but opted for a mug of hot mulled wine instead.

A thin man brushed against Dot's rib and pain shot through her side. She cursed him under her breath, primarily because the pain almost caused her to drop her mulled wine. The man seeped into the jagged shadow of the Scott Monument and sat behind a cardboard sign:

> *Homeless and hungry*
> *Ex-soldier, please help.*
> *God bless. Merry Christmas.*

The man's clothes contained holes and were too thin for the cold weather. His shoes were wet and the soles were worn through. He picked up a small Tupperware box and shook it so that the few coins inside rattled about.

Dot watched dozens of people curve around him like he was a rock in a stream, avoiding his gaze. It was as though he was invisible to them, like they couldn't see him, or wouldn't allow themselves to.

He placed his Tupperware on the ground and leaned forward,

burying his head in his hands. As if summoned from the spiced steam of the stalls, a second man sprinted past and lifted the Tupperware from the ground, tucked it into his jacket pocket and evaporated in the busy crowds.

The thin man looked up briefly, utterly defeated.

Dot felt her heart crack. This guy looked as though he could use a bit of luck for once.

'Hi, I saw what happened. Are you okay?' Dot asked calmly, not wanting to add more anxiety to his situation.

The man looked up at Dot, his face unshaven and eyes mistrusting. 'I'm not great.'

'Can I help?'

He shook his head, breathing warm breath into his cupped hands. 'It's cold, and I've nowhere to stay. I'm just trying to get enough for a hostel room to stay off the street. If I can get enough, I want to catch a train to see my kid in Glasgow. I've not seen him in a long time and . . .'

Dot nodded and knelt beside him. She took an envelope from her bag and handed it to him.

He opened the envelope and peered inside, quickly holding it against his chest. 'Woah!' He looked about nervously. 'What is this?'

'It's yours.'

He looked confused but unzipped his coat and placed the envelope into an inside pocket, zipping the coat up again.

'Are you sure?' he asked. 'It's a lot. Nobody's ever given me anything like this before. The most I ever got from one person was twenty quid.'

'I'm sure,' Dot said. 'I got lucky recently – thought I should pass some luck on.'

'Thanks . . . I . . . Now, I can get the train. I can go see him for Christmas.' He sniffed back a few tears and wiped his nose on his sleeve.

'That's nice, good for you. Is there anything else I could do?'

He shook his head and stood. 'No. Thank you.' He held his hand out.

'Would you like a hug?' she asked, sensing he was still quite shaken and upset.

He smiled. Dot hugged him, and he hugged her back.

'Family's important, you know?' he said. 'I haven't got anything except them, and a couple of friends. Family and friends – we keep each other going. I'll get them all something with this money, too.' He looked around nervously. 'I'd better go. If someone finds out I've got this much, they'll come for me.'

'Okay. Merry Christmas,' Dot said.

He hugged her again and whispered: 'Thank you. God bless, and Merry Christmas,' before walking away, blending into the crowds and disappearing.

★

Home, Dot couldn't shake the man's words from her head: 'Family and friends – we keep each other going.'

She had no choice over her family, but Dot wished that she hadn't lost contact with Grace. They'd been friends, almost inseparable for the years they worked together, until retirement. While Dot had spent her wages almost as quickly as she received them, Grace had saved her money and moved to Texas to start a new life with an old flame. Dot's loss was Texas's gain. Damn lucky Texas.

What would Grace's life be like now that she'd lived in Texas for more than a decade? Did she eat burgers and fries instead of

183

fish and chips? Did she wear a cowboy hat and stirrups? Did she ride a white horse and lasso cattle, or chase vermin from corn crops with a shotgun?

Dot searched for her special shoe boxes of letters. She rifled through hundreds of documents before arriving at the small change-of-address note that Grace had sent to her a few years ago. The note Grace sent had no personal message attached but, Dot assumed, Grace couldn't be too sore with her anymore, could she? People didn't send change-of-address notes to people they hated, did they?

Dot felt sick as their final words to one another replayed in her head:

Grace had said she was sorry but had to do what was best for herself.

Dot had said Grace's home was here, her friends were here, she had to stay!

Grace said she needed to be with Angela.

Why couldn't Angela move? Why was Grace having to make all the sacrifices? Why was Angela such a controlling bitch?

And that was enough. Grace and Dot separated in fury and silence, never to speak again.

But now, Dot felt like she'd given up far too easily on a friendship that was worth saving. Maybe, just maybe, Grace would give her a second chance. After all, they were best friends, and Grace was one of the very best people Dot had ever known, assuming America hadn't changed her too much.

Dot took out her nicest pen and paper and began to write slowly:

My dear Gracey

No, too over-familiar, especially considering how things

had ended and the years that had passed since they last spoke. She crumpled the paper into a ball and started again:

> *Dear Grace,*
> *I'm sorry for what happened between us, it was all my fault. I miss you so much and hope your life has turned out to be everything you wished. If you ever come back, even just for a holiday, I'd love to meet again. And if not, then I hope you will write back, though I understand if not.*
> *My love, always,*
> *Dotty*

Dot added her home address and email address to the letter, placed it inside an envelope and sealed it with a kiss. She stuck as many stamps as she could onto the envelope and marched to the post box along the street. She posted the letter as quickly as she could, so she couldn't change her mind, and crossed her fingers.

26

Home & Away

Dot examined the shop owner's laminated face on the postcard she'd received. Behind the owner and his wife, snow-capped mountain peaks contrasted against the impossibly blue sky. The owner's wife, Chaha, was bathed in warm sunlight and her face was a picture of ecstasy. Dot was pleased that they hadn't sold the voucher, that Chaha had defeated the mortgage-obsessed miser – good for her.

Dot wondered whether she might like to go to Nepal. She'd been reading about dream holidays and bucket lists online, and a lot of people listed 'Climb Mount Everest' as one of their must-do items. But she would rather smother her face with raspberry jam and stick her head into an ants' nest than climb a mountain. Even though she might appreciate the view from the top, she had never found any pleasure in exercise and was suspicious of anyone who claimed to genuinely enjoy tired legs and sweaty pits.

Perhaps she could hire a helicopter to fly her to the peak of a mountain, check out the view with a thermos flask of tea and a few ham sandwiches, and then fly back down again. That was more her mountain-climbing level, plus it had the added benefit of including ham sandwiches and zero exercise.

No, Dot had never been particularly interested in extreme sports or energy-sapping excursions, even when she and

Charles were much younger and had managed to save enough money to travel abroad.

While their friends were busy wiping up baby vomit or changing dirty nappies, she and Charles had been enjoying foreign cuisines, walking unknown streets and listening to exotic music while watching the world turn. Maybe – if they were feeling particularly adventurous – they would visit a museum or historic landmark, but it was usually a means of whiling away the hours between meals. When it came to enjoyment, the tummy always won.

Since her living room's deforestation, several of Dot's photo albums had voyaged from the darkness of her big cupboard to the light of her coffee table. She opened two of her holiday albums and slipped into their memories of her travels with Charles: Paris in spring, when they ate nothing but cheese, bread and red wine; Berlin in winter, where her obsession with Christmas markets first began; Athens in autumn, where they were chased by stray dogs and took refuge in an olive oil shop. Charles had called it a slippery escape and they vowed never to return, even if it angered the ancient and vengeful deities of olive oil.

She explored photos of her weekends away with Grace, when they would visit random little locations of disinterest, including a pencil museum, a kitchen gadgets museum, a gas museum and umpteen model villages. They had no genuine interest in mining the information contained within the museums, but they appreciated the randomness of the attractions, and that someone out there took such an interest in innocuous things. It taught them that not everything in life had to be serious, or even important.

The recent postcard and her deep dive into her holiday photos had caused Dot's travel bug to awaken from hibernation. She was tempted to book a taxi to the airport where she might board the first flight to somewhere sunny, but she didn't want to go alone, and it wouldn't be appropriate to ask Max to go with her. Plus, Christmas was fast approaching (she couldn't miss that!), and there were still plenty of items to strike from her bucket list, so any travels could wait until the new year.

As if reading her mind, another golden envelope landed on the mat at the front door. She rushed to open the door, but only caught the imprint of Max's bike tyre on the thin layer of snowy slush on the ground. She ripped open the envelope:

> *Dot*
> *You are cordially invited to a day at the fair.*
> *Your ride arrives at 7 a.m., Wednesday. Don't be late!*
> *– Bucket Master*

★

A taxi collected Dot at stupidly early o'clock, driven by the same woman who'd taken Dot to the zoo and suggested that Max might be her grandson. But Dot didn't hold a grudge and tried to count a few more sleepy sheep as the taxi thundered towards its destination.

'Hello? You're here!' the driver eventually said, waking her from an in-and-out snooze where reality and dreams had collided into an Eton mess.

Dot got out and tipped generously. 'We really should stop meeting like this. You must be exhausted at this hour.'

The driver yawned. 'Work's work. It looks like you're having fun, and I appreciate the tips.' With that, she put her foot to the floor and drove back towards the city.

Dot's bleary eyes cleared. She was stood at the entrance to a funfair, its rides dormant behind tall, painted wooden walls.

Tinkling carousel music swam out from behind the walls, dreamlike. She half-expected her dad to walk out to greet her in his soldier's uniform.

'Good morning, Dot,' an otherworldly voice boomed from the loudspeakers on the walls. It was Max's voice, although slightly distorted by crackling. 'Welcome to Dot's Fun Land! Please enter through the turnstile and make your way to the helter-skelter.'

Dot clapped her hands with excitement, running to the turnstile where she was given a big badge and a red balloon by a member of staff. She continued towards the helter-skelter, which towered in front of a big top tent, taking toffee popcorn and candyfloss from more staff members as she passed by a glorious fountain, its water dancing to the rhythm of the fair's music.

It was only 8 a.m., so the sun hadn't fully risen, but the fair was brightly lit by miniature hot air balloon lanterns that hung on strings. As Dot neared the towering slide, the rollercoaster came to life and its carriages slithered along the tracks like snakes. Bumper cars flashed their lights and honked their horns; the swing-chairs lifted into the sky and flew gracefully on their chains; the pirate ship swung on its mighty oceanic arc with a *Yo ho ho, me hearties*.

'Nearly there!' Max's voice echoed over the speaker system.

Dot arrived at the entrance to the helter-skelter and Max approached, chomping on a toffee apple. 'A toffee apple a day keeps the doctor away,' he said.

'What's going on?' Dot asked, placing a cloud of candyfloss into her mouth. 'Where is everybody?'

'The fair has opened early, just for you,' Max said, grinning.

'What do you want to ride first?'

Dot *eek*ed. She used to dream of being at an empty funfair with her school friends. They wouldn't have to queue or worry about bullies and big boys talking down to them.

'Can you read my mind?' Dot asked, thinking about crème brûlée to throw Max off her psychic scent.

'If I could, I wouldn't,' Max said.

'For moral reasons? You wouldn't want to intrude on someone else's privacy?'

'No, I just don't want to go inside there.' He pointed at her head. 'I have a feeling it would be terrifying.'

Dot chuckled. 'Okay, what first?' She looked at the rides as they repeated their motions.

'It's up to you, it's your funfair.'

Dot looked at a sign, which pointed the direction to a variety of rides and amusements.

'What's *Musical Mirrors*?' she asked.

'It's like a hall of mirrors with music. You're meant to dance as you go through so your body changes shapes.'

'Ooh, that sounds fun – let's dance!'

Max shook his head. 'I don't dance. I told you that, right? Max doesn't dance.'

'Speaking in the third person? You must be serious. Why don't you dance? Were you traumatised by the tango? Mauled by the macarena? Shaken by swing?'

'No, I just really don't like dancing. It's not me.'

'Understood. The rollercoaster, then!' Dot dashed off, her heart thumping excitedly.

The ride's huge sign roared at them. It showed an ox-headed man with a golden axe and furious red eyes. Beside the ox-headed man it said: *Dare you ride THE MINOTAUR?*

'I dare!' Dot shouted defiantly, turning her way through the labyrinth of the queue barriers until she reached a waiting ride carriage.

She sat in the front carriage so she'd get a proper view of the dips on the track, to really build the anticipation and rattle her bones.

Max sat beside her. 'You know this is the scariest seat, right?'

'Yes, that's the whole point. You've a lot to learn.'

The coaster lurched forward, turning sharp corners, climbing high before quickly descending its dips. Dot enjoyed it well enough, though it cricked her neck and didn't thrill her as much as she had hoped it would. It wasn't the ride's fault, per se, but it lacked atmosphere and noise.

'It wasn't quite the same without other people screaming,' she said to Max as they got off the ride.

'My turn to pick. How about the bumper cars?'

'One of my favourites. It'll give you another chance to out-drive me, after your abysmal effort at the track.'

'Okay, Evel Knievel, show me how it's done.'

They hurried to the bumper cars. Dot chose a purple car and drove straight for Max, smashing into the side of his vehicle. The impact stung her neck but she continued, racing away from Max to lure him into corners before circling around to pound his car again.

The ride eventually ended, and Dot was pleased with the number of times she'd managed to smash into Max, though he'd given as good as he got.

'I missed colliding with the kids,' Dot said. 'The look of fear and excitement in their eyes, just before the realisation that I have them trapped and there's no escape from my bumps.'

'You're a sadist,' Max said. 'But, yeah, I agree, it's not the same.'

'It's not your fault,' Dot said, concerned that she'd hurt his feelings. He'd clearly put a lot of work into organising their experience.

Max checked his watch. 'It's not long now, anyway.'

'Until what?'

'Until the park opens. We're only alone here for an hour, before it opens properly. Come on.'

They walked to the front of the park, where Dot could see queues of schoolchildren forming behind the turnstiles. Max and Dot ate their snacks and waited, the queues growing fatter and louder, until a bell rang out and excited kids poured into the park.

'That's more like it!' Dot said as circus music blared from the big top tent.

*

Dot and Max sat on a wooden bench in the big top tent, surrounded by primary schoolchildren. Worn-out teachers watched over their swarms of kids with world-wearied eyes, as though they were actively counting down the seconds until their wine-soaked winter holidays.

The tent lights dimmed and some of the kids screamed. A spotlight illuminated a ringmaster, who was dressed as Father Christmas and introduced everybody to Santa's Circus Extraordinaire. Everybody cheered as snowflake-costumed acrobats swung from the ceiling on tinselled ropes.

Dot clapped along to the jolly music as clowns performed their comedy act, tripping over one another and throwing pails of fake snow into the crowd, causing the schoolchildren to scream and laugh. Max looked frosty at first but eventually melted and laughed along with the slapstick gags.

Once the elvish jugglers, snowman fire-eaters and

gingerbread sword-swallower had finished their performances, the ringmaster returned and wished everyone a great day at the fair. The kids began to file out of the tent even more excited than when they arrived.

A little girl, about six years old, wearing an antler headband and with a red-painted nose, tripped on the steps of the tent's seating area and fell towards Max. He caught her mid-fall, stopping her from tumbling down.

'Are you okay?' Max asked the girl.

The girl looked sheepish but nodded and rubbed her red nose.

'Be careful, okay?' Max said softly, smiling. 'I know reindeer can fly, but it's not Christmas Eve yet.'

'I'm not a real reindeer!' The girl smiled and nodded. She ran off to join her friends outside the tent, leaving Dot and Max sitting on the wooden benches.

'That show was kinda lame,' Max said to Dot. 'But funny.'

'I had fun,' Dot said. 'It's better with the kids here.'

Max zipped his coat up to his chin. 'Well, I guess it's not *what* you do, but who you do it with that makes the difference. Those kids were loving it.'

'You're so cute. You like kids?' Dot asked. 'You seem really good with them.'

'Oh, yeah. I have a lot of little cousins I helped with, and a few people I know from school had babies.'

'You mean the teachers?'

Max shook his head. 'No, like two of my friends. And a few other girls, even one who was just thirteen, I think. Do you have kids?'

'No, they weren't really my thing.'

Max blew into his hands to warm them. 'I'd like them someday, I think, but not yet.'

'Probably a good idea to wait until you're ready – you're still really young. When I was your age, most of the women I knew had kids or were trying.'

Max hesitated. 'Can I ask you something? You don't have to answer.'

He seemed nervous. Dot prepared herself not to act surprised at what might follow.

'Yes, what?' Dot asked.

'What happened to you? Your face, I mean. It's much better now, but when we met at the park you were pretty . . . scabby.'

'I was mugged at the cemetery near my house. Then I was so afraid to go out that I locked myself away for a while.'

'Shit, sorry.' Max said. 'Did the police catch them?'

'The police are busy,' Dot replied. 'They told me not to get my hopes up. But the muggers took my special silver locket.' She tried not to let the memory of that night reignite in her, but it was hard to keep it suffocated. 'I'm fine, really, but I sometimes hear their voices in my head, their hands and boots when they took it . . .' She rubbed at her throat, where they'd torn the chain from around her neck. She thought instead of her locket, imagining its smooth metal between her fingertips, and it calmed her. 'My dad gave it to me when we went to the fair together. It was our last day together before he . . . left. And it had a photo of him inside. I wish I had that; I don't mind about the rest of the things they took.'

'It sounds important. Maybe I can ask around.' He stood. 'I know a few people who buy and sell jewellery, though I've not seen them in a while.'

'Fences?' Dot asked. It hadn't occurred to her before now that Max might know how to find stolen goods. A crack of hope widened within her, like an opening door.

'Yeah. I can ask them. You were mugged a while ago now, so your locket's probably been sold or thrown away already, though. Was it worth a lot?'

Dot touched the scabs on her face. 'Only to me.'

'I got you. I'll put my feelers out and see what comes back.'

'Thanks!'

Dot liked the idea of Max looking out for her. She imagined him swooping down from the sky, red-caped and ready to crush her enemies.

'You're made of pretty tough stuff,' Max said, walking towards the tent exit. 'Fighting off muggers, smashing up cars. You're always up for whatever I have planned. Do you ever sleep?'

'I eats me spinach.' Dot flexed her thin arms.

'Maybe I should try some.' He placed a hand over his mouth and yawned.

'Have you got a lot to do?' she asked. 'You seem tired.'

'I've got my community service four days a week, and I have to keep applying for work or I lose benefits. And the bucket list takes a lot of time.'

Dot could read between the lines, and she felt bad for being so thoughtless.

'I'm sorry, Max,' she said. 'I had been so ravelled up in my own things that I hadn't even thought about how much you have to do. And you don't have a paid job at the moment, yet I've been forcing you to work for free! You ought to have called Amnesty on me by now.'

'No, it's okay, I just mean . . . Well, yeah, okay. I am struggling a bit. I'm not workshy but doing all of this means I've not applied for many jobs. I just thought I should say something, because I probably can't keep this up forever. Not at this rate, anyway.'

'You shouldn't have needed to say something, this is my fault. Right, from now on you're being paid a wage. And I'm back-paying you.'

Max held up his hands as if being robbed at gunpoint. 'I didn't mean that!'

'I know. But you're not my slave, and you're doing a great job. I hadn't appreciated how much of your time my bucket list would take. You deserve to be paid, Man Friday. Besides, I bet all the other millionaires have private assistants.' She held out her hand. 'Consider yourself hired!'

He beamed and shook her hand. 'Thanks. And while we're talking about the bucket list, I've thought of something we can add to it, since I won our car race.'

'Erm, *I* won the race,' Dot corrected him, although she knew she was driving on black ice.

'You almost wrecked your car and yourself. The reason I didn't cross that line is because I had to check you were okay. So, let me add something to the bucket list. It's a good one, I'm sure you'll enjoy it. And I notice you've been holding your neck today, so we need to take it easy, just until you're fixed up. Eat more spinach in the meantime.'

Dot rubbed her neck as they continued out of the tent, into the cold air outside. 'So, what are we doing next? Where are we going?'

Max pointed to the clear sky. 'Space: the final frontier . . .'

27

What the Stars
Have in Store

Dot drifted through the vacuum of space, her limbs light as air, her mind as blank as newly fallen snow. She twirled with her arms stretched out, floating past planets and stars.

'Okay, Missus Hindley.' The workman's voice broke through Dot's daydream as his installation team left her home. 'That's your new security suite fitted. Doors, windows, motion sensors and lights. It's Fort Knox in here now. It'll be hard for anyone to break in, and if they do then our security team will be alerted. We've installed the panic buttons in your bedroom, kitchen and lounge, too.'

He produced a user manual so thick that Dot instantly regretted her decision to install the added security. She had just wanted to be safe at home, not to read the complete and unabridged works of Security Shakespeare.

The workman placed the tome on Dot's coffee table, wished her a nice day and followed his team outside.

Whether or not the new security features would protect her completely, Dot instantly felt more at ease. It was as though a suit of armour had been placed around her home. Sure, the random red buttons and lock-down shutters over the windows might make her house look like the base of an evil super villain (actually, that appealed to her a little, and she let out a small maniacal laugh), but it was otherwise quite unobtrusive.

She moved her kettle in front of the red button in the kitchen, her bedside table in front of the button in her bedroom, and shifted her telly slightly so that the button in her lounge was hidden from view. Out of sight, out of mind, she told herself. Plus, she didn't want any visitors to accidentally push the buttons and for a security team to burst through her door. After all, who could resist pushing a red button? It was practically impossible.

Finally, she placed her heaviest rolling pin beside her bed, just in case an intruder made it into her fortress.

Dot checked her emails, hoping that Grace might have received her letter and replied, but she only had the usual messages from African princes who wished to share their vast wealth with her. She'd been tempted to respond to keep herself entertained, but figured that would only result in more junk emails and potentially – although she had to admit the chance was slim – causing offence to absconded African royalty.

The online community forums were alive with the usual complaints about potholes, bin collections and noisy cat sex. The posts held no real interest to Dot now her life was busier, but she stopped at one post titled *Christmas Tree in the Commons*. She read the opening message:

> *SallyRiley (1 week ago)*
> *Has anyone seen the huge xmas tree in the commons near the 24 hour corner shop (closed right now, any idea why?) It's BEAUTIFUL! Who put it there?*

And a reply:

BigJohnProud2Bbri69 (1 week ago)
Certainly wasn't the council! Looks good, but how long until kids steal all the decorations and pull it down?

Another reply:

MuchAdo (1 week ago)
Kids aren't touching it. Saw a few robins in the branches, it's lovely SallyRiley. I think it's the old woman who won the lotto.

And another:

BigJohnProud2Bbri69 (5 days ago)
Went to check it out. Nice tree but a fire hazard. Mrs Moneybags is a bit of a showoff, isnt she? And I saw a lot of pigeons. Flying rats spread disease & might be nesting in the tree. I'm not a lotto winner, but I bet the council won't come to get rid of it. Hazard to the area, and who put Mrs Moneybags in charge?

Which prompted this:

Beam-Me-Up-Scotty-Too-Hotty (5 days ago)
I've got an air rifle.

Dot's fingers were poised over the keyboard, ready to defend herself. She was glad to see some people had appreciated her efforts, but a little dismayed that she had gained a nickname and a reputation as a Maker of Hazards. She continued to read:

SallyRiley (4 days ago)
Guys chill out. It's a Christmas tree and birds are normal. No need to get trigger happy, no need to call the council. I think it's just

a nice gift from an old woman, let it go. Seriously.

Unsurprisingly, Big John was not impressed:

> *BigJohnProud2Bbri69 (4 days ago)*
> *Mrs Moneybags puts up a huge tree in a PUBLIC SPACE and I bet taxpayers have to pay to get it removed. Who asked us if we wanted a tree? Sick of the rich elites doing whatever they want. This country's becoming a dictatorship. If I wanted that I'd move to CHINA. They'll line us all up and shoot us next if we disagree.*

And, of course:

> *Beam-Me-Up-Scotty-Too-Hotty (4 days ago)*
> *I've got two air rifles.*

The chat descended into a debate about communism and capitalism and their various evils, then broke down into a slagging match where the forum members called one another Hitler and Mao. Such was the way of the community forum, ever since Dot could remember. She vowed not to visit the forums again, especially as she was now the target of vitriol.

Dot jumped at the sound of something being posted through her letterbox, and she raced to her front door, hoping that Grace might have replied. But there was only one piece of post: a golden envelope.

She quickly opened the door but, yet again, was too late to catch the infamous Bucket Master.

She tore open the golden envelope and read the note excitedly:

Space awaits!
Wear warm clothes, scarf and gloves.
It's cold out there and remember:
In space no one can hear you scream!
Your ride arrives Wednesday, 9 p.m.
— Bucket Master

★

Wrapped up like a pig in a blanket, Dot waited for her taxi to arrive. 9.05 p.m. came and went. 9.10 p.m. followed with no signs of a taxi on the street. Had she misread Max's invite? She checked it again. No, her ride was simply late.

A quiet metallic jingling sounded outside, growing louder with the musical *clop clop* of something heavy on the ground. Dot opened her front door.

A wooden stage carriage, covered in fairy lights, rolled down her street pulled by two large white horses. The horses snorted, blowing white clouds from their nostrils, the bells in their braided manes jingling and tinkling. Their leather reigns were held by a man in a Victorian-style grey coat, vest and top hat, and he waved at Dot as the carriage came to a stop outside her house.

'Good evening, ma'am,' the driver said, his voice thick and sweet as honey. 'Please climb inside, our magical journey is about to begin!'

The horses' pearl-white hair was so beautifully groomed and tied, with lights flickering on the strands, that they looked unreal. Dot felt like she was a princess in a fairy tale.

She giggled to herself and opened the carriage door.

Max was inside and on his phone. He quickly put it into his pocket and waved Dot inside.

201

She got in beside him, grinning like a cat who'd been given double cream in a field of catnip.

'You like?' Max asked.

'Oh, I like! I love it!' Dot said, her body overflowing with energy. She wrapped her arms around him and kissed his cheek. 'Thank you, Bucket Master.'

Max peeled away, wiping his cheek with the back of a gloved hand. 'You're very welcome.' He rang a silver bell on the wall, and the carriage began to move away. 'I figured this might be your kind of thing.'

'You figured right. You really are one of the best people I've ever known, do you realise that?'

Max blushed. He opened a thermos flask and poured two cups of steaming hot chocolate, passing one to Dot.

She took a sip. Its rich chocolate danced on her tongue, and its strong alcohol warmed her throat and tummy.

'Hot and boozy,' Dot said, 'just how I like it. So, where are we going?'

'Up!' Max said. 'You'll see. Enjoy the ride.'

They sat in silence as the carriage continued along Dot's street. Children rushed out from their houses to see the horses, and the driver tossed candy canes down for them before explaining that they had to return home because he had a very special journey to go on.

The carriage sped up and began to ascend a slope, pushing Dot back into her seat. She looked out of the carriage's slatted windows but it was too dark to see anything other than the shrinking lights of the streets below.

Eventually, the carriage stopped.

'This is it,' Max said. 'Space.'

They got out of the carriage, and Dot could see that they were on a dark hilltop.

'We'll be back soon,' Max said to the driver, leading Dot a little further up the hill, illuminating the ground with an electric torch so that they didn't stumble.

The hill was quiet, except for the briefest whistles of wind.

'I used to come here,' Max said, 'when I ran away from home or school. It's quiet, and nobody thought to search for me up here. And it has a great view.'

Turning off his torch, he looked up at the dark sky, and Dot stared up with him. A quilt of stars – hundreds, maybe thousands – shone above them, clearer than Dot had ever seen them before.

Max pointed to a cluster of stars. 'See that constellation? The three bright stars in a line? That's Orion, the hunter.'

'I see it!'

Max took a laser pen from his pocket and pointed its red beam into the sky at two other stars.

'And there's Gemini, the twins.' He moved his laser back to Orion, lifting its beam higher to highlight another constellation. 'That's the Bull's Eye – it contains the Crab Nebula.'

'How do you know all this?' Dot asked, equal parts mesmerised and impressed.

'I came here so often that I decided to get a book from the library so I knew what I was looking at. It was like I was here all alone, in secret. Nobody to bother me. Nobody to say anything . . . well, you know, shitty. It was like I had this little pocket of the universe all to myself. And' – he cleared his throat – 'I wanted you to see it, too.'

'Thank you, Max.' She didn't know what else to say.

'And I got you this little present.'

He took a small book from his pocket and handed it to her: *Songs of Innocence and of Experience*, by William Blake.

Dot ran her fingertips over the book's dog-eared cover. 'It's just like the one I had in school!'

'Yeah, I got the oldest copy I could find.' He laughed.

Dot flipped through the pages of the book, noticing something handwritten in the front:

> Dot
> *Thank you for everything. Keep burning bright.*
> BM

'That's so lovely, thank you, Max,' Dot said, so touched by his sweetness that she felt a little teary.

It had been so long since someone had shown any interest in her, let alone given her such a special and personal gift. Now that she thought about it, the last time something so special had been given to her was when Charles had died and Grace dropped by with home-cooked meals and flowers and a few photos that she'd taken from before his diagnosis, when they were all happy.

'You know I've been alone a long time,' Dot said slowly. She'd not opened up like this before, and worried that it would be too much for Max, or that she'd make him feel awkward, or that she'd seem overly emotional about his gift. But he looked at her calmly, and it reassured her to continue. 'And – without wanting to bring the loveliness of tonight down too much – I didn't think I had a lot left to look forward to. Even if I had all this money, it wouldn't have been the same without you.'

'It's been cool to hang out,' Max said. 'I wouldn't have done any of these things without you, either. I know you won the money, so it's not like you're some big business tycoon, but you've helped me to see what my life could be like, that I can escape. Maybe I can work hard and do well, maybe I could help people like me and my mum, who've had a hard time.'

'You can do it,' Dot said. 'I can see it in you.' She looked up at the stars again; it felt like they were looking back at her and winking. 'I don't really believe in fate and horoscopes, but my mum did. And after everything that's happened to me lately, I wonder if maybe there's a little bit of truth in it, like maybe we do have a destiny.'

Max hummed quietly.

Dot continued: 'It feels like something wanted us to meet when we did, that something special made me choose your shirt number for my lottery ticket.'

'You are fully capable of deciding your own destiny. The question you face is: which path will you choose?'

'Who's that, a philosopher? Heraclitus?'

Max raised a hand, palm towards Dot. He spread his fingers so that the little finger remained in contact with his ring finger, and his middle finger stayed in contact with his index finger.

'Doctor Spock,' Max said. '"Live long and prosper."'

'I intend to, Doctor.'

'I'm not sure I believe in destiny or fate, either,' Max said. 'But then I met you and everything changed. I haven't had any real friends for ages, and then randomly I start chatting to this weird old lady—'

Dot cleared her throat to correct him.

'I mean, one day I met this really . . . unique woman in the park, totally randomly, and she *got* me. If you looked at our lives summed up on paper, then we shouldn't click at all, right? But we do. So, maybe there is something true about fate, after all.'

'Could be!' Dot grinned.

'But if fate does exist, then it's not all good. Sometimes it feels like the decks are stacked against me, you know?'

Dot nodded.

'But I want to fight against it,' Max said with determination. 'I'm not going to let people get to me anymore. I can change things – I feel like there's something strong inside me now, trying to break out. Like, a fire that wasn't there before.' He took a long, deep breath. 'Speaking of which, I think it's the right time . . .' He turned on his torch again, running its light along the ground until he found a thin rope. 'There.'

Max dipped his hand into his jacket pocket and took out a lighter, which he passed to Dot.

'Light it,' Max said.

'Just here?' she asked, bending to reach the end of the rope.

'Yes, then let's hurry back to the carriage.'

Dot held the flame against the rope then stepped back as the flame grew, burning the rope, and joined Max beside the carriage.

'The horses are okay with loud noises, right?' Max asked the carriage driver.

'No problem. Like I said on the phone, they're trained,' he replied.

A small ball of white light rose silently into the pitch-black sky, like a star over a manger. It stopped and hovered, then splintered with a *BANG*, cascading outwards. Each fragment exploded again, creating a dozen spheres of twinkling lights that rained down like pixie dust on the streets below.

'Fireworks!' Dot exclaimed, clapping.

A barrage of fireworks rocketed into the sky, whistling and screeching, spinning and erupting robin-red, holly-green and star-white, until the entire sky was filled with light and noise.

As Dot watched the display, *ooooh*ing and *aaah*ing, she felt like a little girl again.

She watched Max's smiling face, lit by the cracking lights, and thanked her lucky stars that she'd met him.

28

Running Down the Wing

Lottery number 7

(Max is eight years old)

Max's dad told black lies, Max's mum said, and Max needed to keep his eyes peeled and his head on straight and his feet on the ground. It all sounded very Mr Potato Head to Max and, besides, his dad was fun. Sure, he didn't come around as much as Max would like, but he was always in a good mood with Max, even when he stank of whisky and cigs, or even when he'd lost his horse wins, or even if his mum was being a right old dragon and needed to learn to keep her mouth shut.

Even if all those bad things had happened, Max's dad always smiled when he saw Max, and he always asked how he was and if he'd been good. Yes, of course Max had been good. And his dad would smile and say: 'That's ma boy!' like in an American movie.

But anyway, Max's mum was warning him about his dad's black lies again, which meant his dad was coming over some time soon, so Max was happy. He and his dad loved to watch the footie together, and they were both Man-U fans – so, whenever Man-U played, Max put on his number 7 shirt. Number 7 was his favourite player of all, the best player ever to play football, probably: Ronaldo. And when Max wore his number 7 shirt, he felt like he was Ronaldo. And that was pretty great.

So, because his mum was warning him about black lies, Max got ready for his dad to come over by putting on his Ronaldo shirt. The door *ding dong*ed and Max ran to answer it.

'Maximus!' his dad yelled, picking him up and hugging him. 'How's life in Rome?'

'Life's good in Rome,' Max said as usual, turning his head away so he didn't have to smell the stink of whisky and cigs. He wasn't exactly sure why his dad talked about Rome so much, but he knew Rome had good pizza so it must be a brilliant place to be.

'And have you been good?' his dad asked.

Max nodded so quickly that his neck hurt. 'Yes, of course.'

'That's ma boy!' His dad twirled around, stumbling a little, and put Max on the floor. 'Is the old dragon in?'

That was his dad's nickname for his mum. It was their little secret, just a white lie – although sometimes his mum really was like a dragon when she got mad.

'Mum's making bacon,' Max said, pointing to the kitchen.

'Is she now? Wait here.'

Max's dad walked along the hallway and into the lounge, where the TV was blasting Max's favourite cartoon: Spider-Man. If Max couldn't play for Man-U when he was older then he wanted to be Spider-Man, or maybe Batman. He wanted to be a hero, more than anything.

His dad tapped on the kitchen door.

'Don't come in, I'm cooking!' his mum roared from inside the smoky kitchen.

But his dad went in anyway and closed the door behind him. Max could hear them talk in muffles, sometimes louder and sometimes more quiet. After a while, his dad came back out to the lounge. Max could see through the crack in the door, and his mum was wiping her eyes with the sleeve of her towel dressing gown.

'Is mum okay?' Max asked.

'She's fine.' His dad pulled the kitchen door shut again. 'Smoke in her eyes. But you and me are doing something special today!' He turned off the TV before Spider-Man had finished saving Mary Jane from the Green Goblin, which was disappointing. 'I'm really glad you wore your Ronaldo shirt today, because you'll never guess what . . .'

Max's heart thumped so hard that he thought it might burst out of his chest, like in the film his dad and his dad's friend had been watching one poker night: *Alien*.

'What?' Max asked.

'We're going to see him play!'

'The real Ronaldo?'

'Yep, the real Ronaldo. So, get your shoes on, all right? And go wait at the car for me.' He tossed the car keys to Max, who caught them in the air like Spider-Man might catch the Green Goblin's grenade. 'Great save. I won't be long.'

Max got his shoes on fast and ran out the house, across to the lifts. He pushed the sticky button and, after a long time, the lift clattered and chugged to the top of the flats. He held his breath and got into the lift, because it smelled of dirty toilets and cigs, and rode it all the way down to the ground.

At the bottom, Max pushed the button on his dad's car keys. The car beeped and its lights flashed. He got inside and turned on the radio, pushing the buttons to skip through the boring news and weather, until he got to some fun music he thought his dad might like. Then he waited until his dad came down and got into his car.

'The old dragon's a bloody pain in the neck, isn't she?' Max's dad said.

'Mum?'

Max's dad nodded and started the engine, and he was breathing deep and his face was a bit red. He was probably just as excited as Max was, Max supposed, to see the real Ronaldo in real life.

'Well, let's go,' Max's dad said.

He made the car do a screechy wheel spin in the car park before they zoomed off, both singing as loud as they could: 'Viva Ronaldo! Running down the wing, hear United sing, Viva Ronaldo!'

★

The football stadium boomed with music and voices, and people swarmed near the guarded gates. Meaty burger and onion smells filled Max's nostrils and his tummy rumbled, but he barely even noticed he was hungry because he was so excited.

He stared up at the huge stadium – which looked a bit like the special white shell he found on the beach, which he could hear the sea inside of if he held it to his ear – and imagined the players inside, stretching their legs and talking about the big match. He imagined them around Ronaldo, smiling and laughing, patting his back and telling him what a great player he was. Max wondered if Ronaldo ever got nervous, like Max did when he had to see the headmaster at school after fighting with Dean Scott, or when new friends came to his house to see his mum.

'All right, we're going through the VIP entrance,' his dad said.

Max knew VIP stood for *Very Important People* and thought that his dad must be really important. He'd thought his dad was just a regular guy, with regular pals, but maybe he was wrong. Maybe his dad was a secret agent, like James Bond, or maybe he was best pals with Ronaldo and kept it a secret until now.

Either way, Max's dad led him through the crowds and around the side of the stadium, towards the back. A few big men stood near a metal fence, chatting. Max's dad shook their hands, and they stood aside. One of the men pulled on the metal fence and it opened up like he was peeling foil off a chocolate bar.

'Quick, in,' Max's dad said, turning sideways to slide through the gap in the fence. He reached out for Max's hand. 'Hurry up.'

Max took his dad's hand, and his dad pulled him through the gap. A man pushed on the metal fence and it closed up so neatly that it was almost impossible to know the gap was there, unless you knew for sure. Max felt a little flutter of happiness, like he'd been let in on a secret, like he was one of the guys.

Max's dad pulled his hand and they walked around the back of some boring grey building, then around the side of a truck that sold T-shirts and bobble-heads of famous footballers.

Max hadn't been inside the stadium before and didn't know what to expect. It was full of mostly men, and he could hear singing. He whispered, joining in on the tune he recognised: 'Viva Ronaldo! Running down the wing, hear United sing, Viva Ronaldo!'

Singing the song made him feel like he was part of the group, part of this huge family that all loved Ronaldo. This family looked out for each other, he hoped, if anyone ever got in trouble. Like, if Dean Scott ever tried to fight Max again, one of his football family might appear from nowhere and knock his block off or frighten him away. And if the headmaster called Max to his office to tell him that he was in trouble, maybe one of his football family would meet him at the door to check he was okay. Maybe one of the family would say: 'Forget the headmaster and Dean Scott, they're idiots. Let's go play footie instead.'

Yeah, it felt great to be at the stadium with his dad. And as they walked up the steps leading to the seats around the pitch, and the singing got louder and louder, Max felt like he was walking into Heaven, and the angels were singing so loud that his ears rang like the bells of Heaven. Their words were so loud that they smooshed together, and it sounded like they were chanting Max's name, like they were calling him onto the pitch to play and save their match.

With his special shirt on, Max marched up those steps and was ready to play, ready to save them all. They would hold him up in the air and call out his name – Max, Max, MAX! – and he would be their hero.

'All right, this way,' his dad shouted, pulling him towards the very back row.

Max looked down at the pitch, which was like a beautiful green gem. Around him, people waved their scarves and drank beer and yelled. Nobody really looked at him, except his dad. It was cold out, and a lot of people wore big winter coats, but Max only had his Ronaldo shirt on. Max's dad took off his coat and put it on Max so he was warm. He was a great dad.

'Thanks,' Max said. His dad's warm body had heated up the coat, and it felt good except that it stank of cigs.

His dad bent down and cupped his hands around Max's ear.

'The game's going to start soon, okay? When it starts, you have to help me out. See that man's coat pocket?' He nodded to a fat man in a big winter coat.

Max nodded.

'When he's not looking, you reach into that pocket and take out something. Feel for something big and heavy, not a tissue or a coin. Then take it out, and drop it into your coat pocket, all right?'

Max hesitated. 'Why?'

'It'll help me out. And if you get something good, I'll buy you a McDonald's on the way back. Something heavy, got it?'

Max wasn't sure. He looked up at his dad, hoping he'd change his mind.

'That guy took something from me, and I need it back. But if I try, he'll see me. But he won't see you – and if anything happens, I'll come get you. It'll be easy. Just dip your hand in quickly. Give it a try, for me.'

'Okay,' Max said, feeling sick from not having any lunch and from not wanting to go anywhere near the man. But he didn't want to let his dad down, especially after he brought him through the VIP gate to see Ronaldo.

'Do it quickly, just walk by,' his dad said, nudging him away. 'I'm here.'

Max walked up to the man. He felt like his legs might turn to tentacles or jelly, but he kept walking and tried not to think all that much about anything. It was noisy and busy, and they were at the back of the stadium and nobody was looking at all. He dipped his hand into the man's big pocket and his fingers touched something hard. He gripped it and took it out, kept walking and dropped it into his own coat pocket, like he'd been told.

Max felt sure that the man or someone else would have

214

seen him. He gulped and took a deep breath, feeling his heart pounding like a roadworks drill in his chest. But nobody was looking – they were all just watching the pitch and chatting to each other, singing and waving their scarves.

Max's dad waved to him and did a 'come back' curly finger, so Max walked a different way around – not wanting to pass near the fat man again – back to his dad.

'You did it!' His dad grinned. He looked so happy that Max couldn't help but grin back. His dad dipped his hand into Max's pocket and took out a phone. He put the phone in his backpack. 'That's it, perfect. There are a couple more people who did bad things, and I need my stuff back, okay? You're great at this – I'm really proud of you, Maximus.'

His dad had never said that he was proud of him before. He'd said he loved him, and he thought he was really great, and he'd told him he was a little brat once or twice, and that his mum was an old dragon and he'd better be careful not to turn out like her . . . but he'd never said he was proud of Max before. Max felt big, like he'd been pumped up like a balloon. Like he was Spider-Man after saving Mary Jane.

'When's Ronaldo playing?' Max asked.

'Ah, crap. I just heard someone say that Ronaldo's not playing today,' Max's dad said. 'I'm really sorry, I thought he was going to play. Maybe next time, all right?'

Max could have cried then, but he didn't. He was still all pumped up from his dad saying he was proud.

'Is he okay?' Max asked. 'Is he sick?'

'He's not well, but he'll be fine. The match is about to start, and I still need your help.' He pointed to two men. 'Next is that guy, and then that one. Okay?'

'Okay,' Max said, hoping the match would still be worth

watching. Everyone in the stadium seemed excited, so he felt excited too.

'That's ma boy!' His dad nudged him away as the players marched out onto the pitch.

Max watched the players come out but didn't forget his mission. He dipped his hand into another man's coat, took out something heavy and dropped it into his own pocket. He wandered away quickly, then as the ref blew his whistle for the match to begin, Max dipped-and-dropped the final guy his dad had pointed out.

He walked back to his dad, who took a wallet and another phone from the coat and smiled. 'You can have a Happy Meal *and* an ice cream. Good lad.'

Max beamed. He reached up, wanting to be lifted onto his dad's shoulders like he'd seen some other kids do, but his dad shook his head.

'You're too big for that now. You're a proper man, got it?' He pointed to two more men who were busy yelling at the players. 'Just a couple more, that's all. Then we'll watch the match.'

Max did the dip-drop two more times but didn't go back to his dad straight away. Instead, he watched the game and his dad's smiling face. It was so exciting and everyone was so happy, especially Max.

29

Life's Not Always Carrots

Dot's elation hadn't subsided since the fireworks and stargazing. She fluttered about the house, decorating it with colourful foils and garlands, singing Christmas songs and ordering the most hideous Christmas jumpers she could find online.

Her whole body felt lighter, and her rib, knee and neck barely hurt any more. Smells were stronger, her sight seemed clearer, sounds were sharper. She wondered whether she might be imbued with Christmas magic, or was de-aging like Benjamin Button. She hadn't felt so chipper in years.

Spurred by her good mood, Dot explored her photo albums and carefully removed the best photo from her wedding – the one of Charles and her laughing together, believing they were alone at the side of the church. The picture had, for a long time, been a reminder of what she'd lost, but now she felt ready to see it on her wall again.

She would never fully get over Charles being gone, but she didn't *want* to be completely over it, either. He was the most important part of her life, and his absence shouldn't be ignored. But instead of the familiar pain she'd felt, instead of the void he'd left, she felt happy to see his face and to think that the future might hold something important for her again. Not another man, but another Dot.

She put a new screw into the wall, placed the photo into a silver frame and hung it.

'Nice to see you again,' Dot said to herself. 'It's been a long time.'

Dot's phone buzzed and there was a text message from Max: *You free today? Community service rescheduled. (Gentle) bike ride?*

She hadn't any other plans, and the photo hanging had reminded Dot of her wedding day bike ride: the wind in her hair and lungs, the blood pumping through her legs, the butterflies in her stomach.

She texted Max back: *Yes. But I've no bike, go to bike shop first?*

He replied: *No need. I'll be with you in 20 mins.*

The sky was suspiciously sunny for early December, but it was cold and Dot changed into comfortable, warm clothes anyway. Her doorbell rang and she opened it to Max, who was wearing his number 7 football shirt, like when she'd first seen him. His bike leaned against the wall of her house, beside a second bike with pink ribbons, a bright brass bell and a woven basket.

'Did you steal that?' Dot asked with a hushed voice, hoping her neighbours wouldn't be able to identify Max when questioned in court.

'No, I pulled it out of the pond,' Max said. 'I asked around but nobody claimed it, so I fixed it up. And now, it's yours.' He grabbed the bike's silver handlebars and rolled it towards Dot. 'I know some great, easy routes. So, hop on, test the saddle. You can ride a bike, right?'

'Of course I can!' Dot snatched the handlebars from him and climbed on, a little unsteadily. 'It's been a while since I went on a good long ride. But you know what they say, you never forget how to—'

Dot's weight shifted: she lost her footing and careened

towards Max, who reached out and nudged Dot back into an upright position.

'You never forget how to fall off?' he asked.

'I'll be fine once we get started. I just need the momentum.' She placed a foot on the ground to steady herself and squeezed the brake, then rang the bell. 'You really took this from the pond and fixed it? It's good as new!'

'Yeah. I told you, I'm good with bikes. I thought we'd head onto the tracks near the hill, then to a farm, if you're up for it?'

'I'm up for it. If you think you can keep up.'

Max sighed. 'How about we just cycle at a nice, steady pace and nobody gets hurt this time?'

Dot peddled, riding onto the pavement, and circled the Christmas tree on the common.

'See, you never forget!' she called out to Max, hoping she wouldn't fall off – partly because she didn't want to risk injury, but mainly because she didn't want to seem like a fool for showboating. She considered doing a wheely but knew it would be pushing her luck.

Max rode alongside her. 'Come on, we don't have all day. I'll lead, I know the best routes.' He tossed a brown paper bag into her bike's basket.

'What's this?' Dot asked, trying to look nonchalant while concentrating on following him as he rode away from the tree.

Max picked up speed. 'Treats. We're going to visit some friends, so keep up!'

★

The treetops looked like they'd been sprinkled with icing sugar, and the crisp winter air felt fresh in Dot's lungs. Geese honked as they passed overhead, and the hilltops loomed over the distant forests and sparse houses. If she ignored the occasional hatchback on the road, the scene looked like an old-fashioned Christmas card picture.

'I'd forgotten' – Dot panted as she rode on the cycle path beside the woods – 'how pretty it is . . . out here.'

Max slowed, allowing Dot to catch up.

'Yeah, it's nice. And we've not much further to go. Just over the potato field.'

Dot's voice rattled as she rode over the uneven field, its earth upturned: 'Maybe I'll treat us to some fish and chips with plenty of salt and sauce – we've earned it.'

Just about managing to ride straight with one hand, Dot used her free hand to open the brown paper bag in her basket. It was filled with sugar cubes and carrots.

Then her front wheel plunged into a hole. She turned her handlebars and squeezed the brakes to regain control. Her bike came to a sudden halt as Dot's foot planted against the earth, sending a sharp spike of pain into her knee with a quiet *crack*.

Dot screamed out in pain, managing to put her weight on her other leg to stop herself from falling.

'FUUUUUUDGE FUCKITY SHITTING FUCKBAGS!' Dot shouted, her curses echoing over the fields and rebounding from the hillsides to surround her in a wall of fucks.

Max's bike screeched as it turned sharply and he sped towards her.

'What? Are you okay?' He held her arm to support her weight. 'Your knee?'

'Yes, my fu . . . dging knee,' she growled, testing whether she could stand on it. She could, though it hurt. 'It's not too bad. I can walk.'

'Should I call an ambulance?' Max asked, taking out his phone.

'Don't. I'm all right.' Her knee was already beginning to feel less painful and she was embarrassed at her outburst. She raised her foot and twirled her ankle. 'I think it's fine now. Just a bit sore.'

'I've never heard you swear like that. I thought you didn't swear, like it was against your religion or something.'

Dot snorted a half-laugh. 'There's a time and place for it. Like many things, the less often you do it, the more special it becomes.'

Max bit his lip. 'If you say so. But you're really okay? You had me worried.'

'I'm really okay,' Dot said.

'We're almost finished, so why don't we leave the bikes and walk the rest of the way? Then we can pick them up on the way back, if your knee's up to it and if you can resist screaming about fudge.'

'No more fucking fudge. I've used up my annual swearing quota.'

Max examined Dot's bike. 'The chain's come loose.' He fiddled with it, swiftly returning it to its necessary position. He leaned their bikes against a stone wall, taking the paper bag of sugar cubes and carrots from Dot's bike's basket.

'You probably terrified the farmer,' Max said. 'He must have thought he was being attacked by potato-stealing, foul-mouthed marauders.' He led them slowly along the wall and turned past a few leafless trees, coming to a field surrounded by a wooden fence. 'Here they are, some friends.'

At the opposite end of the field, Dot could make out the silhouettes of three horses. Max called out to them, shaking his paper bag of treats, and the horses ran towards them.

Dot quickly realised that the horses were much larger than most. They had long necks and sloping shoulders, and their legs were heavily feathered below the knee. They towered over Max and Dot.

'Shire horses, beautiful,' Dot said, taking a carrot from the bag and holding it to one of the horse's flapping lips.

The horse bit the carrot in half. Dot stroked the side of its head, and it rubbed against her, demanding the rest of the carrot.

'How's your knee now?'

'*Stable.*' Dot smirked, pleased with her quick quip. 'It just dislocated for a second, but it's back in place now. All the troops are back in their barracks.'

'Does that happen a lot?'

'More than I'd like. But I'm a tough nut.' She took another carrot from the bag and held it out to the third horse, who sniffed it several times before taking a small bite, as if testing drugs for purity. 'I'm at that age now where I get letters about which coffin I'd prefer, or offers for a free clock when I alter my last will and testament.'

'Sounds thrilling.'

'Exactly. I'm on the old fogies mailing list. They think I'm a hazard to myself.'

'You seem fine to me.' Max placed sugar cubes into his palm and allowed a horse to trade them for a handful of saliva. 'Except maybe for your random dislocating knee. And I could help if you need it – I don't live far away.'

'That's sweet . . .' Dot felt like the day was growing heavy. Her previous exuberance and lightness had mostly evaporated, though she enjoyed the company of a good horse. 'But you've plenty to get on with. And I don't want to feel like you're my carer. We're friends, right?'

'Yeah, we're friends. But friends help friends, too.'

'That's true.' She looked to the hills in the distance. 'But I'm not over the hill yet. I want to keep adding to my bucket list, and there's plenty more to do while we still can.'

Max held his fist out and Dot bumped her fist against it, as she'd seen a few kids in the area do.

She tipped the paper bag upside down, and a few granules of sugar fell out.

'That's your fill for today, kiddos,' Dot said to the horses. 'Life's not always carrots and sugar cubes.'

*

'And why do you want this job?' Dot asked, adopting a very serious and gruff voice, imagining herself as a hard-headed business leader in an expensive suit, interviewing a potential apprentice with more ego than talent.

'Really?' Max asked.

'Really.'

'Money.' Max smiled but, on seeing Dot's expertly practiced sneer, straightened his imaginary tie. 'I mean, I think I have a lot to offer. I've wanted to work in data management for a while now. I'm hard-working, a quick learner and willing to put in the hours to climb the ladder.'

Dot tapped her fingernails menacingly on the table. 'Good. I like your hustle.' She examined her notepad. 'Now I see you've been out of work for some time. Why is that?'

'Well . . .' Max sighed. 'Should I tell them the truth, or not, Dot?'

'Who're you talking to, young man? You are confusing me, the uber wealthy and powerful Lord Saccharine.'

'Dot, I'm serious!' Max looked suddenly deflated. 'Should

I tell them I've been doing community service, or pretend I've been on a gap year, like all the rich kids they normally interview?'

'It's up to you,' Dot said. 'Maybe they'll appreciate the honesty.'

'They don't, usually. When they realise I've no past experience, they put two and two together and get seventeen. I think I should lie. I'll say I was in hospital.'

'Or you could say you were doing some volunteer work, helping in your community. That's pretty much true, isn't it? It's just a white lie. Tell you what, just put me as your reference – I'll convince them to give you a shot.'

Max cracked his knuckles. 'I hate this. I don't even want a stupid job in data management. I don't even know what data management is!'

'I don't think any normal person really knows what it is. We should probably find that out before the interview, otherwise they're sure to notice.'

Max groaned and rubbed his forehead. 'I think I'll cancel. This is crazy. I'm forced to apply for jobs I don't want or I'm accused of being a *drain on society*. Why can't I just get a break in a job I'd actually enjoy?' He took a deep breath and leaned back. 'Sorry. Thanks for your help. But I've done this a hundred times and I never get a chance. I'm just so tired of it.'

'I understand, Max. But don't give up. You'll get there eventually. You've so many skills to offer. If you can get to the interview, I'm sure your personality will help get you through sooner or later.'

'Was it this hard when you were applying for jobs?' Max asked, eyeing the kettle. 'How about a cuppa? Hot and sweet, right?'

'All right,' Dot conceded. Max knew tea was her Achilles

heel and had learned to use her weakness against her. 'Maybe we need a break. We've been at this for a while now.'

They walked to Dot's kitchen and Max filled the kettle.

'You'd make a good nurse, actually,' Dot said. 'You're caring and patient. Mostly.'

'Nah, that's not for me,' Max said. 'I can't look at vomit. It makes me want to hurl. And I'd look no good in the white skirt.'

'Fair enough. It's not for everyone. And to answer your question: it was easy to get into, even easier to get out of. But people had different expectations back then. They expected me to train, pop out a few kids and then retire by the time I was about twenty-six, or sooner.'

'So, it's better now?'

'Not really. Just different. Some things are better, some are worse, by the sounds of it.'

'Well, sitting at a computer screen must be easier than wiping arses,' Max said, grimacing.

'Not for me. It was a tough job at times, but it wasn't all bad. I had some good colleagues. One in particular, who was a good friend and helped me to get through the worst times.'

Max tossed teabags into mugs and retrieved milk from the fridge.

'Oh, who?' he asked.

'Grace. We trained together – we were a bit like sisters.'

'What happened, then?' He gulped awkwardly, as if realising he might have made a misstep. 'Sorry, is she dead?'

'No! At least, I don't think so. I hope not. She moved to Texas with her wife.'

'She sounds cool.'

Dot couldn't stop herself from smiling, briefly remembering how close she'd been with Grace, how they'd looked out for each other all those years. Grace had been there for Dot when her mum died and when Charles was sick, and countless other times when they needed each other.

'She was cool, really cool,' Dot said. 'All the girls secretly wanted to be like Grace, I think. She was stunning, and very loyal. She didn't take any nonsense from anyone, either.'

'So, why are you talking about her like she's dead? What happened?'

The kettle hissed and its insides bubbled, ready to erupt.

'We fell out. It was my fault, really.'

'That's a shame. Seems like you were close, and . . . well, I've learned lately that good friends can be hard to come by. But they're worth hanging onto once you've found them, you know?'

The kettle clicked. Max poured the hot water into the cups and waited for the tea to brew.

'You're a very smart guy, you know that?' Dot asked.

Max added sugar and milk to their tea, then passed her a cuppa and smiled. 'Thanks.'

'And you're right.' She raised her cup in the air. 'Here's to friendship.'

'To friendship!' they said in unison, chinking their cups together before returning to work.

30

Back from the Dead

New email received!

From: Grace Young
To: You
Date sent: 10 Dec — 4:37 a.m.

My Dear Dotty!
SO GREAT to hear from you. It's been WAY too long & I'm sorry too — can we forget all about how we left things & just pretend it never happened? I think that's best. As Mark Twain said, 'Forgiveness is the fragrance that the violet sheds on the heel that has crushed it.' I love that quote, let's live by it.

Texas has been good to me (the BBQs have been TOO good, I'm as big as a house now) & I love the heat & people here. There's no BS, you know? I wish you could see it all, I just know you'd love it here too. So many cowboys! Remember the time Charles dressed as a cowboy because he thought we were going to a fancy dress party, but it was a party with formal dress? That was HILARIOUS. He was a good man, and I think about you both a lot. I think he would have gotten on with my better half — she's a dope too!

I hope things are great for you. Maybe not my place to ask, but did you ever meet anyone else? Did you move, or are you still in the same house? I remember your moving-in party — I drank so much I fell asleep in your garden & you didn't find me until the next morning. We were wild back then, weren't we? Love it.

Anyway I really do hope you're well & happy. If I'm ever back then we HAVE to meet up. I've got a new hip & I set off the metal detectors at the airport. It's a HOOT.

Much love,

Gracey

XxXxX

PS: Did you hear Matron died last year? I don't like to speak ill of the dead, but I hope the worms are hungry.

In response, Dot typed reams, as though her fingers were possessed. She was so excited to finally be in touch with Grace again, and so happy that any grudges were forgiven, that she let the words flow like wine and clicked *Send* without a second thought. She felt like she'd reclaimed a lost treasure, like she'd won the lottery all over again.

The local paper landed on Dot's doormat, its front page promoting *FREE Eggnog Cinnamon-Spiced Babyccinos For EVERY Reader.* There were also stories on council debates over potholes and the homelessness crisis sweeping the city, and there was a feature on . . . Dot blinked, then blinked again at the paper's feature on the mysterious Christmas tree that had brought a community together — her Christmas tree!

She read the article and it held about as much journalistic integrity or interest as a damp sock, but she enjoyed the fact that readers would find out about her tree — and perhaps be encouraged to do something cheerful themselves. The article was full of bizarre errors and purposeful misinformation, claiming that the tree appeared overnight as if from nowhere. It quoted locals saying that the tree had made them feel great, and the article suggested that the tree must, therefore, have a magical happiness-evoking aura about it.

Well, they could dream. There was no harm in that.

Another feature, although with fewer colour photos accompanying it, told of a movie scene being filmed in the nearby soon-to-be-refurbished shopping centre. The movie, *Spree*, was a horror based on a group of shopaholic mums who were trapped inside stores with flesh-eating zombies. The filming was taking place that week, and the movie producers were looking for members of the public who might be willing to take on the roles of the undead creatures.

It was perfect! Dot's bucket list still had a few items remaining, and she was yet to fulfil the *Movie marathon* item that she'd included for Max's sake. She picked up the phone and called the number that was printed.

'There will be some make-up applied,' the producer said. 'It might take an hour or so, but the scene is a short one. And there will be some fake gore. Is that okay?'

'Sounds lovely,' Dot replied. 'Tip top.'

'And do you have any acting experience?' he asked.

She didn't want to lose this chance. 'Oh, plenty. We've both walked the boards and appeared in the background of all sorts of things.' It was more a misdirection than an absolute lie. Dot hadn't appeared in any kind of performance before, and she was fairly sure that Max hadn't either, but they had both walked along her new laminate flooring, as well as appearing in the background of photos and memories.

The producer seemed pleased as punch spiked with Prozac. Dot noted down the details and sent a text to Max.

★

'You look absolutely horrifying,' Dot said to Max. 'When are they going to put on your make-up?'

'Ha ha ha,' Max said, his skin grey, with rotting sores on his cheeks and forehead. He slumped towards her with his arms stretched out, rotten teeth gnashing. 'Braaaaaains.' He tapped and inspected her head, then looked disappointed. 'Looks like Zombie Max is going to starve with these slim pickings.'

Dot couldn't stop staring at her reflection in the camera lenses and shop windows. Though the shopping centre had been closed years ago, the film's production team had made a good job of redressing some of the old shops to look like they were in business once again.

'Okay, zombies!' the director shouted. 'Walk slowly towards the camera on my mark.'

He turned to his main actresses, two beautiful women in tracksuits and with 1980s perms, each pushing an empty pram, and nodded.

Someone shouted a countdown, followed by: 'ACTION!'

Dot lumbered towards the camera, her dodgy knee having prepared her well to recreate the effects of her character's rotting muscle tissues. Several other zombies around her moved more quickly towards the cameras and actors.

'Cut!' the director called. 'Zombies, some of you are moving too fast. Back to our starting spots, please.'

Dot leaned on Max's shoulder and whispered: 'Amateurs.'

'I think they're trying to get their faces seen on camera,' Max whispered back. 'But my character is more hesitant. Zombie Max is contemplating everything he's lost: his wife and children, his country, his ability to walk without his guts falling out.'

'Zombie Dot is contemplating the moral complexity of eating human flesh,' Dot said, repositioning a stick-on bloody mound above her lip. 'What does it mean if we must become monsters to survive?'

The director piped up: 'Zombies at the back, stop talking. Ready?'

Dot and Max gave the thumbs-up, then slouched their shoulders to adopt their most convincing undead poses.

'ACTION!'

Dot hobbled towards the camera while Max turned away, as if distracted by something off camera. It was excellent acting, Dot thought, and she wondered whether she'd missed her calling as a Hollywood starlet or a key feature in a Broadway show like *Zombie Hamlet*, *Zombie Cats*, or *Zombie on a Hot Tin Roof*.

I've got the guts to die. What I want to know is, have you got the guts to live? Dot thought, trying not to laugh out loud. She'd have to share that one with Max when the next cut was called.

She didn't have to wait long before the director called for a halt.

'Zombies at the front, move to the back. The two zombies at the back, come here,' the director instructed.

'Uh oh,' Max said as he and Dot walked towards the director. 'Did we mess up?'

'I'm not sure, let's pick his brains.' Dot chuckled.

'Good job, you two,' the director said. 'Keep doing what you're doing. I want you two up-front for the next scene. Just follow Jane and Colette.' He nodded to the two main actors and they smiled at Dot and Max. 'Don't rush at them, just walk as you were, okay? We'll use this shot in the final cut, all going well, so you ought to be in the film.'

'Awesome!' Max said, his prosthetic loosened jaw seeming almost to fall off as he smiled at the thought of the promotion.

The director gave them further details on where to stand and where to look, and they took their positions. Dot could hear the other zombies moaning in the background, but they were moaning about their distance from the cameras rather than their uncontrollable impulse to consume flesh.

Cameras rolling, Dot and Max slowly pursued the main actors as they ran and tripped and screamed for help. Dot could already tell that the movie wasn't exactly *Schindler's List*, but it was a blast, nevertheless.

★

'I miss my eroding jaw,' Max said glumly as he slotted coins into the photo booth.

Outside the booth, the chatter and footfall of supermarket shoppers muted the beeping of the checkout tills. Having finished with filming, Max and Dot were keen to memorialise their first screen appearance with a photo, and the nearby supermarket (not currently zombie infested, but operating as normal) had a photo booth.

'I asked if I could keep my bloody mound,' Dot said, checking herself in the booth's screen. She looked deeply unwell, but not quite as dead as she had before the make-up artists had removed the more expensive zombie facial features after filming.

'What did they say?'

'Sorry but they needed them for other actors in other scenes. It's a shame, I was expecting them to give us both full-time jobs!'

'I know!' Max pushed buttons on the booth's display screen. 'I genuinely think they were impressed with us. I looked at you and I didn't see Dot, I saw Elderly Female Zombie 2. You were completely convincing.'

'Maybe I should change my name to Elderly Female Zombie 2,' Dot said, grimacing for the camera.

The booth showed their snap and asked if they'd like to try again. Max selected *Yes*.

'I want to look sadder,' Max said. 'After everything Zombie Male 4 has gone through, I think he deserves to have his inner turmoil captured properly, you know?'

'Absolutely.' Dot pulled a pained expression and the booth flashed, immortalising their mortified image.

'Perfect,' Max said, pushing a button to print the photos.

They waited outside the booth and glared at children as they passed, laughing and waving at any who looked alarmed.

'This was one of the best days yet,' Max said.

Dot leaned against the exterior of the booth. 'It's not exactly the movie marathon I had in mind when I added it to my list, but I can't wait to see us on the big screen.'

'My mum's going to freak out when she sees it. I'm not going to tell her; I'm going to wait until the movie's out, buy it and then show it to her. She loves zombie movies.'

'You make a good brainless man-eater,' Dot said. 'I'm sure you'll make her proud.'

The photo booth beeped and Max took their snapshots from a tray filled with warm air. The photos were ludicrous and Dot couldn't stop laughing. She laughed so hard that she thought she might, quite literally, crack a rib.

Max snipped the reel of four photos into two sets of two, passing a set to Dot.

'I'm keeping this,' Max said, placing the photos carefully into his phone case. 'It's one of the best things I've ever done. Cheers for finding it and inviting me.'

'My pleasure. I'm glad I could pay you back a little for all the things you've planned. There's not a lot left on my bucket list now – we've done well.'

Max frowned and opened his mouth to speak, but his phone rang. He held up a still-bloody finger and answered his phone.

'Hello? . . . Yeah . . . Mm-hmm . . . Yeah . . . What, really? . . . Definitely!' He grinned like an undead capuchin. 'Yes! Thank you!' His eyes were so wide that Dot suspected his eyeballs might pop from their sockets. 'I won't let you down. Thank you! Bye!'

He hung up.

'What is it?' Dot asked, his obvious excitement infecting her.

'It was my probation officer, the guy from the park. He said he spoke to the board and because of my good behaviour, they've reduced my community service. I'll be finished in a week!'

Dot raised her hand to receive a high five, and Max didn't disappoint.

'Fantastic. Well done you!' Dot said, truly happy for him. 'You deserve it.'

'Thanks. And they asked if I wanted to transfer for the last bit, because the park's pretty much finished now.'

'Transfer to where?' Dot asked.

'My first choice, which was to work with the kids' groups.' He hugged Dot, squeezing her so tightly that all the air left her lungs. He released her. 'It's perfect. I can put it on my CV, and maybe they'll recommend me for some work with kids afterwards.'

'You'd like that?' Dot asked.

'Yeah, they're fun. I used to go to those groups when I was little, when my dad was locked up and my mum was struggling, so I know what they do to help them. They're great.'

'Good for you, Max,' Dot said. 'I knew you could do it.'

31

Rhythm & Blues, Coladas & Shrooms

Dot opened her important drawer and checked the bucket list:

> *The Bucket List*
> 1 *Build a snowman = DONE*
> 2 *Afternoon tea = DONE*
> 3 *Go dancing*
> 4 *Day at the fair = DONE*
> 5 *Movie marathon = DONE*
> 6 *Ride a horse = DONE*
> 7 *Fire a gun = HUH?!*

Dancing — it was the perfect activity to celebrate Max's happy news, except for the fact that he claimed to hate it, of course.

But Dot was sure she could convince him otherwise. She texted him to ask if that was okay, and he said he knew it was coming sooner or later, and he had a few ideas. He asked for a few days to arrange things, and did she have any new items to add to the list?

That relieved her. With Max's new opportunities, he might

be offered work and find new friends, and Dot had been concerned that he might forget all about her. But asking about new items to add to the bucket list meant that he didn't intend to stop, even when presented with the glitz and glamour of a normal life.

Dot took the time to recuperate and recharge. She'd felt like an excitable Labrador lately, rushing from one bucket list event to the next, without much time to just sit. She ate buttered crumpets and drank tea, listened to the radio, wrapped a few gifts to leave under the community tree for the local kids, and exchanged emails with Grace. It felt almost as if they'd never fallen out, never been apart, except for the fact that that there was so much to catch up on. Grace had done so many things with her life that Dot's years seemed empty by comparison — other than her winning the lottery and spending her recent days with a young man with a criminal past, of course.

Have you seen Harold and Maude? Grace asked in one of her emails. *You saucy old goat!*

Dot hadn't seen the movie despite Max having mentioned it before, so she rented it online.

Oh, God no! Dot replied to Grace. *It's nothing like that. Nothing at all. We're friends!*

Grace had found Dot's recent antics hilarious, and said she was jealous. She told Dot all about her wife and the ranch, the big barbecues they had, their horses and road trips. They shared more memories from their ward, their nights out, their trips to obscure museums and galleries, but Grace also bore bad news among the good.

I've not been too well, Grace wrote. *Chemo. It helped to keep me alive but it kept me sick, too. And it's damn expensive here, you wouldn't believe it. But I got great news last week, the Big-C has gone into remission. For now, at least.*

Dot didn't hesitate to offer to help pay the medical bills, but Grace explained that – thankfully – they had good medical insurance and were coping with their payments. And there was no way that her wife would take charity – no way, José. But she appreciated the offer.

In between her email correspondence with Grace, Dot's twinkly-eyed, Paddington Bear-coated neighbour, Jacob, dropped by for a cuppa and a chat.

Jacob sipped his tea and leaned back on Dot's extra comfy sofa. 'What you did with the snowmen and the Christmas tree really cheered people up. It cheered me up, too, and got me chatting to a few other folk on the estate, people I'd never spoken to before. We've been setting up a special group.'

Jacob explained that they'd called themselves the Clean-Up Crew. It consisted of Jacob, the couple with the noisy baby, the two kids from the local primary school (who'd taken and redistributed Dot's plants around the estate) and their dad. They were seeking more members to help with small local projects, to bring a little more community spirit and pride to the area.

'Are you in?' Jacob asked. 'You started all of this, after all. You can't bow out now, you know.'

How could she refuse his offer?

So, the rest of Dot's week filled itself with Clean-Up Crew activities. They walked the streets together, delivering food parcels to people who were struggling, cleaning up litter and writing to the council in the hope that they'd invest some time and money into supporting the group's efforts.

'I doubt the council will show any interest,' Jacob said. 'In all these years, they've left this area to rot. There are more potholes than there is road.'

But, to their great collective surprise, when Dot called their local councillor and asked for an appointment, they agreed to hold a hearing with the entire Clean-Up Crew in the new year.

With several bags of rubbish collected and a council appointment on the horizon, Dot's street already felt much friendlier and cleaner than it had in years. She'd almost forgotten about her impending dancing session with Max, until a golden envelope fell through her door:

> *Put on your dancing shoes!*
> *Meet outside The Jazz Bar, Friday, 9 p.m.*
> *– Bucket Master*

★

Max stood outside The Jazz Bar's red door, dressed in a tuxedo. A busy stream of people leaned against the infamous Edinburgh winds as they weaved in and out of the surrounding shops and cafés.

'Nice monkey suit,' Dot said to Max as she approached. He looked taller, stronger, but more gentile in his black suit and crisp white shirt. 'You scrub up well for an orangutan.'

'You too, for an old bird. Nice dress, though I hope the sequins don't attract magpies.'

Dot curtsied. She looked and felt great, despite how busy she'd been lately. The chilling cold on her bare legs reminded her of her late nights out on the town with Grace and Charles, under-dressed and overexcited in anticipation of drinking and dancing.

'Thank you,' she said. 'Should we head inside? I fancy a strawberry daiquiri.'

Max shook his head. He took his phone from his pocket and swiped the screen. 'Not just yet.'

'It's freezing out here, and it's my round.'

'Hold your horses, just wait a couple of minutes. I'm expecting someone.'

'Who? A Sinatra impersonator? He's my favourite.'

Max glared at her. 'You're worse than my two-year-old niece. Be patient!'

Dot walked on the spot to keep warm, watching Max as he surveyed the surrounding area.

A metallic beat sounded. Dot turned to see a man tapping a steel drum with a wooden stick. He hit it again, picking up his rhythm.

'Is this who you're waiting for?' Dot asked, her feet tapping to the jaunty rhythm of the drum.

'Partially.' Max smiled, nodding his head to the drum beat as it quickened.

A woman in a scarf and wool hat stepped out from the passing crowds, shaking a maraca. She stomped her leg and a tambourine strapped to her thigh let out a bright metallic rattle. The woman hummed a deep note.

Passers-by stopped, looking up from their phones and gathering around as the percussion grew louder. Another woman in an ugly sweater emerged from the crowd, playing an acoustic guitar, followed by a trilby-headed man with dreadlocks who tooted chaotically on a trumpet.

More people stepped out from the crowd, stamping and humming, walking closer as they grew louder. They danced, waving their arms and whooping, and, as their voices merged with the notes of the musical instruments, Dot recognised their tune: Louis Armstrong's 'Winter Wonderland', but with a jazzy twist.

Onlookers tapped their hands and feet as the music and dances continued. The performers grasped hands with some of the members of the thickening crowd and danced with them.

A tall, handsome young man approached Dot and held his hand out to her.

Dot looked at Max, who was busy filming it all on his phone.

'What is this?' Dot asked.

'Dance! It's a flash mob!' Max said, waving her away with his free hand as he continued to record.

Dot took the handsome young man's hand, and he pulled her into the dancing area, gently turning her with the music, moving her hands in his. She felt the rhythm pulse through her as she danced, her blood pumping through her body in time with the beat of the drums.

'Winter Wonderland' bled into 'I saw Mommy Kissing Santa Claus' and that moved jauntily into 'It's Beginning to Look a Lot Like Christmas' – all songs that Dot had enjoyed when growing up and that she'd almost forgotten about.

The handsome young man returned to the crowd and picked up a flute, playing it and leaving Dot to the music.

Dot panted for breath but didn't want to stop.

She held her hand out to Max.

'I don't dance,' Max said, lowering his camera phone.

'Oh, come on, you grinch!' She grabbed his hand and pulled him away from the door of The Jazz Bar, moving his hands with hers. He resisted dancing, looking around nervously. 'Come on, Max, show me how it's done!'

Dot twirled him around, passing under his raised arm as the music quickened into 'Jingle Bell Rock'.

'I like this one,' Max said, finally moving with a hint of enthusiasm.

More of the onlookers joined the dancing mass, until it was so busy that Dot could barely move for happy faces. She accompanied another older woman who had joined the group on her own. Dot looked back at Max as he danced with a beautiful young red-headed woman, laughing and smiling as the music eventually ended and the musicians disappeared into the crowds as if they'd never been there.

Dot said a quick farewell to the people she'd danced with. She found Max leaning against the wall of The Jazz Bar, his face red and sweaty.

'And you said you didn't dance!' Dot said. 'Except maybe when there's a pretty girl involved?'

'Maybe,' Max said coolly, unable to hold back a cheeky grin.

'I don't blame you, she was a stunner. Did you get her number?'

His grin widened but didn't say anything, which to Dot clearly meant *Yes*.

'Let's go inside,' Dot said, pushing the door to The Jazz Bar. 'Dancing's thirsty work.'

*

Earthy cello music washed over Dot and Max as they descended the steps into the basement bar. Dim lights hung from the ceiling on long wires over small round wooden tables. The bar was almost empty – except for a waistcoated barman, the cellist and two women who whispered to one another beside black and white jazz posters – but it felt like the kind of place that might be filled with ghosts playing ethereal trombones.

'Sit, I'll get the drinks,' Dot said, eager to check out the bar's cocktail menu. 'Any preferences?'

'Lager. Pint of,' Max said.

'Dull. I'll Schwarzenegger it.'

'Okay, I'll give you a hand when the drinks are ready.' Max walked towards a corner table, which held a single unlit white tea candle and was surrounded by old sofas.

Dot turned sharply and adopted a bad Schwarzenegger accent. 'I'll be back.'

Dot inspected the drinks menu: espresso martinis, Long Island iced teas, fresh mint and lemon mojitos, Singapore slings, rose gin and tonic, an expensive list of wines – everything sounded wonderful, but she wasn't the drinker she once was, and she'd be drunk as a teetotal skunk if she didn't pace herself.

But she knew where to begin.

'Two piña coladas, please,' she said to the barman. 'And don't forget the umbrellas.'

She sat on a bar stool and soaked in the atmosphere while the barman got to work mixing coconut rum with pineapple juice, shaking it with coconut cream and ice, and topping it with toasted coconut shavings.

By the time her drinks were made, Dot's dance-thumping heart had finally slowed to its usual pace.

The barman placed her two milky-yellow drinks on the bar. 'Sorry, we're all out of umbrellas.'

Dot pouted.

The barman held up a *wait a moment* finger. He searched beneath the bar and found two sparklers. He placed one into each of the drinks and lit them, sending shards of white light bursting out.

'Better?' the barman asked.

'Much better,' Dot said, paying and thanking him.

Max appeared beside Dot and snickered at her drink choice, the sparkles reflecting in his eyes.

'They're a little flamboyant,' Max said.

'Have you tried one before?' Dot asked as she and Max walked to their corner table, placed their drinks down and sat.

'No, it's very retro,' Max said. 'Reminds me of some old comedy I saw about a market trader who used to put whole bananas in his drinks. We used to watch it at Christmas.' He removed his sparkler and held it at a safe distance, then took a sip of his drink. 'Actually, it's delicious. I take back any criticism.'

'Coconut and pineapple, two of our five a day!' Dot removed her sparkler and painted her name in the air before its glittery burn faded.

Dot leaned into the soft, worn leather of the sofa. Max sipped his drink, eyeing the two women near the jazz posters as they tried to pretend that they weren't looking over at him.

'Do you reckon people think we're weird?' Max asked.

'Who'd want to be normal?' Dot said, sensing something uneasy was about to leak out from his lips, and it wasn't the piña colada.

'Me, sometimes. But, I mean, do people think we're strange for hanging out together?'

Of course she knew it was strange, and it hurt a little that Max might feel embarrassed by her company.

'They probably think we're related,' Dot said. 'Do you care?'

'Not really.' He clinked his glass against hers, took a sip and stared into his drink. 'I worry I'm not *normal*. Like, I don't get on with anyone my age. People expect me to be working and hooking up with girls, partying.'

'Do you want to do any of that?'

His voice dropped. 'Not really.'

'Okay, I'm putting on my old-woman hat now. So listen up, because I hate wearing it.'

Max stared up at her expectantly. 'Shoot.'

'Max, the only thing that really matters is that you're happy and you try not to hurt other people along the way. It's the only thing in life you can really control, because other people can't do that for you. Forget about what people expect you to do, because if you try to reach everyone else's expectations then you'll always lose. The only way to win is to make sure you're doing what you want to do. Even if everyone else says it's stupid, if it makes you feel happy . . . if it makes you feel like *you*, then it's probably the right thing to do.'

'Is that what you've done?' Max asked, straightening.

'No. Not really. I used to, but things changed – they fell apart and I didn't know what I wanted or who I was anymore. But I'm trying to change that; I'm trying to be Dot 2.0. Anyway, do what I say and not what I do. I'm better at giving advice than I am at taking it.'

'Thanks, I'll try it.' Max placed his cocktail down on the table. 'And I'm starting now . . . I'm getting myself a beer. You want one?'

Dot nodded. She liked that he was being more forthright with her, that he felt comfortable enough to speak his mind and do as he preferred.

Max walked to the bar and ordered drinks. One of the two women who'd been sitting near the music posters joined Max at the bar and spoke to him. He returned with two pints of lager and passed one to Dot.

'You're Mr Popular today, aren't you?' Dot said, *cheers*ing with Max.

'Not exactly. She wanted to know if I had any coke.' He gulped half his beer down in one. 'I hate that. Happens quite a lot: people see me and assume I'm a dealer.'

'Are you?'

Max's nose wrinkled. 'No! Never touched any of it, other than a bit of weed. Have you?'

'Not a drop. I could have lost my job if anyone found out, and my husband was never into it. But . . .' A gleam appeared in Dot's eyes. Why the hell not? What did she have to lose now, except her last remnant of sanity? 'I'd be interested. Nothing heavy, maybe just something trippy.'

'Like mushrooms, or acid?'

Dot nodded. 'Oh, I *love* mushrooms!'

'I'm not sure people eat them for their earthy flavour. It's more for the effects.'

'The *magic*! Even Sherlock Holmes dabbled, to free his mind. If it's good enough for Holmes, it's good enough for me.'

Max sighed. 'You're a liability, you know that? I don't want to. I've enough going on without hallucinating pink elephants or something.' He leaned in and lowered his voice. 'But, if you really want to try it, I know some people who can make a home delivery.'

'Well, I was looking for something new to add to the bucket list.' Dot took a long drink and picked up her purse, ready to roll. 'It's something completely different, it's *so* Dot 2.0. Make the call.'

32

A Mug

Max's call had been quick. It seemed as easy as ordering pizza; the delivery would be made within the hour. Drug dealers really did provide a quality and timely service – hopefully without pineapple – and Dot was impressed.

But she was also a cocktail of excitement and nerves in the taxi back to her house.

As a nurse she had seen the damage that some drugs could do to her patients, but she'd also seen their healing effects. And, if the rumours were to be believed, drugs were responsible for some of Dot's favourite music. She'd never heard of anyone coming into the hospital with a mushroom-related problem, which reassured her, and surely magic mushrooms (being natural and barely illegal anymore, as far as she was aware) would be unlikely to cause any seriously negative side effects.

Home, Dot put some gentle music on the record player to settle any remaining nerves. She filled the kettle and waited for it to boil. This felt right – more like an experiment or an unknown voyage than a risk. Where would the little fungi take her? What might she see? She'd spent more than seven decades on Earth, and she was growing increasingly excited to explore another plane.

'The internet says you might feel a bit sick, giddy or confused,' Max explained, scrolling on his phone.

'Nothing new,' Dot said, bolstering herself and not wanting to worry him.

'Well, I'll stick around for a bit, just to make sure you're not making any calls on the giant porcelain telephone, or freaking out over the size of your hands.'

'I have perfectly well-proportioned hands, thank you!'

'You might get giggly, too. Are you sure about this?'

The kettle whistled and Dot poured two mugs of tea. Max seemed much more anxious than Dot felt, but the more he read online the more he seemed to relax.

'I'll just take a little bit,' she said to reassure him further. 'A smidgen. You'll barely even notice that I'm' – she tried to recall some drugs lingo from the shows and movies she'd seen – 'tripping my balls off.'

'Your balls? Have you already taken something?'

'Relax. I'm a big girl, I can take care of myself. You don't need to stay if you don't want to.'

'I'm staying,' Max said sternly. 'Just to make sure you're all right. Maybe if you enjoy it, I'll have a go, too.'

'So, you're using me as a guinea pig? Charming!'

He nodded. 'Squeak squeak, Dot. Squeak squeak.'

They waited, listening quietly to the chill-out music until a knock sounded at the front door.

'That's them!' Dot said, her heart revving up to fourth gear. 'You get it, you know them.'

Max placed his tea on the coffee table and walked to the door while Dot lurked in the living room. She didn't want drug dealers knowing her face, in case they saw her in public and asked her if she'd like another . . . she searched her movie memories for more drugs lingo . . . hit.

Dot held her breath and listened, like a kid trying to overhear her parents after bedtime.

'Hey, Maxipad, here's your stuff. You coming out?' a man's gruff voice said from the hallway. 'We've not seen you around in a while.'

'Nah, just staying here,' Max replied, and Dot could hear the gentle rustle of money exchanging hands. 'Thanks, guys. Appreciate it.'

'You sure you don't want something stronger?' another man's voice sounded. There was something familiar about it, something that sent a wave of panic through Dot.

'No, this is all. Cheers,' Max said.

'When you coming back?' the other voice said, and Dot was sure she knew its timbre. It wasn't friendly.

'I'm trying to stay low, keep out of trouble.'

'Man, this is your place? You've got some decent stuff. You sure you're out?'

Dot's head throbbed. She knew the voices; her body knew them.

'Yeah, I've got something else on, right now,' Max said.

Something else on? Did he mean *her*?

'Fair play,' the man said. 'You've got my number if you want some work again.'

Dot peered around to see their faces, to confirm her worst fears. Stood at her front door, smiling at Max with dead eyes, were the men who'd mugged her.

She ran into the kitchen and shut the door.

'I'm calling the police!' Dot shouted. She searched the drawer for her rolling pin but remembered it was upstairs, so she drew a bread knife from the knife rack. 'Get out of here!'

'Who's that? What the fuck you up to?' one of the muggers growled.

Were they coming for her? Were they already inside her

home? Would they find her, recognise her and finish the job they'd started in the cemetery?

Dot shoved the kettle aside and pushed the red security button.

An alarm blared.

'They're on their way!' Dot yelled. Her head was woozy and she felt breathless, like she'd been kicked to the floor again.

There was no lock on the wooden kitchen door, so she held the handle up to try to prevent anyone from opening it.

'Fuck this, we're out of here,' one of the muggers said. 'You coming, Max?'

Dot heard footsteps exit her home and the front door closing shut behind them.

A gentle knock sounded on the kitchen door, followed by Max's voice: 'Dot, what's wrong? What's going on?'

He knew them – they were his friends. Was he in league with them? Did they work together to batter and rob vulnerable people? Did they find out where their victims lived and burgle them? Had Max just been trying to get close to her so they could rob her again, or was he trying to stop her from talking to the police?

Her thoughts continually swarmed and stung; she couldn't swat them away.

'You go, too, Max,' Dot said. 'Get out, now! The police are coming.'

'Why? What's happened?'

'Just go!' Dot felt her knees buckle. She let go of the kitchen door handle and sat with her back against the door, her breath quick and shallow. 'Just go.'

Max tapped again but Dot couldn't make out his words through the pounding of blood in her ears.

Eventually he stopped trying and Dot sat alone for what

felt like for ever, cold and shaking in her sequin dress, until the house phone rang. She ignored it, but it rang again. She listened for Max's voice or footsteps but could hear no signs that he was in her home anymore.

Convinced that everybody had left her house, she got to her feet and answered the phone.

'Missus Hindley? This is John from Fort Knox Security. We received an alert. Are you okay?'

'I'm okay . . .' Dot steeled herself. She didn't want a bunch of men flooding her home. 'It was a false alarm.'

'Are you sure? We can send a team. Just say *Yes* if you need help.'

'No, really. It was an accident – the kettle hit the button.'

'Okay. Well, I'm glad I called. Good night.'

Dot hung up. She triple-locked the door and checked the windows were sealed before slumping into her chair, exhausted and confused.

All this time Max had been friends with the men who attacked her. He was one of them, a thief and a predator. He'd betrayed her and she couldn't trust him. She'd been so stupid – why would anyone like Max want to be near her, if not for her money?

As the clock ticked and the night deepened, Dot felt herself sinking into the darkness.

She was alone again.

*

The chain was on the door. The windows stayed locked and closed.

Dot watched the street through the slats in the window's security blinds. Cars rolled by slowly, and she wondered whether the muggers might have returned to scope out her home, now they knew where she lived.

She needed a bigger rolling pin.

Dot ignored yet another call from Max and deleted his texts without reading them. She'd been duped into believing their friendship was genuine. Now it made her feel sick just to see his name.

She tried not to obsess over his potential schemes, over the crimes he might have committed and the people he might have hurt. He hadn't seemed like those two brutes, but how well did she really know Max, anyway? She'd seen that he was unable to control his anger, that he was willing to hurt people for the wrong look or word.

He had mentioned selling his bike because he needed the money. He'd said he might not be able to continue with their bucket list because he was strapped for cash and time. Had he been trying to manipulate her? Was he only interested in getting her money from her?

Damn him! She'd trusted him. She'd been so naïve to let a stranger get so close to her.

She took slow breaths to steady her racing mind and heart. Deep down she knew she might be overreacting – she'd seen patients with trauma and knew that their fear or anger could take over in the wrong situations, but she couldn't deny her fear of Max, how betrayed she felt.

Dot's neighbours had tried to check in on her, ringing her doorbell and calling her, but she ignored them. She'd rather they thought she was on holiday than hiding away in fear. She didn't want to see anybody anymore. If she couldn't trust Max, then maybe she couldn't trust anyone.

'Dot, are you in there? We just want to make sure you're okay,' Jacob's voice sounded through her letterbox.

'I just want to be alone,' Dot eventually said, realising that her silence might only cause them to call for the police. It wasn't uncommon for people her age to be found injured or dead at home, after all. 'Please, leave me alone.'

Jacob and the others put up a little resistance but obeyed her wishes.

After that, life began to return to how it had been before she knew Max, and Dot felt comforted by her mundane past. It was almost surprising how easily she slipped back into her old habits and routines. Almost.

The mornings became colder and quieter. The lights came on at number seven later than usual. The young couple walked back and forth through their kitchen, rocking their noisy baby to settle its screams. Dot felt like screaming, too, and wished she had Charles to coddle her in a thick blanket and safe arms.

The old black cat ran along the garden fence outside number eleven and looked up at the Christmas tree in the common, stalking birds within its branches. Dot placed a bet with herself that the cat would be successful in its hunt, but it was useless and gave away its position well before it got close to landing a strike.

A gritter lorry trundled along the street, scattering its crystals. Snow was expected, then. Dot unwillingly thought of the time she and Max built a snowman in her front garden, how the street was lined with snowmen looking into one another's houses like stalkers or cat burglars. If more snow arrived and more snowmen appeared, she might sneak out in the dead of night with an extension cord and a hairdryer to melt their ever-watchful faces into puddles.

Even the community Christmas tree, which had made her so happy, now made her feel like an idiot. Each blink of its lights seemed to say: *You let him in, You let him in, You let him in.*

It was safe for Dot to say that she wasn't the happiest of bunnies.

To make matters worse, the sugar pot was empty and she had no butter left for her toast. She ate it dry, with savoury tea, staring into Christmas Town. She pushed various buttons to bring the town to life, watching its inhabitants skate and sing, its Ferris wheel turn, its colourful lights twinkle.

'Why are you all so cheery?' Dot asked the inhabitants.

She pushed her finger against one of the skaters to stop them from turning. Their painted cheer grated on her, like they had no consideration for how she was feeling, despite everything she'd done for them.

The skater clicked against her finger, trying to continue on its never-ending cycle. She gripped the skater between her thumb and finger and snapped it from its holding. It felt good to make a difference, to be able to change things, to have the power to stop or destroy them.

The town's big festive tree was next. Dot held it between both hands, bending it at a right angle until its lights stopped twinkling. Then she pulled the heads off the carol-singing snowmen and yanked the Ferris wheel from its holding, pulling off its carriages like grapes from a vine.

'You did this!' Dot uttered as she continued to smash and break Christmas Town, hurling its residents at the walls and windows, snapping the candy cane factory to smithereens, until the entire town was destroyed.

She sat on the floor, amongst the fragments, and cried. Charles's handsome wedding day picture smiled at her from the frame on the wall.

If only Charles was around, she'd have all the companionship she would need. They would be safe and happy together.

He would protect and reassure her, and none of this mess would have happened.

33

Somewhere, the Odds Are Different

Lottery number 50

(Dot is fifty-five years old)

Dot took the tiller of the boat, turning the small, rickety vessel away from the coast. She liked the isolation – just her and Charles *at sea* together. Bobbing on the water under the Tunisian sun, she could let herself believe they were the only people on Earth. When the shore was far enough away that she couldn't make out the shapes of civilisation, she shut down the engine.

Charles looked over the side of the boat, down into the clear water, his face thin and rugged with stubble. He looked the part of a salty sea dog, his grey-flecked hair swept back by the wind, the blue ocean reflecting in his eyes.

He smiled at Dot and opened his mouth wide. A maggot writhed on the cushion of his tongue. He plucked it out with his fingertips and skewered it on his fishing hook, decimating Dot's dreams of him as a rugged, sensual (maggot-free) seafarer.

'The heat makes them wriggle more,' Charles said.

'What girl doesn't dream of meeting a man with a maggot in his mouth?' Dot asked, taking a rod. She opened the bait box and picked up her own victim, piercing the maggot on her hook. 'However did you hook a catch like me?'

'I got lucky.' Charles cast his line. 'Let's make this interesting, shall we? Whoever catches fewer fish buys dinner?'

Dot opened the cooler and took out a beer, passing it to Charles.

'But you're the birthday boy,' Dot said. 'Birthday boys don't buy their own dinner. Even old birthday boys like you. And I'm definitely going to win because I can sing to the fish and draw them to me.'

He cracked open his beer and clinked the can against Dot's. They each took a long, cool drink.

'You're right, beer does taste better when we're abroad,' Charles said.

Dot settled her can on the seat of the boat and cast her line into the sea. She fixed her rod onto the boat's grip so that she didn't have to hold it until she caught a bite.

'I think it's the contrast,' Dot said. 'The cold can complements the warm air. If I drink a cold beer back home, I just get a mouth of river water followed by the shivers.'

Dot didn't want to upset Charles, especially not today, but his recent results had been the only thing she could think about. She'd hoped the trip away would somehow help her to forget, at least for a time, but it hadn't. She'd woken up every morning, drenched in sweat, and cried while making breakfast for when he woke. As if sensing her missing from his side, Charles had been getting up earlier than usual, but he'd been strong for her, chirpy even. She knew he was putting on a brave face to alleviate her worry.

Charles adjusted his line. 'You're right, you need the heat

and the cold to make it work.' He paused to sip his beer. 'Sometimes, we need the bad parts to help the good parts to feel special. Or am I just being a sap?'

'You are.' She kissed his head. 'But I like it.'

Dot wasn't entirely sure she bought into Charles's philosophy, but she wasn't about to argue with it. She'd been keeping her fear and anger balled up, praying that it wouldn't seep out. *Why him?* she asked herself each morning and night.

And, though she wasn't especially religious, she desperately wanted someone to reply; she needed an answer. If God was real, how could He let this happen? Where was the justice for a good man, when so many bad people lived easy, painless lives?

Death didn't discriminate, and she'd seen so many people come through her ward who deserved much better than they got, and others who deserved much worse. There was no logic to it, no way to solve the puzzle. It didn't hold water.

She only had his odds: fifty–fifty.

And since knowing the odds, she weighed everything against them: they were a hair better than in black jack (odds of winning were forty-nine per cent). Black or red on the roulette wheel were around forty-eight per cent. Giving birth to twins was just one in two hundred and fifty. Four-leaf clovers were one in ten thousand. The odds of being struck by lightning in your lifetime were one in around fifteen thousand.

Comparatively, Charles's odds were good. But it still felt like their whole life, her universe, hinged on a coin toss.

'It's nice out here, isn't it?' Charles said, watching his line. 'There's nothing else to think about, just this water, this rod and us.'

'I wish it could last for ever,' Dot said.

'It'll be okay, you know.' Charles turned to face her, his eyes determined. 'I'm going to fight this. We'll fight it together, like we always have.'

'But what if we lose?' Dot felt sick as the words left her mouth.

Saying it out loud felt like admitting defeat somehow, or at least that defeat was a real possibility. It didn't feel like a fair fight – it was like putting Charles in the ring against a fighter with a horseshoe in their glove. How could they fight this? It wasn't something they could control – Charles would either survive, or he wouldn't. His fate wouldn't be decided through a lack of trying.

'You'll be all right.' Charles slotted his rod into the boat's grip and placed his hand on hers. 'You're strong. It's one reason why I love you. You've never let anyone tell you who to be, or what you can't do. Even without me—'

'Please don't say that.'

Charles sighed, holding her hands tighter in his. 'Even without me, you'll be okay. And I don't intend to go anywhere anytime soon. Fifty–fifty, the doc said. And I read that reducing stress might help. And that's what we're doing, right? We're enjoying ourselves out here, relaxing, improving the odds.'

Dot smiled weakly, feeling her façade break. She took a deep breath and fixed her gaze on his.

'Yes,' Dot said stoically, like she'd learned in the hospital. She couldn't let her patients see her upset, and the practice had paid off. She took another long drink of beer but it didn't taste quite as refreshing as it had before, the can having warmed a little. A distant raincloud had passed over the sun, chilling the air.

Their silence was interrupted by a gentle *whirrrr*.

'I've got a bite!' Charles yelped, lunging to his rod. He held its butt to his waist and the tip of the rod curved towards the water as its line tightened. 'It's a big one!'

Charles's face reddened as he reeled his catch in, widening his legs to distribute his weight and anchor himself. He grunted as he pulled the fish towards the boat, taking quick breaths when the fish fought to escape.

'Do you need help?' Dot asked, reaching for his rod.

He turned the rod handle away. 'No chance! I know your game – you'll claim it's your catch. Sneaky little Dot!'

'I would not!' Dot protested, laughing.

A separate *whirrrr* sounded from Dot's line. She grasped her rod and began reeling her catch in, but she could already tell that the fish was a weakling and she'd have no trouble landing it. Still, as she liked to joke with Charles, size wasn't important. It was the number of fish she caught, and not their weight, which would settle their bet.

'I'll race you!' Charles said. 'Whoever reels in last, buys the drinks.'

'No fair, you got a head start,' Dot said, knowing that she was seconds away from victory. 'But fine. Cocktails, all right?'

'Done.' Charles panted as he reeled faster.

But Charles's efforts were useless, and Dot reeled her tiny fish in effortlessly.

'It's just a tiddler!' Charles laughed, watching the tiny fish flounder as Dot brought it aboard.

'A bet's a bet! Piña colada, please.' She removed the fish from the hook and held it for Charles to see. 'He's called Moby.' She tossed the fish back into the sea and yelled: 'Watch out for Captain Ahab, little one!'

'Mine's coming, fetch the net,' Charles grunted. 'Ah crap, no!'

His snapped line flailed in the gentle wind that blew over the boat. He stood stormy-faced and fishless.

'One—nil,' Charles said. 'And it was a big one – a shark, probably.'

'Well, it doesn't look like we'll be having fish and chips and sauce tonight,' Dot said, putting an arm over his shoulders and kissing his cheek.

Charles leaned into her. 'Like our wedding day, remember that? Your mum was furious that we'd disappeared.'

'That was a good day.' Dot drifted back, remembering herself in her white dress and clutching flowers, walking into the church on her uncle's arm to see Charles, ever so handsome, waiting for her with a massive, nervous grin on his face. 'Do you want to do it again?'

'What?' Charles asked, staring out to sea as the clouds moved and the sun lit his face.

'Get married again.' She held his hand and twisted the ring on his finger. 'I wanted to ask the first time around, but you beat me to it. So, now it's my turn, all right?'

He nodded and chuckled. 'All right.'

Dot slid the wedding ring from his finger and bent down on one knee. 'Charles Hindley, will you marry me and my chips obsession all over again?'

'I will,' Charles said.

Dot stood, placed the ring on his finger and kissed him just as she had on their wedding day.

'Good,' Dot said, staring at an arc of lights that curved through the distant sky. 'Look, a rainbow, just for us!'

They held each other, the salt air warm on their faces and

their boat bobbing gently over the endless waters, looking at the rainbow.

Charles sang to Dot sweetly and quietly about making wishes to stars, lands beyond rainbows and daring to dream.

34

Stomping Grounds

Dot hadn't intended to get itchy fingers before she arrived at the garden centre, but old habits die hard. A fly trap going missing here, a miniature fern disappearing there – what difference would it make to anyone?

With Christmas Town obliterated and its inhabitants tossed into the rancid hell of her wheely bin, Dot had felt like she needed to cleanse the air, and she had space for new green friends. So, the garden centre beckoned her inside like a siren on the shore.

Dot perused the green aisles, avoiding the security guard. When he was in sight, she lost him behind the sheds and gazebos, then circled around the outer edges behind the larger plants and trees, so that she would have plenty of time before he saw her again. It was a game of cat and mouse, and this street mouse was ten times as wily as the unwitting tomcat.

'Squeak squeak, Dot. Squeak squeak,' said Max's imagined voice in her head, intruding.

She'd found it hard to shake Max from her mind. Every now and again, his words would pipe up unexpectedly and she'd have to push them aside by thinking of song lyrics or movie quotes. But movie quotes reminded her of Max, too.

Imaginary Max was persistent, and Dot found herself

unwittingly running through little segments of conversations with him, hearing his retorts to her various excellent jokes and observations, until she was able to quash him into silence.

But back to the crime. Dot wasn't going to be too greedy – she was out of practice, not having stolen anything from the garden centre for a while now. She worked her way back to the bonsai trees, for old times' sake, then checked she wasn't being watched. She swiftly placed a healthy-looking tree into her big handbag and moved on.

She didn't intend to hang around but was curious to see who was at the garden centre café. Would the young waiter be there, the one who'd been so happy about Dot's generous tip? Dot didn't intend to become friends with him, not after her experience with Max, but she wanted a moment of adoration and appreciation. She wanted a little injection of gratitude to boost her morale, which had taken a distinct turn towards the dumps recently.

Dot approached her usual table at the café, noticing the two old crones she'd seen so many times before. They were hunched over a single pot of tea, whispering to each other as they eyed passers-by, but didn't seem to notice Dot. The waiter Dot hoped would be there, wasn't. Instead, an older man with a moustache and beer belly was serving tables with all the efficiency and enthusiasm of a coma patient.

'Excuse me,' a strong male voice sounded behind Dot. She turned to see the security guard looming over her. 'Would you mind showing me what's in your bag?'

Dot felt like her heart had stopped. Maybe she should fake a cardiac attack and drop to the floor, she considered, but she simply froze and stared up at him, clutching her bag.

'I . . . no, why?'

'I have reason to believe you have stolen items in your bag,' the security guard said. 'I'll need to take you to the security office.'

Dot couldn't speak. A thousand excuses jumbled in her head, but her mouth made no sense of them. She gasped and uttered fragments of words.

'Excuse me, young man,' a croaking voice sounded behind the guard. The smaller of the two old crones was stood behind him with crossed arms, and the other glared at him from their café table. 'Might I have a word?'

'I'm busy,' the guard said.

'I'm sure you are!' the taller crone said, joining her friend's side. 'You just love to pick on old women, don't you?'

The smaller crone nodded. 'Well, we won't stand for it this time! It's' – she raised her voice – 'DISCRIMINATION! Perhaps we should speak to the manager about this. It isn't the first time you've been caught following women around, is it?'

They both glared at him. His shoulders drooped and he looked more like a scolded boy than a grown-up guard.

'I . . . well . . .' the guard uttered, his jaw slack. He turned to Dot. 'Okay, I've decided to give you a chance. But this is your only warning, okay?'

Dot stood silently, mortified at being caught. Even if she'd wanted to run, she knew she couldn't. Her legs were at least thirty-five per cent gelatine.

'Give me the item and I'll return it,' the guard said. 'I won't mention it to management, but I don't want to catch you doing something like this again. One-time warning, you understand?'

'Of course. Yes, thank you,' Dot said shakily. She opened her bag and handed the bonsai tree to the guard, who returned into the main body of the store.

Dot approached the crones' table slowly as they returned to their seats.

'Don't worry, dear,' the smaller crone with the hoarse voice said. 'It happened to us once.'

The larger crone raised her teacup to her thin lips. 'We girls have to stick together, don't we?'

'Yes,' Dot said quietly. 'Thank you.'

'It's nearly Christmas, after all,' the larger crone said. 'We know you're a good egg. The young waiter told us what a nice thing you did for him. And we know how hard it is for people like us sometimes, especially at this time of year.'

The smaller crone poured more tea. 'We all make mistakes now and then, don't we?'

'Yes, I suppose we do,' Dot said.

Deeply embarrassed by what had happened, Dot wished she could click her heels to return home in an instant, though perhaps a broomstick would have been more appropriate. She felt wicked for having treated the two women so poorly in the past (free tea aside).

Perhaps she ought to compensate them for their kindness . . .

'Have you girls ever been race car driving?' Dot asked.

★

The women's laughter pinballed through Dot's head as she walked homeward. She had told them about her bucket list, how she'd eaten every dessert in a swanky restaurant and made a snowman, decorated a huge tree with her neighbours (they'd read about that in the paper), raced cars and been to the funfair, helped the community as part of the Clean-Up Crew, ridden in a carriage, stargazed and let off fireworks, fed horses, been a starlet in a zombie movie and danced in a flash mob.

Lumped together like that, she realised how busy she'd been and how exciting her life would have seemed to her pre-lottery self.

'That's a bit much for us!' the women at the café had replied. 'But good for you, giving those young'uns a run for their money.'

Dot walked the route that took her past the abandoned skate park, noticing kids sat on the rails and ramps while listening to angry-sounding music on their phones. They looked thoroughly bored and chilled to the bone as snow began to fall in fat flakes – the angry music felt justified. Similar to Max's life, perhaps theirs hadn't been a cakewalk either, and Dot felt fortunate that hers had its fair share of happy memories, especially with Grace and Charles, and during the last few weeks.

None of that changed what had happened between her and Max, but she thought about what he'd told her about his friends and family – how sincere he'd seemed about wanting to improve his life and help his mum, and his belief that good friends were worth holding onto.

On the one hand, Dot had to take care of herself. She had to make sure she wasn't being taken advantage of, and that she wasn't putting herself at risk. And Max could be a risk, despite all the great things they'd done together. But on the other hand, she missed him, and the crones' words about everyone making mistakes had resonated with her.

If the crones could forgive her, could she forgive Max?

She continued towards home, past the community Christmas tree, staring up at the angel at its peak.

Her head kept her afraid, but her heart told her otherwise. There was great kindness in the world, if she was willing to seek and see it.

35

The Fragrance That the Violet Sheds on the Heel That Has Crushed It

Dot tried to call Max, but there was no reply.

Maybe she'd scared him as much as he'd scared her, then. Perhaps he felt as betrayed by her as she had by him. Time was the great healer of wounds – she'd seen that on her wards – but it could also cause scars. She'd allowed her broken friendship with Grace to go untreated for far too long; she couldn't let it happen again.

The snow outside her windows had grown so heavy that she felt like she was living inside a marshmallow. The journey out would be arduous, but at least she knew where Max lived, approximately.

Dot grabbed her thickest coat from the hook, almost strangled herself with her scarf, pushed her feet into her thickest boots, took a deep breath in preparation for her heroic voyage into the cold and unforgiving wilds, but stopped. What was she doing? This was all so unnecessary.

She ordered a taxi and boiled the kettle. As the kettle heated, heavy *thud*s sounded at the front door. Her ride was quicker than she expected, so she rushed to answer.

'Dot . . .' Max said, leaning against the wall of her house, panting.

He lurched forward and she caught him. He was heavy in her arms and she helped him stagger inside. His face was blue with cold and black with bruises, red with blood.

'What happened?' Dot asked, aiding him to her comfy chair.

He sat with a pained groan, his lip torn and his nose askew. 'I got it.'

'What? The beating of a lifetime? I'm calling an ambulance.' She picked up the phone.

'No, stop.' With scraped knuckles, his shaking hand reached into his coat pocket and he pulled out a silver chain. A metal oval was attached to it. 'Is this yours?'

Dot hung up the phone and took the locket, opening it carefully. Inside, her dad smiled back at her.

'Yes!' Dot said, unable to stop a tear rolling down her cheek. 'How did you find it?'

Max's bleeding lip turned upwards. 'Those guys had it, I got lucky.'

'Lucky?!' She bent down to his side, lifting his face with her hand. He looked pulverised, but the injuries weren't as severe as they first appeared. Still, he might need stitches. 'They beat seven shades out of you.'

'Ten shades actually,' he laughed, crying out in pain. 'I counted.'

'Wait here.'

Dot rushed to her kettle and made tea for Max, telling him to drink it slowly. She dug out her first aid box and some clean towels, then returned to his side with a bowl of warm soapy water.

'You're an idiot, you know that?' Dot said, cleaning his wounds with the towel and water.

He winced. 'I thought this would show you I wasn't working with them. I'd never do that. I just sold them bikes one time and we swapped numbers.'

'You're an idiot for putting yourself at risk like that, Max.' She dabbed harder to remove dirt from a cut on his cheek, and he yelped. 'No piece of jewellery is worth this.'

'I had to get it back for you. When I worked out what they'd done, I couldn't let them get away with it.'

Dot felt like Max had walked over her grave and then stomped on the flowers.

'What did you do?' Dot asked, filled with dread and hoping that his answer wouldn't get anywhere close to her worst fears.

'I gave as good as I got, but there's two of them. Anyway, they won't be bothering you again. I threatened them with the police, said I had a bunch of evidence and you as a witness. I said I'd forget it all if they left town.'

'And they did?'

Max nodded slowly as Dot wiped blood from under his nose. 'They hadn't been here long, they're drifters. They steal what they can and do some drug deals, then move on when things get too hot to handle. They didn't want to stick around and risk getting caught.'

Dot kissed his forehead. 'Thank you. I'm not sure you did the right thing, but I appreciate it. Just don't do anything like that again, okay?'

'Okay.'

She stared into his eyes, adopting her *I REALLY MEAN THIS* face. 'Promise me.'

'I promise. I don't want anything to do with people like them. I don't want to be like them or . . . my dad. They only care about themselves, and I'm not like that. Do you believe me?'

'Of course I do.'

'Do you trust me?'

'Yes,' Dot said confidently. Max had said enough now to prove that he wasn't in league with her muggers, and that he had no intentions of becoming a brute. He'd opened up to her, and she felt ready to confide in him. 'It's hard, but I do trust you. It's been difficult for me to trust people. I lost my husband and best friend, and I didn't want to be hurt again. Deep down I think I knew you weren't trying to hurt me, but I've had years of worry to fight against. I kept expecting the worst in people, until I met you.'

Max smiled briefly. 'I just don't want you to hate me. You're, like, the only person who ever gave me a chance. Just give me one more.'

How could she refuse? 'I will. And now you trust me, let me call an ambulance.'

Max looked out of the window, which was meringued by heavy snowfall. 'I'm just beaten up, it's not that serious. And there's a snowstorm out – other people need an ambulance way more than me.' He stood shakily but straightened up and looked much more like his usual handsome self. He examined his face in the wall mirror. 'If my mum sees me like this, she'll freak out. Can I stay the night and work on my excuses?'

'Okay, I'll make up the spare room. It's been a long time since anyone used it. And in the morning, we're going to A&E to get you checked out. Deal?'

Max smiled, leaned in and wrapped his arms around Dot. 'Deal.'

★

In the hospital waiting room the next morning, Dot couldn't stop staring at her dad's picture in the locket. While it was still idiotic of Max to risk so much to retrieve it for her, and it was only a piece of metal and a slip of paper, she felt like a missing part of her had been returned.

The waiting room was sparsely decorated in tinsel, had a Christmas tree with fake presents under it, and the reception staff had pinned thank-you cards to the walls. Dot missed those positive parts of her old job – it was always nice when patients were grateful, and she'd had some happy times with friendly colleagues like Grace.

She remembered the time a man arrived on Christmas Eve with a particularly festive problem: a carrot was stuck up his anus. He claimed it was an accident, but on retrieving the root veg (carrots were one of Dot's favourite root vegetables up until this experience) they discovered that the carrot was wearing a condom. The staff had referred to the patient as Rudolph, and whenever another accident of the anus was admitted, they would refer to the situation (away from Matron, management or the patient themselves) as *A Rudolph*.

The kids' reindeer song never quite sounded the same to Dot and her colleagues again.

Other, less anal, memories flooded back to Dot as medical machines bleeped, trolleys trundled and staff chatted in codes and acronyms. She smiled and squirmed at the memories before returning to the ghosts of Christmas present, and her lack of actual Christmas presents.

The return of her locket had felt like a particularly special gift. It had been years since Dot had been given a Christmas present or bought one for anyone else. So, Max was the perfect candidate to receive her first gift in a very long time, and she wanted to make sure he liked whatever she chose.

But he already had one of the best bikes money could buy – what else could she get for him? It wasn't a conundrum that would be easily solved, and Christmas Day was less than a week away.

Despite the weather and the time of year (when Dot knew A&E was particularly busy with revellers and carrot enthusiasts), Max was in and out of the hospital quickly, and he didn't need stitches, after all.

As they left, Dot asked Max: 'So, what did you ask Father Christmas for this year?'

'I'm expecting coal, to be honest,' Max said. 'I've not been a very good boy.'

'You've been good enough, I'm sure. Saint Nick is very generous. So is Saint Dorothy, Patron Saint of Bucket Lists.'

'Then, will she be generous enough to forgive me for bringing those guys to her house?'

Dot waved her hand slowly in front of Max's eyes, like she imagined the pope might. 'You are forgiven. Now what will you ask Saint Dot for?'

Max walked a little awkwardly, wincing with pain. 'You got me the bike already. And we've got the bucket list. Have you added anything new yet?'

'Not yet.'

'Then let's do something today. I feel like celebrating – those arsehole muggers are gone, you've got your locket back and we're friends again.'

'Bestest fwends?' Dot asked in a little girl's voice.

'Bestest fwends,' Max repeated in his regular deep voice. 'And I think we should make some New Year's resolutions. One: that we don't fall out like that again. We talk things through first, no big secrets or plot twists.'

'Agreed,' Dot said, pleased with how forthright and mature

272

he was being with her. 'And two: you stay out of trouble. No more crime. And while I'm at it, no more crime for me, either.'

Max nodded. 'And three: we keep the bucket list going. Even if we get busier, we'll make time for it.'

'Sounds good to me.' She stopped walking and held out her hand.

Max shook Dot's hand and his eyes brightened. 'I almost forgot.'

He took a plastic sandwich bag from his pocket. Inside were little posh-looking mushrooms, like Dot had seen in some of the snazzy farmer's markets around the city.

'You kept them?' Dot asked, beaming as she waved down a passing taxi. 'I'm up for it if you are. A little shroom party? And yes, I have been memorising the lingo.'

Max laughed. 'My mum warned me about women like you.'

<u>36</u>

Tea, Toast, a Trip
& a Tango

'How should we do this?' Max asked, scratching a scab on his ear.

'Don't scratch,' Dot scolded, slapping his hand. 'You'll scar. Do you want more of my special cream?'

'That sounds wrong. And no, thanks.' He stopped scratching and returned his attention to the bag of magic mushrooms on Dot's kitchen worktop. 'Any ideas? The dealers said these were really good and wished me a Merry Tripmas. I believed them. Should we just swallow them?'

'No, let's be a bit more creative,' Dot said, boiling the kettle. 'It's our bucket list, after all. How about shroom tea? I read about it.'

'All right, I'm game.'

Dot took a loaf out of the bread bin. 'And maybe some shrooms on toast? It's a bit like afternoon tea.'

Max laughed but looked a little nervous. 'Why not.' He sat at the kitchen table. 'I've never done these kinds of things, though I'm pretty sure mushrooms are safe.'

'It feels quite naughty, doesn't it?' Dot said, sawing two slices of bread from the loaf. 'But I like a bit of naughtiness. It makes me feel like I'm breaking the rules, like we're not just doing what we're told, you know?'

'Yeah, I kinda like that, too. But remember the pact: no crime. And, theoretically, this is a crime.'

Dot *pff*ed. 'Barely. It's just a little thing, not really hurting anyone else. The pact is for real crimes like stealing cars or murder.'

Max stared at the mushrooms as if they were taunting him. 'It's a slippery slope.'

'You know, considering you're an ex-con, you're a bit of a wimp,' Dot said jokingly.

'I'm hardly an ex-con. I was made to clean a park and help some poor kids.'

Dot dropped the bread slices into the toaster.

'We ought to prepare the area,' Max said. 'I saw it on TV. It helps us to visualise things and might help stop us taking a bad trip.'

'Like what?' Dot asked.

'Leave it to me. You keep preparing the tea and toast.'

Max exited the kitchen and Dot could hear him cluttering about while she loaded a shroom tea recipe on her phone. She combined the mushrooms with hot water, ginger and lemon juice, allowing them to stew. Then she cooked the remaining mushrooms in a little butter and garlic, placed them on top of the toast and sprinkled them with parsley.

They looked and smelled like any other mushrooms – were they truly a magical variety?

'Tea is served! Dot chimed, bringing the tea and toast out to the lounge, where Max was flicking through TV channels.

Max looked at the toast and laughed. 'Have you been watching *MasterChef* or something? What's with the green stuff and the sauce?'

'If we're doing this, we do it right. I pimped it right up!' Dot said.

'You ought to cut down on the hardcore gangster rap.'

'I can't, I'm addicted.'

Max turned down the TV volume. 'Do you even know what hardcore gangster rap is?'

'Not a clue, but it sounds exciting.'

Max flicked the TV to a kid's channel, where colourful suns floated around the screen to serene music. 'This will do. It's meant to keep little kids happy, so it should work for us.'

He sat on the floor, where he'd placed cushions stolen from the sofas and pillows pilfered from the beds.

'Why's all this here?' Dot asked, sitting on the ground and passing him a mug of shroom tea.

'I'm not sure. I just saw it in a movie once. I guess we might want to lie down at some point.' He sniffed his tea, and they *cheers*ed their mugs, both taking a sip at the same time. 'It's not bad, a bit like hot toddy minus the whisky.'

'And a bit more earthy,' Dot said. She took silver cutlery from her sweater pocket and handed a set to Max. 'Toast time.' They each cut a square of toast topped with mushrooms. 'Down the hatch!'

They both ate, and Dot was impressed by her quick-action cookery skills. The mushrooms were beautifully buttery.

'Hey, that was pretty nice,' Max said. He raised a hand in front of his face and wiggled his fingers. 'Nothing yet.'

'Me neither,' Dot said, watching the suns on the TV laugh as they transformed into baby faces and floated out from the screen, hovering in the air like huge baby-faced fireflies.

'Maybe I got duped,' Max said, drinking more tea. He brushed at his shoulder, then looked up at the ceiling. 'Damn. It's snowing again.'

The marshmallow floor wrapped around Dot as she lay back, absorbing her in its sweet vanilla scent. The baby-faced fireflies danced in the white space around her, their laughs chiming like silver bells. Golden sands sprouted around her feet; the bells and laughter softened into the gentle crashes of ocean waves; perfectly blue waters lapped at Dot's toes, tickling them.

Dot was on a tropical beach, under the cooling shade of a coconut tree. The sun was warm on her face, and someone's fingers touched her hand.

Charles was beside her, lying on a towel.

'Hey, good-lookin',' he said softly, smiling.

His skin and teeth were perfect. His naked chest was muscular, and he was in his mid-twenties. He glowed with a faint, golden light. He sat upright and great white wings unfolded from his back, the feathers made of such shiny ice and snow that Dot could see her reflection in them.

She was young, too. Her skin was smooth and her body was light and alert. Charles wrapped his arms around her and she felt his warmth radiate through her, filling her with a feeling of peace and happiness like she'd never felt before.

She wanted him to never let go.

Charles's wings flapped and he lifted Dot into the sky. She looked down at the perfect waters below, the sunlight shimmering on the surface like the scales of a fish. As they flew higher and higher, she could see that the ocean was in fact a vast fish – perhaps a cod, she wasn't sure – and its colossal glassy eye watched them ascend through the pink and white candyfloss clouds.

'Where are we going?' Dot asked, her voice lighter than

usual. It was how she used to sound, and she felt like singing, so she did: 'Wheeeeeere aaaaare we gooooooiiiiiing, Chaaaaarles?'

Charles kissed her lips into silence, and it felt like their first kiss outside the cinema all over again. She closed her eyes and held him until they passed through the clouds and landed on top of them, standing on them as if they were made of mattresses.

An ornate pearl-white gate — which stretched so high and so far that Dot couldn't see its ends — barred the way to an endless meadow of wildflowers and tree-topped hills.

Charles opened his mouth and string music flowed out from his lips. His voice tinkled between the notes: 'Shall we dance?'

'Oh yes, let's dance!' Dot replied, taking his hands in hers.

Charles rocked her gently, turning her under his arm, holding her close to his chest so that she could feel his heartbeat merging with hers. She felt so warm and wanted, so utterly, endlessly happy. She could almost cry.

He was back. She had him back.

They danced and the baby fireflies swirled around them, but the music slowed and grew quiet. Charles stopped dancing and took a step away.

'Don't stop, ever,' Dot said, reaching for him.

His icy wings fluttered and he drifted away from Dot, towards the pearly gate. A golden tear ran down his cheek, along his neck and chest.

'Don't go!' Dot begged.

'Dot, it's okay,' Charles said. 'You're fine.'

'No, please. Don't leave me again.'

'Dot . . . you're okay.'

He smiled so sweetly that she felt herself melting. Her fingers stretched like uncooked bread dough, drooping down to her feet, and she began to sink through the clouds. Her comfy chair hovered among the sweet candyfloss. A pillow flew by and honked like a migrating goose, followed by a sofa cushion.

'I love you,' Charles's voice echoed around her.

'I love you,' she said back.

As she opened her eyes, Max's blurred outline floated towards her from the opposite side of the room.

'You're okay, Dot,' Max said, the clouds drifting away to reveal his face.

She was in her living room, though the walls were thick with clouds and the baby fireflies danced around the telly. She sat upright, her body old and aching again.

'What's . . . ?' Dot started.

'I've got you,' Max said, helping her to sit. 'Are you okay?'

'I'm okay,' Dot said, trying not to be too distracted by the sands receding at her feet, and the waters splashing against Max's legs.

'What did you see?' Max asked.

'Heaven,' Dot answered, smiling.

37

Merry Christmas,
Dot & Max!

Max tried to explain that the mushrooms had probably been spiked with something much stronger, but Dot was having none of it.

Despite how trippy and random her shrooming experience had seemed, Heaven felt so real. It was as though someone had put their hands inside her brain and reconnected some worn wires, like she'd been reset. A veil had been lifted.

She wasn't sure she would go so far as to say she'd been touched by God (she wasn't completely convinced that God existed, and if God did exist then the holy books and various interpretations made by humans left a lot of room for improvement), but it felt like she had been. And since seeing Charles again, she felt different, more peaceful. It was as though she'd been made a promise that there was something else out there, something full of love for her, something always watching out for her. It was like she'd never be alone again, and she came to think that maybe she never had been alone, not really.

Dot poured Irish cream into big mugs, creating a fifty–fifty ratio of booze-to-coffee, then added some sugar for luck.

She placed three filled mugs on a tray and carried them to the living room.

'I hope it's not too early,' Dot said, 'but I fancied starting the day off with a boozy beverage.'

'It's never too early for booze on Christmas Day!' Max said cheerily, pulling his ugly Christmas sweater over his head. 'This is about the ugliest sweater I've ever seen, Dot. Thank you!'

'Don't be so rude, Max!' his mum said, taking a mug from Dot's tray and sipping it. 'Oh, it's so good! I love Irish coffee. And Irish men.'

Max grimaced. He took a mug and clinked it with his mum's and Dot's, and they all had a drink.

'Geez, Dot!' Max said, gasping. 'How much booze is in this?'

'Not enough?' Dot asked.

Max's mum laughed and coffee spurted from her ruby-red lips.

'I love your lipstick,' Dot said. 'Where did you get it?'

'The market, just a quid. I love a good bargain, me!'

'Amen to that!' Dot clinked mugs again. 'So, Max, what's first on the moviethon? The king's speech?'

'Absolutely, it's a classic Christmas thing to do,' Max's mum said. 'It's like eating sprouts: whether you like it or not, you just do it!'

'Well, the king's not due to start for a while yet,' Max said, 'so I thought we'd start with *The Muppet Christmas Carol* instead. Have you seen it?'

Dot shook her head, feeling even happier with a little boozy cream inside her.

'It's a classic,' Max's mum said. 'We used to watch it when you were little, didn't we, Maxi?'

Max grinned, loading the movie up on the telly. 'You'll love it, Dot. It has scares and songs and Muppets. What's not to like?'

Dot had cranked up the boiler to make the house roasty toasty, and they sat in the tropical heat of her lounge, laughing as the Muppets sang and danced.

'I will live my life in the past, the present and the future,' Scrooge said triumphantly, and Dot caught Max smiling at her in the reflection of the screen.

They cheered when Scrooge finally changed his miserly tune and asked a passing rodent what day it was, sending it away to buy the prize turkey for everyone to share around a festive table.

'That reminds me,' Dot said. 'I couldn't be bothered to cook.'

'No Christmas lunch?!' Max cried cartoonishly, but with a genuine hint of alarm and disappointment.

'Of course there's Christmas lunch, but it's been Schwarzeneggered.'

'Schwarzeneggered?' Max's mum asked.

'It's what we do,' Max said. 'We pump things up, make them bigger and better.' He looked to Dot. 'What did you do?'

Dot smiled and tapped her nose. Max tried to prise the secret from her, but she was unwilling to confess it. By the time he'd chosen and loaded the next movie for their moviethon, the doorbell rang.

Dot answered and allowed the catering staff into the house. They quickly decorated Dot's table with a red tablecloth, a mistletoe centrepiece, silverware and gold-trimmed china plates. A huge roasted turkey, root vegetables (not carrots), greens, potatoes, pigs in blankets, stuffing and gravy followed, and Dot invited Max and his mum to sit at the table while the caterers cleared away and left the house.

Dot put a record on the player, and they tucked in.

'This is beautiful,' Max's mum said as she ate, chestnut stuffing falling from her lips.

'What's for pudding?' Max asked when they'd finished, gulping down red wine. 'They didn't leave one.'

'I made a trifle,' Dot said.

Max stood from the table and walked to his coat on the hook. He pulled a small, wrapped gift from his coat pocket, and handed it to Dot.

'Small but promising!' Dot said.

'It's just a little something.' Max watched with intent.

Dot opened the wrapping carefully to find gold. 'Hooped earrings,' she said enthusiastically.

Max smiled, and Dot passed an envelope to him.

He tore it open and stared at its contents, his eyes flitting across the page and his mouth agape. 'Dot, I . . .'

'What is it?' his mum asked.

'Planning permission,' Max said, turning to the next page. 'And an operating agreement.' He stared at Dot, confused. 'I don't get it.'

'Maybe this will make it clearer, then.' Dot placed a golden envelope on the table.

'A bucket list event?' Max asked. 'You know, only the Bucket Master is meant to have access to those.'

Dot slid the envelope towards Max. 'Well, for once, I'm the Bucket Master. And you've been given a task.'

He opened it and read it aloud:

Max
You asked for one more chance, you got it.
Run your own business. Be happy.
Starts: next year
With love from The Bucket Master (a.k.a. Dot)

38

Fire a Gun

Max looked great in his new suit and shiny shoes. The spring air was crisp and clean, filled with birdsong from the nearby trees. A small but enthusiastic group of locals and journalists had gathered in the skate park for the reopening, with several kids clutching their bikes and skateboards.

Dot noticed Chaha and her husband from the corner shop in the crowd. On a nearby bench, the two older women from the garden centre were chatting idly while keeping an eye on proceedings.

Dot waved to Max from the crowd and he smiled at her. Poor soul, he looked like he was about to run away screaming for mercy, but he took a deep breath and his nerves seemed to settle, just as they had practised.

'Welcome, everyone,' Max said loudly and confidently. 'I'm Max Campbell-Brown, the new manager of Three-Sixty – a community-orientated skate and bike park.'

The two older women from the garden centre had joined the crowd and finger-waved to Dot. A few members of the crowd clapped quietly at Max's words, but Dot let out a loud, solitary whoop. The two older women joined in with her, and the rest of the crowd applauded more loudly, adding to the whoops.

The clamour settled and Max continued. 'We've a lot of work to do, bringing the park up to standard and installing new ramps and other features, but today I'm pleased to open The Bike Shed.' He gestured to the new custom-built building behind him. Tools were laid out on a table in front of the building. Max glanced at his papers and looked to Dot.

Dot smiled and gave a thumbs-up.

Max continued: 'The Bike Shed is a unique feature of our community park. Here, I will personally teach kids how to fix and maintain their bikes. We will run a bike-maintenance service for paying customers, and we'll also renovate lost and reclaimed bikes, which can then be sold or donated to people who need them.'

The crowd clapped much louder than they had before. Several kids whispered to one another excitedly. Looking around, Dot noticed Jacob at the centre of the crowd, surrounded by other members of the Clean-Up Crew.

Max checked his paper again. 'We have already partnered with local businesses for sponsorship and will be working with community charities who help disadvantaged kids and young people. Thanks to our kind sponsors and also our local supporters such as the Clean-Up Crew, who helped to get the council on board with this project' – he smiled at Jacob, then at Dot – 'we will also be expanding to create a green space for rest and relaxation, as well as running local events for people to get to know their neighbours and forge strong community relationships.'

Max walked to an object covered by a white sheet. What was he doing, and what was underneath the sheet? Dot hadn't rehearsed this part with him, and he hadn't mentioned it to her.

'To formally open the park and welcome you all, I wish to unveil something special. But I need some help.' He looked out to the crowd. 'Dot, would you please help me?'

What was he up to? The sneaky thing! Well, she could hardly say no, so she walked out of the cheering crowd.

'What is this?' she whispered to Max.

'You'll see,' he whispered back. He addressed the crowd again: 'Dot, can you please remove the sheet to officially open the park?'

Dot pulled the sheet away to reveal a white-painted wooden bench, its sections each carved into the shapes of birds. A bronze plaque was screwed into the back rest:

In loving memory of Charles Hindley
A place to meet new friends

Dot refused to cry in front of so many people. There was just no way, no chance whatsoever.

Max handed her a tissue as she bawled.

'We'll be having a celebration barbecue now,' Max said to the crowd. 'So, please grab a plate and chat to someone you don't know! If you have any questions about the park and what we are doing, there are leaflets, or you can come and talk to me. I don't bite!'

The crowd chuckled and began moving towards a smoking barbecue behind The Tool Shed.

The kids from the local primary school – who'd distributed support packages around the neighbourhood, including Dot's rehomed plants – rode their bikes over to Max.

'Can we come here?' the older kid asked.

'Of course,' Max said. He knelt, examining the kid's bike. 'Nice bike. But did you know your brake's a bit worn out?'

The younger kid nodded enthusiastically. 'Mine too, look.'

'We'll have to fix that. I'll show you how – it's really easy!'

Max said. 'Grab a hotdog first. I'll show you in a few minutes, okay?'

The kids grinned. 'Yeah!' They rode their bikes towards the meaty smoke.

'You little sneak!' Dot scolded, wiping the last of her tears and snot away. 'Making me cry in front of all these people.'

'Do you like it?' Max asked. 'The bench was made by a local retired carpenter.' He pointed to Jacob, who smiled and waved to Max while his frog-wellied grandson ran circles around him. Max waved back. 'We're going to use him for some of the other benches and tables.'

'I love it,' Dot said. 'And I think Charles would have, too.'

Max put an arm around Dot's shoulder, leading her towards the barbecue. 'Good. Let's get you something to eat. Do you prefer your sausages to be raw or cremated?'

'Oh, cremated, please!'

They joined the queue for food and Max answered questions about the park from interested locals, several of whom wanted to know how they could be involved. Dot listened to Max answer confidently as he smiled and joked with them. His mum ambushed him and planted a big kiss on his cheek, leaving a ruby-red lipstick print on his face.

The boy had done well, really well.

Dot grabbed her burnt sausage and sat on Charles's bench, watching Max as he showed the kids how to improve their bikes. The women from the garden centre café passed by, placing a comforting hand on Dot's shoulder and saying: 'Well done, dear,' before leaving her alone.

A gentle wind blew through the park, carrying the voices of its people and the songs of its birds. Dot closed her eyes and let the spring sunshine warm her face, the buzz of voices softening into a sleepy drone in her head.

A dog barked, breaking Dot's respite, and she could feel its busy nose sniffing her legs.

'Clyde, leave her be!' Bonnie snapped, pulling Clyde away from Dot.

Dot opened her eyes and chuckled. 'Oh, let him sniff.' She scratched behind Clyde's ear. 'He deserves it.'

Clyde sniffed at Dot's hotdog, so Dot tossed her burned sausage on the ground and watched Clyde gobble it down as though he'd never been fed.

'I read in the papers that all this was going on today,' Bonnie said. 'I didn't know you were involved.'

'I'm not, really,' Dot said. 'But I know Max, the mastermind behind it all.'

'Well, it's busy, and I recognise a few folk from around the big park. They seem nice.'

Dot looked around, surprised that she knew so many of the people in the skate park. It wasn't her lottery money that had caused them to appear. It wasn't her lottery money that had cleaned up the streets or brought so many people here to show their support. It wasn't really the money that had changed her life – it was the people. And most of all, it was the time she'd spent with Max.

If Bonnie and Clyde hadn't rescued her, she never would have met Max and everyone else around her. None of them might have spoken to each other, let alone become friends.

'You know,' Dot started, aware that Bonnie wouldn't fully understand the impact she'd had, 'if you and Clyde hadn't found me when you did, none of this would have happened.'

Bonnie smiled. 'Ripples in a pond, aye Dot?'

Clyde rose on his hind legs, placed his front paws on Dot's knees and licked her hands.

'We'd better keep moving,' Bonnie said, trying to get Clyde

to sit, 'or he'll never leave you alone. You've made his day with that sausage.'

'Thank you both, again,' Dot said.

'See you soon, we hope.' Bonnie led Clyde away, trying desperately to pull him in the opposite direction to the barbecue.

Dot leaned back on the bench, watching Max chat to an array of locals, his mum looking on proudly from afar. Dot took a deep breath of sausagey air, and let the bird song wash over her again, content.

'Excuse me, are you Dorothy Hindley?' a voice sounded behind her.

Dot turned to look at a suited woman. 'Yes?'

'Oh good. I was just talking to Mr and Mrs Jain, from the corner shop. They pointed me in your direction. Could we do a little interview for our website?' The woman gestured to a man with a video camera. 'It's local news. We're interested in sharing your story.'

'It's Max's park,' Dot said. 'You should interview him.'

'We will. But this all started with you, didn't it? You won the lottery, am I right? How did you come to know Max?'

Dot told their story: how they'd met in the park and she'd chosen her final lottery number from Max's football shirt; how they'd been doing a bucket list together; how Max found her stolen locket (although she missed out the parts about Max being on community service or taking a beating from drug dealers). The camera man filmed it all as the journalist asked questions.

'I hope you don't mind me asking this next one,' the journalist said. Dot anticipated her age-based question. 'But how old are you?'

'Let's just say north of seventy, south of eighty,' Dot answered.

'Isn't it a little dangerous to be taking on all these adventures at your age?'

Dot smiled. 'Honestly? I've come to learn something important, recently: the greater danger is *not* taking on the adventures.'

★

Dot checked her ticket details against those on the departures board. Everything was in order, so she had a little time to explore the airport's alcoholic options, to settle her nerves.

'Everything set?' Max asked.

'I think so,' Dot said, eyeing the laptop carry case in his hand. 'Don't become a workaholic, will you?'

'Of course not! But I can't abandon the park completely while the big renovations are happening. I still need to get in touch with the council to finalise the extension and—'

'I get it, Mr Big Businessman Big Shot.' She punched his arm playfully. 'But remember that life's not all about work – it's about having fun, too.'

'I have fun with my work.' Max punched her arm back, and she pretended it hurt. 'Plus, I'm taking a holiday right now, aren't I? Corfu – the sea, the sand, the feta cheese.'

'Oh, I love some salty feta. Can't get better than feta, so the saying goes. How long until your flight?'

Max checked the departure boards. 'Two hours. Assuming Jo actually finds her way out of the shops.'

Jo – the beautiful young red-headed woman Max had spoken to on the street during the flash mob dance party – emerged from a shop carrying multiple fat bags of shopping.

'Don't look at me like that, Maximus!' Jo said. 'There was a sale. What was I meant to do? *Not* buy everything? That's just rude.'

'I'll be broke at this rate,' Max replied. 'Dot, please tell her . . .'

'You two will have to sort this one out for yourselves,' Dot said, keen not to take sides.

'When's your flight, Dot?' Jo asked. 'Do you have time for a snack, or maybe a little drinky, with us?'

Dot checked the departures board again. 'A451 to Austin, Texas . . . an hour and forty minutes.'

'Plenty of time,' Max said. 'So, you're sure about taking the plunge?'

'Definitely,' Dot said, smiling. 'It's time to complete the list. I have to take a leap of faith – I have to fire the gun.'

Jo smiled at Dot. 'If you're going to Texas, you could fire a real gun, too.'

Dot imagined herself as a sheriff quick-drawing a silver pistol and firing it into the shimmering Texan sky. 'I might just do that, you know.'

Max led them towards an airport bar. 'We have to say cheers before you go – who knows how long it'll be before I see you again?'

'I'll be back,' Dot said in a bad Schwarzenegger accent. 'Let's grab that drink. And this time, you're paying.'

ACKNOWLEDGEMENTS

Massive thanks to the whole Polygon team (especially my editor Edward Crossan, my copy editor Craig Hillsley and cover designer Abigail Salvesen) for backing this book and helping to bring Dot and Max's story into the world. Thank you also to my wonderful agent, Caro Clarke, for their support and vision – for believing in this story. To my partner, Jo, for her reading notes and suggestions, thank you, and sorry for all the puns. And where would I be without my Morale Officers, Pakkun and Eddie – dogs and companions extraordinaire! Bows of appreciation go out to Richard Ridgwell for early copy edits and proofreads. Thank yous are due also to various readers and writer friends along this book's journey (for feedback, or simply listening to me complain), including Finola Scott, Thomas Wood, Stephen and Anne Suess, Jane Yolen, Caroline Hardaker, Cat Hellisen and all my pals from Poetry Gang. If I missed anybody, please accept my sincerest apologies and know that you helped to make this book what it is, including many, many social media friends who advised me on what life was like for a woman in Scotland in the decades before I was born!

And a final thanks to all the gutsy, kind and unique older women I've known – especially my late nans, Jean and Margaret – for breaking myths, smashing stereotypes and being generally ace people, each of whom influenced the character of Dot (and me) in their own ways.

BOOK CLUB QUESTIONS
FROM THE AUTHOR

1.   How much difference do you think winning the lottery made to Dot's life?

2.   What do you think about the way Dot chose to spend her winnings?

3.   What did you think about Dot and Max's friendship?

4.   Do you think Max and Dot learned much from each other? Do you think their different ages helped or hindered this?

5.   Why do you think Dot and/or Max turned to crime?

6.   What do you think Christmas Town and Dot's plant collection meant to her?

7.   What do you think bikes, and mending bikes, means to Max and Dot?

8.   How did Dot and Max's relationships with their dads impact their lives?

9.   What's your view of representations of motherhood in the book?

10. What was your favourite item on their bucket list, and why?

11. Has Dot and Max's story made you think about, or reconsider, your own bucket list?

12. What impact do you think Charles's death had on Dot?

13. Does the book say anything useful or interesting about friendship?

14. Does the book say anything useful or interesting about community?

15. How do you think depression and isolation were presented in the book?

16. What did you first think of Dot and Max when they were introduced?

17. Did you change your opinion of Dot or Max after seeing flashbacks or their lives?

18. What do you think happened when Dot took drugs and saw Charles again?

19. What do you hope Dot will do next?

20. Do you think Dot and Max will remain friends? Why?